She Had No Choice

DEBRA BURROUGHS

Lake House Books
Boise, Idaho
2011

First eBook Edition: 2011
First Paperback Edition: 2011

Although SHE HAD NO CHOICE is based on a series of true stories, the names
were changed to protect the privacy of the people involved.

SHE HAD NO CHOICE by Debra Burroughs, 1st. ed. p.cm.

Cover design by Stephanie Mooney Designs

Visit My Blog: www.Debra@DebraBurroughsBooks.com

Contact Me: Debra@DebraBurroughsBooks.com

DEDICATION

This book is lovingly dedicated to my mother, Juanita,
who, with strength and courage, taught me that I
could do anything I set my mind to do.

ACKNOWLEDGEMENTS

The tireless efforts of my husband, Tim Burroughs,
my editor, Amber Daley, and my beta reader, Buffy Drewett
helped this book to be polished and produced, and they
are very much appreciated.

CHAPTER 1

RUNNING FOR THEIR LIVES

1918, Sonora, Mexico

PANCHO VILLA'S REIGN OF TERROR had ended a few years earlier, but now there was a new enemy to battle – and he was merciless. The Death Angel had knocked repeatedly on the Ramirez family's door over the past few weeks. Now, it was imperative for them to swiftly and stealthily find a way to move what was left of the family to a safer place before he came calling again.

Emilio and his wife, Juanita, hurriedly made plans to flee, covertly receiving word of the time and place for the dangerous escape. They were desperate to get their family out of Mexico quickly, but now all they could do was wait.

The appointed night arrived. Tied about Emilio and Juanita's waists were small pouches filled with as many belongings as they dared to take. She had planned all day, choosing this, discarding that, filling their pouches with dollars they had exchanged for their pesos, a comb, a couple handfuls of beef jerky and an old pocket watch.

This was going to be a perilous journey for the Ramirez family. Emilio and Juanita instructed their children once more, as they had for the past two evenings, that on this trip they needed to stay close together and keep silent. Noise of any kind could draw attention and put them in danger.

"But, Mama, *why* do we have to go?" asked little Sofía.

"We have no choice, mi'ja," Mama replied, putting an arm around her. "One day you'll understand."

Their friend, Señor Vega, agreed to load them in the back of his horse-drawn wagon and take them to the pick-up point. The location was the old abandoned Castro ranch. It was once a working venture, until Pancho Villa's men plundered it during the Mexican Revolution several years before. Now, it was nothing more than a few outbuildings with sagging roofs and jagged, broken windows where lonely tumbleweeds collected. That desolate ranch was where they would begin their journey.

Juanita heard the horses' hooves and wagon wheels crunch the dry ground outside their house and knew Señor Vega had pulled up. Her back stiffened, and she drew in a quick breath. There was no turning back now.

"Emilio, niños. I hear Señor Vega outside. It's time to go."

"Hey, Señor," Emilio called out to his friend from the doorway, as the children somberly filed out of the house. Señor Vega waved back and motioned for the children to get in the back of the wagon.

They reluctantly climbed in, fearful of what lay ahead, sad to be leaving the only life they knew. Mama and Papa had shared with them during the past week how this would be an adventure, a new start for all of them. They had asked their children to trust them.

Juanita took one last look at their home and blew out all the candles lighting the living room. She stood for a moment in the doorway, looking back into the dark house. "Good-bye my friend," she said. "You've been very good to us." She closed the door quickly and walked away, choking back her tears. Drawing a deep calming breath, she held her head high and walked toward the buckboard.

Papa had already helped the children into the wagon. They were quietly talking among themselves, the oldest daughter holding her sleepy little brother on her lap. Emilio could see the pain in his wife's eyes, but speaking of it would only make it worse. So, without a word, he lifted her into the back with their children.

"Remember, niños," he said to the children, "you must be very quiet this whole trip. Understand?" They nodded. They understood to be quiet, but they didn't understand why they had to leave. The youngest were confused and frightened, the eldest sad and nervous.

"And when we get off the wagon, you *must* stay together. You older ones need to watch for the young ones." Then Papa pulled himself up on the front seat next to Señor Vega, and they were off.

Mama watched over her children during the bumpy ride on the back roads. Looking into the dark night, she stared at the cloudless sky with just a sliver of crescent moon and a sprinkling of stars. It seemed to her like a vast wall of sadness with small glimmers of hope shining down on them. She was determined, no matter how she felt, to try to keep a smile on her face for her children's sake, all the while pushing down her own grief and anxiety.

After about thirty minutes, they reached the deserted ranch and found the family named Lopez already there, waiting in silence. The soft moonlight gave them barely enough illumination to find their way and see the silhouettes of the others standing there. The Ramirez family climbed out of the wagon as quietly as they could and shuffled in the darkness over to where the others were standing. Papa whispered his thanks to Señor Vega and shook his hand before he turned the wagon around and left.

In hushed tones, the two families exchanged greetings. Everyone nervously awaited the promised truck's arrival, the vehicle that would take them on the next leg of their journey, one step closer to their freedom. They stood waiting in the faint moonlight, each likely trying to imagine what their new life in the United States would be like.

Emilio wondered if there would be enough work to take care of their family, and Juanita thought about the living conditions. The children were merely concerned with when they would eat next or if they would find friends.

Time seemed to pass slowly. The adults and older children were exchanging nervous looks, even commenting on their wishes for the truck to show up soon. The children were getting fidgety, especially the little ones.

Soon, they heard the faint roar of an engine in the distance. Then, the much-anticipated truck arrived. It was a dark green Buick flatbed, about seven or eight years old, covered with the desert's dust and dirt. It had well-worn wooden railings on each side with weathered canvas tied over it to hide its cargo.

The truck pulled in near to where the people had gathered, coming to a squeaky stop. The driver hopped out and addressed them.

"Everyone, I'm Paco. Let's get loaded up quickly. We don't have much time."

Paco took an old, but sturdy, wooden box off the front seat and walked around to the rear of the truck. He set the box down, stepped up on it and lifted up the canvas flap. One at a time, climbing clumsily into the back, each person stepped on the box then up into the bed of the truck. The stronger helped the weaker, especially the children, until both families were on board.

The driver secured the tattered canvas flap down over the back and picked up the box. He stored it on the front seat next to him, not allowing any of his passengers to sit up front with him in case anyone saw them.

For the most part, they all sat in silence in the back, some resting up for what was ahead, some too anxious to sleep. They sat in their cramped quarters for the next two hours until they reached their destination, near El Sasabe.

The Ramirezes had been told another truck full of people wanting to cross the border would meet them at their drop-off point, and they found it was already there when they arrived. Men, women and children were gingerly piling out of the back of it. As the Ramirez and Lopez families climbed out of their vehicle, their driver told them to huddle around him and listen up. He kept his voice as low as possible, but he was still loud enough to be heard.

"Go out into the desert. Each of you take a hiding place behind the shrubs and rocks. Try to stay out of sight until you're given the signal to run. When it's time, I'll let out a loud coyote howl. Then, you all just run for the fence as fast as you can. Don't look back – just run!"

The families quickly dispersed and found their hiding places, waiting for the coyote howl. Papa took the two younger boys and hid behind a big rock, holding little Marcelo by the hand. Mama and the two girls hid behind a clump of cactus. The older son found his own bush near Papa to shield himself.

Before long, a loud shrill howl pierced the night air and carried out over the flat land. The race was on.

They all ran with every ounce of energy they possessed, crossing the dark Mexican desert with only the light of the crescent moon to guide them. As their shoes were clapping the dry desert floor, the pounding of their hearts was resonating in their ears. Diving in the dirt for the border fence, the hopeful clawed and crawled their way under it to freedom.

Papa could see Mama and little Sofía were struggling. Sofía's little legs couldn't keep up and stumbled a few times. He worried they might be left behind. So, in a firm voice, not more than a whisper, he urged them on. "¡Andale! ¡Andale, muchachas!"

Mama firmly grasped Sofía's hand and held on for dear life, nearly dragging her to freedom as she helped her run. Papa was frantically trying to help the rest of the children under the fence before diving under himself. He made it to the other side, picked up five-year-old Marcelo, and began running, pressing the older children to get moving. "Run, niños, run! ¡Rápido, rápido!"

In desperation, Mama shoved Sofía under the fence ahead of her, yelling at her to run and not look back. Sofía scrambled to her feet and took off running in terror. Mama squeezed through and caught up with her. She grabbed Sofía by the hand and helped her run like she had never run before.

Simply clearing the fence was not enough. The U.S. border patrol could catch them and arrest them for illegally entering the country. It was important that they ran far enough into Arizona land to reach the trucks that were waiting to take them safely to their new lives.

They all reached the other side safe and sound, their hearts pounding in their chests, barely able to catch their breath. They looked around the muffled chaos to try and find their family members amidst the clouds of dust. Fortunately, they had all gotten through without being detected. There were no guards, no lights, and no dogs. It was eerily silent.

Lifting the crucifix she wore around her neck, Juanita pressed it to her lips and gave it a quick, gentle kiss. "Gracias a Diós. Gracias a Diós," she whispered under her breath.

CHAPTER 2

SAYING GOOD-BYE

CROSSING THE BORDER, with little more in their pockets than a few dollars, hope was all the Ramirez family had left. But, hope is a powerful force. It moves people to dream of better lives, and it drives them to take chances they wouldn't ordinarily take – especially when their lives are at stake.

Just a few weeks earlier in Mexico, before their dangerous border crossing, in the simple ranch home the family shared, Juanita lay coiled up in the middle of her bed in the fetal position, crying uncontrollably. She had been there for days, her body shuddering from wave after wave of sobbing.

Her young daughter, Sofía, came into her room and sat on the edge of the bed. Wanting to comfort her in some way, but not knowing what else to do, the little girl softly patted her mother's back.

"Mama, it'll be okay," she said gently, trying to ease her mother's grief. Mama continued to cry, and Sofía kept patting her back. The whole family was in mourning, but of course, Mama took it the worst.

For a mother to suffer the death of her child is painfully heartbreaking, but to lose three children in as many days is unbelievably excruciating. The days dragged on, but no one could console her. Not even little Sofía.

As she sat on the side of the bed, watching her brokenhearted mama cry, Sofía wondered when the sadness would end. It had been days, like a heavy dark cloud hanging over their home. Each day that brought another child's death heaped more grief on top of the other. The priest would stop by to offer comfort and consolation after the death of each child, but he couldn't stay long because there were so many more he had to call on.

Friends and neighbors, in ordinary times, would have come by to offer their condolences and support, bringing food for the family. But, not in these difficult times. They had their own share of grief to deal with.

It was hard for little Sofía to understand just what was happening. She remembered happier times. She wanted life to be the way it was before – days of going to school with her friends, laughing and learning to cook with Mama, helping Papa with the animals, playing games with her brothers and sisters. That was the life she loved. But those days were gone.

Almost overnight, life in their little village changed completely. Men, women, and children started getting sick – a rash, a deep constant cough, and a high fever. Many of the afflicted died right away, some languished for days. Once a vibrant little town filled with life and love, laughter and excitement, it was now a village filled with grief, devastation and heartache. An outbreak of deadly disease took its toll.

The epidemic had spread worldwide, starting in Europe near the end of World War I, killing nearly 10 million people. It was named the Spanish Flu, because it was thought to have begun in Spain.

Mexico was not immune. Likely brought in through the port city of Tampico, disease and despair quickly swept through the country, ravaging town after town. It mercilessly infected Sofía's beloved village, claiming the lives of over half of its residents within just a few short weeks.

Unfortunately, the Ramirez family was not spared. Sofía was eight years old when she lost three of her brothers and a sister to the influenza epidemic. One of the brothers that died was her twin brother, Lorenzo. As one child after another died, Emilio and Juanita suffered indescribable grief. Each time they lost one of their beloved children, it was like a dagger driving deeper and deeper into their hearts.

The small cemetery behind the Catholic Church could not contain the bodies of all that had succumbed to the influenza. The priest was overwhelmed by trying to keep up with all the deaths and burials.

Emilio and Juanita chose to bury their children on their farm. They held a small, private ceremony each time they lost one, with only the family, the priest, and their friend, Señora Ochoa. Others were busy dealing with their own dead.

Many of the surviving children were left orphaned by the epidemic, and the village elders frantically tried to find homes to help these poor children. Those that had relatives in or near the village were sent to live with them. But, for those that did not, the elders tried their best to find families that would take them in.

The Ramirez family had no family nearby. Sofía's parents were consumed with fear, afraid they would contract the influenza and die, too, leaving their remaining sons and daughters orphaned and abandoned. Who would take care of their children, they wondered, if any of them survived? Who would feed the niños? Who would help them with schoolwork? Who would help them say their prayers? Who would hold the little ones at night when they were scared? Mama and Papa asked themselves these questions late into the night, long after the cries of the dying became silent. Their mounting anxiety overwhelmed them.

One day, after toiling in the fields all day, doing his best to stifle his feelings of grief over the loss of his children, Emilio was worn out and headed to the house. As he came through the door, the younger children greeted him.

"Papa! Papa!" the little ones hollered, clamoring to climb up into his arms. Keeping up a strong facade, he bent down and hugged the children. He kissed them on the head and held them close, holding back the tears that wanted to break through. He needed to be strong for them.

"Dinner's almost ready, Papa," his oldest daughter, Maria, said. "Come on, niños, let Papa rest." She grabbed a couple of them by the hand and led them into the kitchen area.

"I'll be back in a minute. I'm gonna check on Mama."

He went into the bedroom to see how his wife was doing. She had stayed in the house, shut up in her room for days, grieving over her lost children. Each day he hoped she was feeling better and would come out and eat supper with the family. But just when she thought she was all cried out, a new wave of sorrow would hit her and the sobbing would start again. Maybe this day would be different.

He gently pushed open the door and saw Juanita lying on their bed. She looked up when she heard the door. Emilio noticed the dark circles around her puffy eyes and how her skin had grown sallow.

"How are you doing?" Emilio asked softly. "Would you like to have something to eat with the children and me?"

"No, I can't even think of food." Juanita answered, sniffling. "I can't stop thinking about the children we've lost. How many more will we lose?"

Juanita buried her face in her hands. She was weak and spent, her strength eaten up by her misery.

Emilio sat down on the side of the bed. He put his arm around Juanita and pulled her in close. The grief and constant worry were getting to both of them. She rested her head on his chest and the tears started to flow once more.

"The only way we're going to make it," Emilio told her, "is to be strong together, for the children. We'll do whatever we have to do to keep them safe. We just can't lose another child to this evil sickness."

"But there's only one way I know to can keep them safe. You and I have to keep from catching the flu ourselves. How do we do that? Tell me, Emilio, how do we do that?"

"I don't know." He paused, searching his mind for an answer. "Somehow we need to get away from here – far enough away to keep our family safe."

She knew he was right. They needed to leave Mexico, escape their disease-ridden village and try to make it into the United States. If they stayed, the Angel of Death would surely come calling again, and they could all die. If they left, at least they would have a chance to survive. But could they do it soon enough?

The Spanish Flu was so deadly that sometimes people were dying within hours of being struck with the disease. They had heard that some victims noticed a rash starting in the morning and death would take them by evening.

The difficult decision had to be made. With their welfare in mind, they chose to take what was left of their family across the United States border into Arizona, where they hoped their chances of survival were better.

Sneaking across the border was not an easy task. It could be very dangerous. Emilio knew some people who had attempted to do this over the years, but he never saw them again. He didn't know if they made it across the border successfully, if they were dead, or if they were captured and jailed.

The next morning, Emilio decided to covertly find out who could help them with their clandestine escape to the United States, trying not to draw attention to himself. Taking one of his horses, he went into town to see what information he could find.

He saw Señor Vega walking down the street, then he ducked into his cantina. Emilio thought he, as the owner of the cantina, would overhear bits of information now and then. He figured he might know someone who could help them make the border crossing. So, he followed him into the cantina and struck up a conversation with him.

"Hola, Señor," Emilio greeted the older man who stood behind the bar.

"Hey, Emilio. How are you doing?" Señor Vega was happy to see him.

"I'm getting by, but this terrible influenza is taking its toll."

"Yes, I lost my wife and both my sons." His eyes were moist and his voice a little shaky. "How about you, amigo? How's your family getting along?"

"Not well. We've lost four children. Juanita cries all the time."

Emilio surveyed the room and saw the cantina was nearly empty. He leaned in and quietly asked his friend if he knew anyone who could give him information about sneaking across the border. Señor Vega said he did know someone, his cousin, Pablo, in the neighboring village of Altar.

"Yeah, Pablo knows a man," Señor Vega told him in a low, quiet voice, leaning on the bar. He looked around to make sure no one else heard him. "He knows a guy who regularly helps people cross the border, but," he paused, with eyes as dark as night, he looked Emilio straight in the eye, "money will have to be paid."

"I understand," Emilio replied. "I'll do whatever I have to."

Señor Vega sensed the desperation in Emilio's voice; he looked haggard, like he hadn't been sleeping well, dark circles forming around his warm brown eyes. So, he proceeded to tell Emilio where he could find Pablo.

Then, he placed a firm hand on Emilio's wrist, making sure he had his attention. "I warn you, keep what I just told you to yourself or there will be consequences."

"Yes, I promise." He knew the old man meant it. "Thank you so much for your help, Señor."

"Good luck, amigo," he said, as Emilio left the cantina.

Raking his wrinkled fingers through his thick, graying hair, the old man poured himself a shot of tequila. He knew what it was like to watch your loved ones die from this deadly disease. His pain was still raw. For a fleeting moment, he thought of going with Emilio and his family. But, since he didn't have anyone left to save, he decided he would stay in the village and take his chances.

Emilio went directly to see Pablo in Altar, about an hour's ride on horseback. He found him where his friend said he would be, working at the general store, waiting on customers. When Emilio walked in, Pablo was on an old rickety ladder, stretching to reach for some spices on the top shelf.

Not wanting to draw attention to himself, Emilio browsed around, waiting for the right time to talk to him. Pretending to look at goods on the shelves, he tried to act natural. But, he couldn't focus on the labels. His mind was consumed with something else.

When the store was finally empty, he approached Pablo and told him his cousin, Señor Vega, had sent him. Emilio rushed to explain why he was there, the words spilling out quickly.

"Hold on, hold on," Pablo told Emilio, keeping an eye out for anyone entering the store. "It can be done, but it's going to cost you, and it's not gonna be cheap. The going rate is $200 for a family."

"$200? Oh, man!" Emilio said, rubbing his forehead with his hand, then running his fingers through his wavy black hair. "I don't have $200."

"Keep your voice down," Pablo warned.

"$200." Emilio repeated quietly, dazed at the enormity of such a figure.

"If you want to get to the United States, that's the price. El Jefe won't do it for less."

El Jefe, the Boss, was the name of the man who organized the escapes. Money was always paid in cash and his real name was never known.

"Do you still want to do it?"

"Yes, yes, I'll find a way." Visions of burying his remaining niños vividly flashed in his mind. "Tell El Jefe we want to be in the next group to go."

"It won't be for two or three weeks. Maybe that'll give you time to raise the money. I'll be in touch with you."

Emilio left the store and rode back to his village. The warm sun was starting to set behind him. He pondered their escape and how he would raise the money. His mind was racing. Where would he get that kind of money? And so quickly! How could he gather it without tipping his hand to his neighbors? It would be hard to keep it quiet.

The children had been especially fussy that day, and Juanita had been unable to complete her chores for the day because of her own restlessness. She was anxious to hear what Emilio had learned, questions burning like fire in her belly.

That evening, after the children were asleep, Juanita began blowing out the candles in the living area, preparing to go to bed themselves. She turned to Emilio and nervously asked him what he found out.

"The children are sleeping now. Tell me, please, what happened today when you went to town? What did you find out? You were gone all day."

"I thought Señor Vega might be a good place to start," Emilio explained. "When I rode into town, I saw him on the street, so I followed him into his cantina. He told me I should go see his cousin, Pablo, in Altar. So I rode over there and talked with him. He said he knew people and could make the necessary arrangements for us to get across the border. The hombre who is in charge is called El Jefe."

"El Jefe? Who's that?" Juanita asked.

"Pablo didn't know his real name. He said no one does. It's better that way."

"What else did he say? Tell me."

"He said it would cost us $200 to get the whole family across the border."

"$200?!" she gasped. "Where are we going to get $200?!"

"Shhh. Keep your voice down."

"But, Emilio, $200?"

"I know, I know, it's a lot of money. I thought about it all the way home. I haven't been able to think of anything else."

"How will we ever come up with that kind of money?" Juanita whispered into the darkness. The moon shone brilliantly through the window, illuminating the whites of her eyes. Emilio could see her fear.

"We'll figure it out, Juanita. We have to."

Emilio and Juanita recognized the danger of being caught crossing the border illegally – they could be shot out in the desert or arrested and put in prison. But, they were more terrified of staying in Mexico and watching their family die, one by one, from the Spanish Flu. They had to decide what was going to be better for the survival of their children.

Later that night, while lying in bed, Juanita told Emilio about what she heard in town that afternoon. "Señora Ochoa told me today that five more people died this week, some of them children. I'm afraid, Emilio, really afraid. How many more days until someone else in our family gets sick? Maybe you… maybe me? Ay, Dios, maybe another one of our niños?"

"I know, I know. I'm working on it, Juanita," Emilio countered, defensively. "I'm getting the money together as fast as I can. I don't know what more I can do. I'm afraid, too." No matter what he said, he could not calm her fears.

He hated to admit he was afraid, too. As a man, he wanted to be strong for her, for his family. He wanted her to understand he was doing everything he possibly could to get them out of Mexico soon. But, it was not an easy thing. It would mean sneaking around, selling his prized possessions, walking away from the home he built and the land he owned. But he would gladly do it for the people he loved.

"I can't stop thinking about the dangers," Juanita said, interrupting his thoughts. "What would happen to our children if we get caught crossing the border? If we get killed or arrested?" Juanita's mind was racing, playing out the scenarios of what might happen.

She looked at him through the tears welling up in her eyes. Emilio put his arm around her, and she rested her head on his shoulder. He drew her in close and kissed her softly on her forehead.

"I don't know, Juanita. I don't want to think about that. I just know our chances of dying are greater if we stay here."

He caressed her cheek in his strong hand. "We *have* to go. We don't really have a choice," he told her, looking deeply into her dark eyes.

The long day had taken its toll on him and he was exhausted, he just wanted some rest. "It's late. Let's talk about it in the morning. Try to get some sleep." And, without another word, he rolled over and blew out the candle on the night table next to the bed. Juanita agreed and closed her eyes, saying a silent prayer for sleep.

* * * * *

Morning came, and Juanita reluctantly agreed with Emilio to move forward. She had tossed and turned all night, thinking of the sweet children she had already lost, weighing the costs. Not willing to lose any more children to this disease, she told Emilio she was committed to move forward with the escape plans and to pay the fee to El Jefe.

They had a little bit of savings. Even though there wasn't a lot of extra money to be gained working their small farm, they had previously set some funds aside they had intended to use to buy seed for next year's crops. Emilio figured he could sell some livestock and farm equipment to collect more of the cash they needed. They couldn't let anyone know they were trying to amass a large amount of money or people would get suspicious and maybe turn them in.

They could not sell their farm. People would wonder why. They would just have to walk away from their home and their land.

Discreetly, and as quickly as they could, they decided they would sell off the animals, a few at a time, and persuade neighbors to buy the farm implements, but it had to be to different people. Getting rid of too much to one person would raise suspicions. They knew that eventually their neighbors would talk to each other and discover Emilio had sold his animals and equipment to each of them, but by that time they hoped to be gone.

Emilio went into town to see Señor Vega and let him know he had connected with Pablo. Emilio walked into the cantina and found his friend in his usual place behind the bar.

"Hey, amigo! Qué pasó?" Señor Vega called to Emilio as he saw him enter. Emilio walked over to the counter and returned the greeting. The cantina was empty, so they were able to speak freely.

"I wanted to tell you I talked to Pablo, and he's making the arrangements."

"That's good."

"I need a favor, though. Would you be willing to pick us up at our house and take us to the pick-up place?"

"When?"

"I don't know yet. I haven't heard back from Pablo, but I think it'll be soon."

"Yes, I can do that for you. Just let me know when."

"Thank you. I really appreciate it."

"Did you hear?" Señor Vega asked him, changing the subject. "The epidemic has already reached los Estados Unidos. But I think it's mostly on the east and west coasts."

"No, I hadn't heard."

"But you're going north to Arizona, aren't you?"

"Yes, that's the plan."

"That should be safe enough," Señor Vega said, trying to assure him.

"I think we'll be all right in Arizona," Emilio replied. But hearing this news caused a measure of fear to rise in him. He hoped his family would be safe. "I've got to get back home. I'll let you know when we need you to pick us up."

"Not staying for a beer?"

"No, thanks. Gotta go."

Emilio mounted his horse and headed for home. He wasn't sure he should share with Juanita what he just learned from Señor Vega. It wouldn't change anything, it would only add to her fears. She already had enough on her mind, he decided.

* * * * *

The date and time were set to make the escape. Instructions were passed along the underground connections to all involved. Pablo came to the house late one evening to tell Juanita and Emilio of the details for their escape.

Emilio heard the sound of horse hooves on the dirt outside and peered out the window to see Pablo dismounting. The glow from the candlelight through the windows lit the wide porch. Anxious to hear what Pablo had to say, Emilio opened the door before he had the chance to knock.

"Come in, come in, Pablo." Emilio's voice was a little shaky, jittery with anticipation. Juanita and the children heard the voices and came to see what was going on.

"Buenos noches, Emilio," he said, taking off his hat and stepping into the humble home. Pablo was a tall, thin man, clean-shaven, in his late thirties, with black curly hair and eyes as dark as the night sky. He wore much more casual clothing than the last time Emilio had seen him working at the general store. This night, he was dressed for riding.

"This is my wife, Juanita," Emilio said, as she stepped forward, "and these are our niños." The younger children were squabbling over a wooden toy, and Maria was unsuccessfully trying to moderate.

"Shhh…niños. Go sit at the table and be quiet," Juanita sternly ordered the children, trying to settle them down and silence their chatter. They could tell from the tone of Mama's voice she meant business and quieted down immediately.

"Pablo, would you like to sit down?" Juanita asked.

"No, thank you." He chose to remain standing with her and Emilio. "I don't have much time, so I need you to listen closely. The escape is set for next Tuesday night. Have your family at the old abandoned Castro ranch about five miles north of here at ten o'clock that night." The children sat silently while he talked, eyes wide, sensing the tension in the room.

"There'll be a truck to pick everyone up," Pablo continued. "Another family will be there, too. I believe their name is Lopez. The truck will be driven by one of El Jefe's men, Paco, and he'll take you to the drop-off point."

"How far away is the drop-off point?" Emilio asked.

"You'll be in the back of the flatbed for about two hours or so. There'll be another truck meeting you there with a couple more families."

"Anything else?" Juanita asked nervously.

"Make sure to tell your niños to be very, very quiet," he said, pausing to look directly at the frightened, silent children. "Your lives could depend on it."

Juanita looked at Emilio. Not a word passed between them, but Emilio knew what she was thinking. Would they all be safe? Were they doing the right thing?

"Oh, one last thing." Pablo was heading for the door, but he stopped and turned, facing them all once more. "You can't bring much with you. You don't want anything to slow you down when you run across the desert. Carrying stuff will just slow you down and maybe get you caught. You all need to clear the fence quickly and keep going. The most important thing is to get yourselves and your niños to the other side."

Pablo turned again and started out the front door. He paused for a moment and looked back at Emilio and Juanita. A lump of hope seemed to catch in his throat as he tried to speak, the reflection of candlelight flickered in his eyes. He cleared his throat and smiled just a little.

"Good luck," he said. And with that he left.

CHAPTER 3

AN UNEXPECTED LIFE

Dear Consuela,

I'm writing, mi hermana, to tell you my wife, Juanita, became very sick and died a few weeks ago. Without her, I cannot take care of all our children. Because you are family, I am sending our youngest daughter, Sofía, to live with you.

She'll be on the 5 o'clock train next Tuesday. I hope you will take care of her and raise her as your own. We move around a lot working on many farms and orchards. I will try to come and see her when I can.

Gracias, Emilio

* * * * *

IN 1922, WHEN THE RAMIREZ family had been in Arizona for almost four years, Juanita became ill and passed away. No one knew exactly what disease caused Mama's death, only that it made a difficult life only more so. The family was heartbroken, but there was little time for mourning their loss. A small ceremony was performed at the grave site, but soon after, the family had to go back to work. The crops would not wait.

Emilio stood over his wife's grave and remembered back to the night he brought her to America – the mad dash through the desert, diving under the border fence, fearing for their lives. The experience had been terrifying, but once across the border and out of danger, they were suddenly overwhelmed with a welcomed sense of freedom.

Their hearts pounded in their chests and adrenalin rushed through their bodies. They felt the joy of being set free from their gripping fear – both of being caught crossing the border and of dying from the influenza. Emilio recalled how they had all hugged each other and their children and danced around with excitement before being reminded by some of their fellow immigrants to keep their voices down and get moving up the road. The main road inclined slightly then splintered off into a narrow road. Two cargo trucks waited there to take them to their new lives.

Emilio recalled the relief he felt riding in the back of one of the trucks with his family. They were now safely across the border, ready to begin their lives anew.

Most of the immigrants who just crossed the border would live their new lives as migrant farm workers. El Jefe had arranged, as part of his fee, for the Ramirez family to work the early summer season on a farm when they first arrived. After that, it was up to them to find their own work at whatever farms or ranches they could.

At the first farm, they harvested lettuce. As the summer wore on and the Arizona sun blazed as hot as a coal furnace, they moved on to picking onions. There were long days of back-breaking work, not just for the parents, but for the children, as well. Climbing into bed at night, their bodies ached from hours of bending over. They hoped the rest would help their sore backs and leg muscles.

Living in make-shift camps, they knew they'd be moving on after the picking season ended. There were tents to sleep in, a lean-to shelter for cooking, and communal outhouses. Life was hard, but no matter what, they tried to remember that they were alive and they were together – at least what was left of their family.

Emilio remembered how Juanita tried to encourage the children with the hope that things would get better for them. She talked with them about her dreams for the future, of having their own home again, working their own land. But now, with Juanita gone, Emilio was not so sure.

A few weeks after Emilio buried his loving wife, he decided it would be best to send young Sofía to live with her aunt, Tía Consuela, in Ruby, just outside of Phoenix. He took Sofía aside one evening after work and sat with her on an old tree stump, trying his best to explain his heart-wrenching decision to send her away.

"Mi'ja, I need to talk to you about something."

"Okay, Papa. You sound so serious. What is it?" she asked.

"Mama is gone now, and we all miss her so much," he began. He wanted to explain to her how he couldn't care for all of his children – especially a young girl – by himself. But the words caught in his throat. He took a slow, deep breath and tried to continue. "With Mama gone, we'll have less money to live on, less hands to work the fields. She was such a good picker, almost as good as me."

"I can work hard, too, Papa. I'll help you."

"Sofía, sweet Sofía…" Emilio looked at his daughter's face and felt awash with sadness. She was a good daughter. Papa knew that she would work hard in the fields if he asked her to. But he wanted more for her than that. "I have decided to send you to live with your Tía Consuela."

"What?" Sofía could hardly believe her ears. "No, Papa, no! Please don't send me away," Sofía was panicked, she could feel her heart quicken its beat.

"She lives in a big house with lots of nice things. She can take care of you and give you a better life than I can," he reasoned.

"I can work. I can bring in money. I'm a good worker, Papa." Sofía pleaded, wiping her tears with her hands. "Please don't send me away!" She had just lost her mother, and now she was losing her father, too.

"She can help you with your education, mi'ja. You can have a better life, not *this* life," he said, motioning with a sweep of his outstretched arm toward the camp and their current living conditions. "Not working in the fields every day. It's for the best, Sofía."

"No, Papa! No!" She continued to cry, sobbing hysterically. Papa's heart was breaking, but he felt it was the best thing for his daughter. He put his arms around her and let her cry. He cried, too.

Tía Consuela was one of Emilio's sisters. She owned a hotel and restaurant in Phoenix. Although Consuela had lost her husband a few years before, she started the business on her own and had made a success of it. Surely she would have the resources to care for Sofía, her father assumed. He wrote to Consuela and asked for her help.

Emilio sent the letter, then took Sofía to the train station a few days later. He did not wait for a reply from Consuela. He didn't want to give her the chance to decline. He felt sure she could do for his daughter what he could not.

The Ramirez's other surviving daughter, Maria, was seventeen years old, and her father decided against sending her away. He needed her to stay to prepare the meals, do the laundry and keep their living quarters clean while he and the three boys worked in the fields. Maria was a dutiful daughter who had learned to cook well from her mother, but she thought Sofía was getting the better life and was jealous. Sofía would have gladly traded places and stayed with her family, but Papa had made up his mind.

The day Sofía left, her father, brothers, and sister reluctantly walked with her to an old green pickup truck Papa had borrowed, and each brother and sister hugged her good-bye. The separation was painful, but they accepted it because Papa had told them it was only temporary.

Sofía had filled her old handmade leather bag with her meager belongings – a pair of pants, a couple of shirts, some underwear, her mama's Bible and a hair brush. Papa lifted the satchel into the bed of the truck and helped her into the front seat.

He paused for a brief moment as he closed her door, looking down at the door handle he was holding, wondering if he was doing the right thing. Emilio knew the move was best for Sofía, but it hurt him deeply to send her away. So he decided he had better get in the truck quickly, before he changed his mind.

Papa's boots made a steady clip-clop as he shuffled through the dust coming back around to the driver's side. He climbed in the cab, forced the key into the ignition and started the engine. Sending his beloved daughter away was heartrending, he tried hard not to let his feelings show. Sofía's brothers and sister sadly waved good-bye as the truck pulled away.

Gray clouds began to form the morning Sofía left her family, and before long, a soft rain started to fall. It was as though the heavens understood the dark heaviness in her chest and the tears that wanted to flow. She looked back at her brothers and sister, feeling like a black cloud was filling her, swollen with moisture and ready to spill out. She could not hold back her sadness anymore and quietly wept for the family she was losing, the end of the only family she had ever known.

The noisy little pickup headed away from their camp, sputtering and chugging down the dirt road toward a patch of bright blue sky. Maybe this was a sign, Sofía thought to herself, a sign that she was heading to a better life.

Sofía and her father shared little conversation. Neither wanted to say what they were thinking.

He likely thought about how, if the influenza had not come to his village, he would still have his loving wife, all his sons and daughters, his farm and his friends back in his little town in Mexico. But the deadly disease did come, and he lost half his children, his farm and all of his friends. He made the difficult choice to bring what was left of his family to an unknown place and work another man's land for next to nothing. And then to lose his beloved Juanita.

If he had not lost her, he could have kept what was left of his family together. Now, to add to his misery, he had to send sweet Sofía away. But he felt he had to do it for her sake, because he loved her.

Sofía was lost in thought, as well, remembering Mama and their life in Mexico. She thought of each of her brothers and sisters, living and dead, not wanting to forget their faces. She tried to burn their images in her mind and keep them with her forever. But it had been more than three years since she came to the United States, and the faces of the dead ones were already fading.

Deep sorrow filled the cab of the truck like heavy gray smoke. Both of their hearts were aching from it. Sofía didn't want to go, and Papa didn't want to send her away. He wanted her to know how much he loved her. He wanted to leave her with some positive words to recall when she was feeling lonely. So, as the truck bumped along the rough, winding road, he broke the silence with a few words of affection.

"Your mama was so proud of you, niña," he told her. "You are such a good daughter and so helpful. She loved you very much. You remind me so much of her, you have her sweet spirit."

"I do?" His words were like warm honey pouring over a slice of her mama's freshly baked sweet bread. Soaking up the sweetness, it was like a salve to her fragile emotions.

"Yes, mi'ja. Just like her." He fought back the tears and his voice started to quiver. He could not go on speaking for fear he would break down and cry.

"Gracias, Papa, for telling me that." She reached out and touched his arm. She would remember his warm, sweet words and always hold them in her heart. A hush once more fell between them.

After traveling half of the day in the uncomfortable, bouncy little pickup, Sofía and her father arrived at the small train station, overheated and exhausted. Their clothes were stuck to their sweaty backs. Papa pulled the truck into the graveled parking area and turned off the engine. They sat for a few moments in silence, watching five or six other people walking toward the train, knowing she would soon have to leave.

The train station was not large. It was an unpainted wooden building, not more than a ticket office and a waiting area with benches along the side. The wood plank platform ran about two hundred feet for loading and unloading passengers and cargo from each train car. When Emilio and Sofía arrived and parked, there were a handful of people hugging and saying good-bye, preparing to board. They knew their time for good-byes had come, as well, but neither wanted to move.

"It's time," Papa finally said. They both slowly got out of the truck. Sofía felt a bit panicked at the thought of leaving her father, Papa just felt sorrow.

He grabbed her bag from the back of the truck, and came around to the passenger side. Sofía was reluctant to climb out, she didn't want to go. But, the train would be leaving soon, and she needed to board. Papa opened the door for her and gently helped his daughter out of the vehicle.

He looked at the bag sadly for a brief moment, then handed it to her. She hugged her father tightly, and he returned the embrace. Neither wanted to let go. But the decision had been made, and the train whistle was about to blow. Sofía gave her papa one last hug, and they said their good-byes.

"Adiós, Papa. I love you."

"Adiós, mi'ja. You'll be all right."

"Papa, I don't want to go. I miss you already," Sofía said, blinking back the tears.

"You need to get on the train."

"Papa, please…"

"Sofía, it's time to go."

"Okay," she said in a weak, shaky voice as she started to walk toward the train. Her long dark hair was braided down her back and her brown cotton dress was wrinkled from the long drive. Papa thought she looked so young, still his little girl. Turning back as she walked away, she called out to him, "I'll write to you, Papa. Write me back. Please, Papa. Please." Her tears fell from her cheeks, making dark spots on her dress.

"I promise I'll keep in touch, mi'ja," her father answered her. "I'll come and see you when I can." She continued walking toward the train, constantly looking back. Fighting to put on a strong front, a single tear escaped as Papa waved at his young daughter as she boarded the train and disappeared out of sight.

He turned and slowly walked back to the truck, his head hung down and his shoulders hunched. Pulling the door open, he slid in behind the steering wheel. Once he closed the door and was totally alone, every emotion he had bottled up came rushing to the surface. He rested his arms on the top of the steering wheel, laid his head against them, and let his tears come pouring out.

After a few minutes, Emilio heard the train whistle, long and loud, and wanted to moan in reply. He wiped his eyes with his dry, calloused hands and watched the train until it was gone. He knew it was time to return home.

The porter helped Sofía find her seat and store her bag. He was a tall, older white gentleman with graying hair who spoke some Spanish, having worked the train routes in the southwest for several years. He watched carefully to ensure no one bothered her and to see she got off at the right station. Papa would be happy to know she had someone watching over her, even if he couldn't.

Traveling on a train was a brand new experience for Sofía. She was only twelve years old and all alone. Coming from the small village, then living in the farm camps, nothing had prepared her for this event.

What would her future hold? She had plenty of time to let her thoughts wander. This would be an adventure, she told herself, a chance for a new and better life.

Papa had told her she would not have to work in the fields anymore, that she would have a fine house to live in and nice clothes to wear. She recalled how he told her she would also have a soft, warm bed to sleep in and good food to eat. He said she would likely go to an excellent school and learn to speak English. It sounded too good to be true; she thought Papa must be exaggerating.

She didn't know for certain what lay ahead of her, but what choice did she have? There was no going back. She trusted her father, trusted that he was doing what was best for her, sending her to live with her aunt. Sweet Papa. She had only been on the train for about an hour, but she missed him already.

As the train rattled down the track, she comforted herself with his words about her mother and with the thought that she would see him and her siblings again soon. These were the things that helped her get through this wrenching separation.

But as time would tell, seeing them again wasn't to be. With her father and brothers moving from place to place as migrant farm workers, Sofía would eventually lose contact with them.

She never saw her sister, Maria, again either. She learned much later that once Maria turned eighteen, she ran off to find her own life. She was envious of Sofía for getting to go to the city and have what Maria imagined would be a new and better life. She resented the fact that she was made to stay in the farm worker camps to cook and clean and take care of Papa and the boys.

But, rather than a wonderful life of privilege with their well-to-do aunt, however, Sofía would soon find herself caught in a life much different from that of Maria's imagination.

CHAPTER 4

A CINDERELLA STORY

1922, Phoenix, Arizona

AFTER A LONG AND NOISEY TRAIN RIDE, Sofía finally reached her destination of Phoenix, Arizona. The train slowly pulled into the station, brakes squealing and steam spewing out. When the train came to a complete stop, she gathered up her few belongings and made her way to the door with the rest of the passengers. The porter took her arm and helped her step out onto the platform.

"Gracias, señor," Sofía said to the porter politely.

"De nada, señorita," he responded. She turned and waved at him as she walked away, and he smiled back at her warmly. She headed toward the ticket office to wait for someone to meet her.

Sofía had never been to a large city. All she had known was a rural life. She had spent the first eight years of her life in their little village until they crossed into the United States. After the crossing, her family went directly to the farms of Arizona.

Everything in this city seemed so strange to her – the sights of large buildings and motor cars, the smells of the locomotive engines and the restaurants, the fancy clothes, the sounds of people speaking English. She stopped for a moment on the platform, drawing in a long, deep calming breath to steady herself.

"Sofía! Sofía!" a female voice shouted.

Her cousin, Olivia, stood up from the bench where she had been waiting for Sofía to arrive and quickly walked over to her. Olivia was sixteen years old, lovely and well dressed. The deep blue silk fabric of her dress, along with the beautiful tailoring and expensive lace that fringed her sleeves and neckline, was a stark contrast to Sofía's drab brown cotton dress with a few buttons in the front and a soft belt that tied at her waist. Sofía felt a little embarrassed at her simple clothing, even though Olivia didn't seem to notice.

Olivia had come with a driver, Ernesto, to meet her cousin at the train station and bring her back to her mother's home to live with them. She smiled broadly at Sofía and her voice was warm and welcoming.

"I am Olivia," she said, as she gave Sofía a quick hug. "I'm so happy you're here."

"Gracias," she replied, shyly. Looking around, she was still trying to take it all in.

"This way, mi prima," said Olivia, pointing to where the carriage was. "I know many people are starting to drive motor cars these days, but my mother won't hear of it. So, we still travel by horse and buggy."

Sofía didn't know what to expect coming to her aunt's home. Her father didn't speak much about his sister, Consuela. From the way Olivia was dressed and the fact they had a driver, Sofía thought Tía Consuela must be very wealthy. She had enough manners, though, not to ask.

The driver lifted Sofía's worn leather bag into the back of the large black buggy and helped the young ladies into their seats, Olivia first, then Sofía.

"Gracias, señor," Sofía said as the driver took her arm to help her up. She felt like royalty. She ran her hand gently over the soft black leather seat. She had never felt anything like it before.

"What must Tía Consuela's house be like?" she thought to herself. "If only Mama could see it." The thought of Mama brought tears to her eyes, so she quickly looked away so Olivia would not see them.

"How was your trip, Sofía?" Olivia asked.

Blinking back her tears, Sofía tried to compose herself to reply to her cousin. She shifted a little in her seat and turned to face Olivia to answer her. Sofía started off slowly describing her trip, not comfortable yet with these new people and her new surroundings. She felt inferior to Olivia in so many ways – her economic circumstances, her dress, her beauty. She hoped it didn't show.

Sofía even assumed her cousin was considerably more educated than she was, since she had not been to school since her family left Mexico when she was eight years old. There were no schools in Arizona for the children of migrant farm workers. But, Sofía hoped she would have the opportunity for more education while living with Tía Consuela.

"Bien...it was fine," Sofía began nervously. "I...I...I've never been on a train before. It was noisy and, um, rattled a lot. I looked out the window sometimes, but mostly all I saw was desert, you know, cactus, rocks and dirt. So, I looked at the people, wondering where they were coming from and where they were going. I sometimes made up stories in my mind of some great adventure they were on or some terrible thing they were leaving behind them. It helped to pass the time."

"What an active imagination you have, prima," Olivia said, impressed with the young girl's creativity.

Before long Sofía relaxed and began describing all the sights and people she saw and the experiences she had. She found it easy to talk to Olivia, and soon the two of them were chatting like old friends.

After about a twenty-minute drive from the train station, they arrived at their destination on the edge of Phoenix. The buggy pulled up in front of a charming white, two-story house with a profusion of blooming rose bushes in the front garden and a freshly-whitewashed picket fence surrounding the large yard. Sofía could not remember seeing anything so beautiful in her life. She realized her mouth was hanging open and quickly shut it.

As the driver helped Olivia and Sofía out of the buggy, Tía Consuela emerged from the massive wooden front door. At almost six feet tall, she was quite imposing. She wore a long, black dress with a high neckline and long sleeves. Her graying black hair was pulled back into a loose bun. She also wore a scowl on her face. Olivia's greeting at the station had been warm and cheerful. Tía Consuela's was cold and direct.

"Sofía, I am your Tía Consuela," she said, from the porch, as the girls quickly strolled up the walkway to meet her.

"You have come a long way. You must be tired. Take your things to the attic at the top of the stairs. That will be your room. As soon as you have unpacked, come downstairs and I will meet you in the living room. Be quick about it." With that, she turned abruptly and walked back into the house.

Ay, Mama," Olivia sighed. "You must forgive my mother," she said, shaking her head sadly. "Since my father passed away a few years ago, life has been hard for her, trying to support the family. It seems all the joy and happiness drained out of her when he died. My little brother, Roberto, and I try to make her happy, but nothing we do brings back her joy. I think she's determined to keep her heart shut so it doesn't get broken again. Come on, Sofía, I'll help you unpack."

Sofía carried her single piece of luggage upstairs to the attic room, and Olivia helped her store her things in the small dresser with peeling yellow paint. The sparse room was furnished with an old single bed with a tarnished brass headboard, a well-worn wooden chair and the little dresser. The thin lace curtains were dingy and the wood-plank floors unpainted. Sofía had thought her room would be nicer from what her papa told her, but this was better than what she had known in the farm camps.

"Come, sit," Olivia said, as she patted the bed beside where she sat. Sofía took a seat and put her hands in her lap, not knowing what else to do with them.

"I'm so glad you've come to live with us, Sofía. We'll be like sisters." Olivia told her. "I have to go to work this afternoon at the hotel, but I'll see you in the morning for breakfast."

"You work in a hotel?"

"Yes, didn't Tío Emilio tell you? Mama owns a small hotel and restaurant that she started after Papa died. We have some workers, and I help out, too. Maybe someday it will be my hotel and restaurant. It's not grand or anything, but we make good money from it."

"It sounds exciting."

"Not really, but it's a living. I have to go now, but we'll talk more later." Olivia got up from the bed and walked out the door. Sofía followed her down the stairs, anxious to explore the rest of the house.

As Sofía reached the bottom of the stairs, her aunt called out to her angrily. "Sofía! Come in here right now!"

Sofía suddenly remembered Tía Consuela had told her to meet her in the living room as soon as she had put her things away. She had gotten so involved in her conversation with Olivia that it completely slipped her mind.

She poked her head into the room. Sofía was in awe of the beautiful furnishings. She had never seen anything like it before – the rugs, the draperies, the crystal lamps, the plush furniture. Maybe Papa was right, Sofía thought for a moment, maybe this will be a good life for me. As she stepped into the room, she caught sight of her aunt sitting in a large leather chair, waiting for her.

"Sofía!" she snapped, and Sofía froze. Tía Consuela's frown told her she was obviously not pleased to be kept waiting.

"When I ask you to do something, you *will* do it. Do you understand?"

"Yes, Tía. I'm so sorry. I was talking with …" she tried to explain but was cut off in mid-sentence.

"Silence! I don't care what you were doing. I will not tolerate disobedience. Since you have just arrived, I will forgive you *this* time." Her eyes narrowed and her lips were taunt as she spoke. Her voice took on a slower, more serious tone. "But if you *ever* disobey me again, you will regret it."

Sofía stood completely still, her heart racing. She had never been spoken to like that before. Mama and Papa had asked her to do many things, and she did them without complaining. She was always a compliant child, always wanting to please.

"I asked you to meet me in here so we could go over a few things. First, you will help Antonia, our housekeeper, with breakfast and dinner each day. Second, you will help at the hotel, cleaning the rooms and the baths. And third, when you are not at the hotel, you will help Antonia keep this house clean when she needs you. Do you understand?"

Sofía was a little confused. This was not at all what she was expecting. She expected to be helpful around the house and do what was asked of her, as part of the family. But she never expected to be coldly treated as merely a worker, a housekeeper, free labor.

"Do you understand?!" Tía Consuela repeated firmly, almost yelling.

"Yes, Tía, I understand." Sofía knew that was the only answer her aunt would accept.

She remembered Papa saying he was sending her here so she would have a better life. Could Papa have been wrong? She missed her mother desperately and had hoped Tía Consuela would be like a mother to her. Unfortunately, Tía Consuela was not pleased that she had no say in taking her niece in, that Sofía was thrust upon her without her approval.

Consuela's relationship with her brother had been strained since he married Juanita. She felt Juanita was not good enough for Emilio. Maybe it was because Emilio and Consuela's family were Opata Indians and Juanita was Española. No one really knew for sure why Consuela disliked Juanita. But, because young Sofía looked so much like her mother, every time Consuela saw Sofía, it only reminded her of the bitterness she harbored against her sister-in-law. Perhaps that's why she treated Sofía so badly.

* * * * *

For the next six years, Sofía lived in Tía Consuela's home, not cared for as a daughter, or even as a niece. She was treated as a servant girl. In the beginning, Sofía struggled with it emotionally. She cried into her pillow every night, hoping things would get better. But, over time, she learned to accept it.

As part of her household chores, Sofía helped the housekeeper clean the house and clear the dishes after meals. She was not used to handling or caring for delicate and expensive things, like her aunt's fine China dishes and fragile crystal glassware. After all, she had grown up with heavy clay dishes and carved wooden cups.

One time, Sofía was clearing the dinner table, stacking the delicate plates, and accidentally chipped one. Tía Consuela screamed at her, startling her, causing her to knock the plates in her hands against one of the dainty crystal goblets and breaking it. This, of course, only made Consuela even more livid. Consuela grabbed Sofía tightly by her arm and dragged her out into the hallway.

"Go to your room, muchacha! There will be no supper for you tonight," Tía Consuela ordered. "Get out of my sight!"

Sofía was never allowed to eat her meals with her aunt and cousins. She ate with the housekeeper in the kitchen after the family was finished eating. But this night she would go to bed hungry.

Tía Consuela was a hardhearted woman and did not accept mistakes. Sometimes Sofía was sent to bed without supper, and sometimes Consuela punished her with a thick leather belt. Olivia and Roberto tried to protect Sofía and sneak her food, but if Consuela found out, she would punish her all the more. Sofía quickly learned to be very obedient, often keeping to herself.

One night she lay in her bed, staring at the ceiling and wondering how much more of this life she could take. "When is Papa coming for me?" she asked herself in frustration. "He promised to come." She rolled over in the bed, buried her face in her little pillow and cried herself to sleep once more.

That night she had a dream that Papa came for her. He sat on the side of her bed and kissed her forehead. "Sofía. Wake up, Sofía. I've come to take you home, mi'ja." Sofía opened her eyes and couldn't believe her Papa was sitting on her bed. She sat up and flung her arms around him, giving him a good squeeze. She felt safe and happy. As she released her embrace, he faded away and she fell back to sleep.

When she woke up in the morning, she was so disappointed that it had only been a dream. It seemed so real, like she could reach out and touch him. She got up, dressed herself, and went downstairs to serve breakfast.

With the dream still vivid in her mind, without thinking, Sofía asked Tía Consuela if she knew when her papa would be coming for her. As soon as the words left her lips, she knew it was a mistake to have said it out loud. She wanted to take the words back, but it was too late.

"You ungrateful girl!" Tía Josephina shouted at her. Consuela's eyes narrowed and her lips grew tight. "After all I do for you, after all I give to you, this is how you act?" She grabbed Sofía by the hair and dragged her into the kitchen where she beat her hard with a large wooden spoon.

That was the last time Sofía would dare to say out loud what she was thinking in her heart. She learned to guard her lips for her own protection.

Sofía washed the breakfast dishes and cleaned the kitchen. It was time to go over to the hotel to start cleaning the rooms and baths.

That afternoon, Olivia and Sofía were both working at the hotel. Olivia noticed some bruising on Sofía's arm and felt badly for what her mother had done.

"Sofía, let's take a break together."

"Okay."

"Let's go sit outside on the bench under the tree." Sofía followed Olivia's lead, ready for a few minutes to relax.

"I am so sorry for how my mother treats you, Sofía. There's no excuse for it."

"Thank you for saying that, but it wasn't your fault."

"I know. I just don't understand what gets into her. She didn't use to be that way. I've heard my aunts say Mama was the life of the party when she was younger. You should hear the stories they tell. They told me my mother had a very good singing voice back then, that she was beautiful, and that men were always chasing after her."

"Really?"

"Yes. One of my aunts, Tía Magdalena, once told me a little story about my mother when she was much younger. When Mama was about twenty, she had a friend named Petra whose husband was always flirting with Mama. Petra and Mama were down by the river washing clothes. They had a big metal tub full of boiling hot water they were using to do the laundry. Petra's husband was very drunk and came stumbling down to the river to find them. He saw my mother and staggered right up to her and began telling her how much he loved her and that he wanted her."

"Ay, Diós! In front of his wife?"

"Yes. Can you believe it?"

"What happened?"

"My mother told him to shut up and have some respect for his wife. But he was so drunk he just kept going on and on. Tía Magdalena told me this was not the first time he had flirted with my mother."

"Did he shut up?"

"No, so Mama told him if he didn't shut up she would throw him in the pot of boiling water. But he didn't listen. He just wouldn't shut up, so Mama pushed him in."

"Ay, Diós! Then what happened?"

"Petra started screaming 'You killed my husband! You killed my husband!' "

"Did she?"

"No, but he did get pretty scalded. Mama told Petra that he deserved it." Olivia giggled a little. "And she told Petra that she was stupid to care. Tía Magdalena said that one did not mess with Consuela."

"Oh, Olivia. What a story!"

It was time to return to work, but this story gave Sofía something to think about while she cleaned the bathrooms. Playing out the story over in her mind made her work less dreary. It even made her laugh a little.

Her imagination was her sanctuary. At night, when she was alone in her meager bedroom, sometimes she made up stories in her head about what her life would have been like if the influenza had not come to her village. She saw herself helping Papa in the fields, making supper with Mama, talking and laughing with her brothers and sisters.

Before the influenza epidemic, before she was forced to leave her village, she used to daydream about marrying one of the boys in her village one day and having lots of babies, just like her mama. She loved being part of her big family. Now, in her sparse little bedroom, as she drifted off to sleep, these stories in her head turned into happy dreams and she was content, at least for a little while.

Morning came, and Sofía realized once more that it was all just a dream. She got dressed for the day and made her way downstairs to help with breakfast and the day's chores. Someday, she thought to herself, she would live out those dreams, and Tía Consuela will not be there to take them away from her.

CHAPTER 5

FREE AT LAST

TIA CONSUELA HAD BEEN IN POOR HEALTH for almost a year. Near the end of her life, Sofía and Olivia waited on her day and night. Two days before Sofía's eighteenth birthday, Tía Consuela passed away. It was 1928.

Sofía tried to feel sorrow for her, as a good niece should, but the feelings wouldn't come. When she thought of her aunt, she was reminded only of the harsh treatment she suffered at that woman's hand for the past six years. Finally Sofía was free, and for that she was elated. But now what? She was exhilarated by her new freedom, but she was also fearful of what would come next.

She had thought and dreamed many times about what she would do with her life when she was old enough to go out on her own. She pondered many questions: How would she live? What would she do to support herself? Would she find love? Would she have a family of her own?

Even though living with her aunt had been so difficult for Sofía, at least she had a place to live, clothes on her back and food every day. She never had to worry about these things, and for that she tried to be grateful. She remembered her mama always impressed on the children to be thankful for what they had.

Sofía knew that once she turned eighteen it would become her own responsibility to provide for herself. She would be free to leave her aunt's house. She was excited to be turning eighteen and for the freedom that would come with it. But she was also afraid of what the future would hold for her. She wanted to talk with Olivia about it, but she would need to wait a few days to let Olivia grieve her mother's death.

Sofía wished Papa was there to help her. Often, she wondered why she never heard from him once he put her on the train, why he never came for her. She thought about her brothers and her sister and wondered whatever became of them. Would she ever see them again? She longed for them.

One morning, shortly after Consuela's passing, Olivia invited Sofía to have breakfast with her in the breakfast room for the first time. Sofía had not been allowed to sit with the family and eat a meal. Olivia never wanted it that way. It was Tía Consuela. She always saw Sofía as the help, not as family.

That morning, Sofía came downstairs to get her breakfast and eat it in the kitchen with Antonia. Olivia saw her out of the corner of her eye and called to her.

"Sofía, come and have breakfast with me."

Standing in the doorway, Sofía paused for a moment. She hesitated.

"Come, sit." Olivia said, gesturing with her hand toward one of the chairs. "Antonia," she called toward the kitchen, "please bring a plate for Sofía."

Sofía was surprised, but she happily went into the beautiful breakfast room and sat down. The room was flooded with natural light that bounced off the yellow and green floral wallpaper. Lovely lace curtains framed the tall windows, diffusing the sunlight. The housekeeper had made some eggs and chorizo with warm flour tortillas, along with a tray of fresh fruit. It all looked delicious.

"I want to talk with you," Olivia started out. "I hope you know I always wanted you to be part of the family, to be like my sister. But my mother wouldn't allow it."

"I know," Sofía said. "It was so hard, though. I was just a child when I first came to live here, and I missed my Mama so much. I still miss her."

"Things will be different now that my mother is gone," Olivia went on. "I want you to eat your meals with Roberto and me. We don't want you doing housework like a servant anymore. You're family, Sofía."

"Gracias. That means a lot to me." Sofía was astonished by this new turn of events and very pleased to hear it.

"I can't take back what my mother did to you, mi prima, but I want to help you. I know that several days ago was your eighteenth birthday. But, because of the funeral and our mourning Mama's death, it didn't seem appropriate to have a celebration. But that is the past. I have asked Antonia to make you a cake and a special dinner tonight."

Sofía's jaw dropped open and she quickly put her hand over her mouth to cover it. She was so stunned. She couldn't remember the last time she was this happy about a birthday. It was probably before the influenza outbreak when she was seven, and her mama made a special dessert for the family to celebrate. Sofía folded her hands on her lap and breathed in deeply. She wanted to savor this day and enjoy every moment of it.

Olivia reached out and touched Sofía's hand. "There will also be a guest for dinner tonight."

"A guest? Who?" Sofía asked.

"His name is Alejandro." Olivia blushed. "I met him in the restaurant a few weeks ago and he's come back several times to see me."

"Oh, Olivia!"

"I've invited him to come and join our celebration this evening."

"You must like him very much to invite him for dinner." Sofía could see a twinkle in Olivia's eyes when she spoke of him.

"I do, Sofía. Wait 'til you meet him. You'll like him, too." Olivia was giddy with excitement. "He's wonderful."

They spent the next hour or so eating and talking about the dinner that night, about Alejandro, and about what each of their futures might hold.

Evening finally came, and Antonia was busy in the kitchen preparing an elaborate meal. Olivia was in her room starting to get ready for her special guest. Her brother, Roberto, had to work at the restaurant but promised to try and stop by to have some cake with them later.

Before she finished getting ready for the evening, Olivia went up to Sofía's room. She decided to give Sofía her birthday presents early. Olivia toted a couple of gift-wrapped boxes up the stairs. Sofía was trying to decide what to wear for her special evening when she heard a soft knock on her door.

"Sofía, it's Olivia. Can I come in?"

Sofía opened the door, and Olivia stepped inside and laid the boxes on the bed.

"What is this?" Sofía asked, her brows knitted together.

"Happy Birthday, cousin!"

"Birthday presents?" Sofía was overcome with emotion. Her tears were threatening to break free. "Oh, Olivia, I never dreamed..." No one had ever given her such beautifully-wrapped gifts. She reached out and hugged Olivia, and the tears spilled out.

"All right, that's enough. You don't want to come to the party with red eyes, do you?"

"No, I just can't help it. You are too kind." She dabbed at her eyes with a handkerchief.

"I just want this birthday to be special. Here, open your presents."

Sofía eagerly opened the boxes. She found a new red dress, made of luxurious silk, and stylish black shoes. Nothing in her wardrobe was ever as elegant or expensive. She held the dress up to herself and twirled around, laughing through her tears.

Olivia had planned to give her gifts to Sofía after dinner, but she thought Sofía might want to wear them tonight, as she really didn't have any nice clothes to wear. She could see giving the gifts early was a good decision.

"I'll let you try the dress on in private, and I'll be back in a little while to see how everything fits." Olivia went back to her room to finish getting ready.

She had laid out a deep green silk dress with black lace trim around the high neckline and at the edge of the long sleeves. Olivia brushed her long black hair and swept it up into a loose bun. She tried her mother's emerald earrings on and decided they looked stunning with the dress, hoping Alejandro would agree.

Olivia was anxious to see how Sofía looked in the red dress and made her way back up the stairs. She knocked lightly at Sofía's door, trying to contain her enthusiasm.

"Sofía, let me in. I want to see how the dress looks."

"Just a minute."

Sofía opened the door and Olivia rushed in.

"Oh, Sofía," Olivia squealed, "it looks wonderful on you. Red is definitely your color. Turn around, let me see how it fits. Yes, yes, it's just perfect." Even the new black shoes were ideal, with two-inch heels that added a couple of inches to Sofía's five-foot frame.

Sofía couldn't stop smiling. "Gracias, gracias, gracias!" She gave her cousin a big hug as they jumped up and down with excitement.

"You are very welcome, prima. Now, let's go downstairs," said Olivia. "Alejandro will be here any minute."

The girls were descending the staircase just as Antonia answered the door. There stood Alejandro, handsome and strong, dressed in a black suit and white shirt. He tugged at his shirt a little and pulled on one of the jacket's sleeves. He looked like a man who wasn't used to dressing up, but he filled the suit out nicely.

"Hello, ladies. You both look beautiful tonight."

"I can see why you like him," Sofía whispered to her cousin. Olivia blushed and redirected quickly.

"Thank you, Antonia. Please let us know when dinner is ready."

"Sí, señorita." Antonia made her way back to the kitchen.

"Alejandro, this is my cousin, Sofía."

Alejandro took Sofía's right hand and kissed it lightly. Such a gentleman, she thought. Not slick, but kind and respectful.

"Let's all go into the living room," said Olivia, as she led the way.

The conversation was light and quick paced. Alejandro and Olivia described how they met and were immediately attracted to each other.

"Alejandro came into the restaurant for dinner after work one afternoon. He had gotten off work late and was too hungry to go home to clean up before coming to the restaurant," Olivia said. "Mama didn't want to seat him because he was so dirty, and she asked him to leave.

"I tried to protest," Alejandro interjected. "I told her I was starving and wanted my dinner right away. Olivia saw the argument starting to flare up and she stepped in to make peace."

"I said to Mama, 'I'll handle this. I think you are needed in the kitchen.'" Mama looked at me, then at Alejandro. She was adamant that he could not stay, then she stomped off to the kitchen."

"I told Alejandro I was sorry, but we could not serve him unless he came back after he had cleaned up. I said, 'I know you're hungry, so let me give you a couple of tortillas to hold you until you return.' Then I grabbed a couple of tortillas off the next table. The customers had left some perfectly good tortillas that would have been thrown out anyway."

"I thanked her and said I'd be back in a little while. I was grateful for the food and enchanted by her kindness and her beautiful smile."

"He went home and showered and changed his clothes. When he walked into the restaurant, I hardly recognized him. I just remember thinking he was so handsome."

Alejandro took Olivia's hand and kissed it.

"That is how we met, prima," she said.

There was a certain sparkle in their eyes when they looked at each other and shared their story. Sofía hoped she would have that someday.

Before long, Antonia appeared in the doorway and announced that dinner was ready. They all went into the elegant dining room and sat down before a veritable feast. Thick slices of savory roast beef on a silver platter, surrounded with shrimp in a spicy cream sauce, Sofía's favorite chicken taquitos, fluffy seasoned rice and mixed vegetables with peppers.

Conversation flowed easily, mingled with occasional outbursts of laughter. Sofía couldn't remember when she enjoyed herself more. She found Alejandro so interesting and full of life.

"Alejandro," Sofía said, "tell me how you came to the United States." Olivia had heard the story before, but the sweet smile on her face told Sofía that she enjoyed watching Alejandro tell it again.

"Well, growing up in Mexico was always a struggle for my family. Finally, when I was about eighteen, my papa was able to buy a ranch near Nuevas Casas Grandes, in Chihuahua. It was during the revolution, when Pancho Villa was taking land away from landowners however he could. Two different times his men attacked our ranch, trying to drive us out."

"Ay, Alejandro. That sounds so scary," Sofía said.

"It was. The second time, we were all forced to flee the ranch. I escaped into the mountains. After about a month, I came down to see if it was safe, but I was captured by some of Pancho Villa's men. They were brutal."

"Did they hurt you?" Sofía asked.

"They beat me up pretty good. Then they held me prisoner in one of the outbuildings. In the morning they were gonna shoot me."

"Oh, no. Then what happened?" Sofía was engrossed.

"Luckily, one of the men guarding me was a cousin of mine. He got the other guard drunk during the night. That hombre had passed out cold, lying against the shed. Then my cousin brought me some women's clothes and told me to put them on. I didn't ask questions. I put the clothes on and a scarf over my head."

Olivia and Sofía both let out a little giggle at the thought of Alejandro dressed like a woman.

"Sí, sí. I know. I'm sure I looked funny. But it helped my cousin sneak me past the other men, and I escaped."

"We're sorry for laughing," Olivia said. "Por favor, go on."

"I never looked back. I haven't seen my mama or papa since. I made my way to the border and crossed into Texas, near El Paso. I found work building the railroad, laying tracks, and wound up in Phoenix."

He looked at Olivia and smiled warmly. He put his hand out and touched one of hers. "Then I met Olivia at the restaurant, and you know the rest."

"Oh, Alejandro, what a story," Sofía said. "And what about you, Olivia? I've never heard how you and Roberto and Tía Consuela came to America."

"That's a story for another time," Olivia answered.

"No, no, Olivia. I told my story. Now it's your turn." Alejandro wanted to hear it again.

"All right, I'll tell you. We came to America because of Pancho Villa and the Mexican Revolution, as well. We were living in Altar, Sonora, when the fighting came to our town. Our papa had died shortly before, so we had very little protection. Soldiers from both sides would come, from time to time, and raid our town of food and…" Her voice began to crack and her eyes began to tear up.

She paused as the memories came flooding back to her. Sofía and Alejandro looked at each other briefly then back at Olivia. She drew a deep breath, calmed herself and continued.

"The soldiers would come and raid our town of food and pretty young women. Sometimes, they raped the women and left them there, right where they had attacked them. Other times, they took the women away with them and we never saw them again. Mama was afraid for my safety."

"I can see why," Alejandro said.

48

"I think Mama was so afraid for me because when I was about twelve soldiers came to our town and one attacked her one afternoon between our house and the neighbor's. Mama was a pretty big woman and fought back hard against her attacker, but she was losing the battle. Our neighbor, Señor Diego, saw what was happening and fired a warning shot into the air and the soldier ran off."

"Oh, Olivia," Sofía said. "I had no idea."

"During one of the raids, when I was about thirteen, Mama hid me and two of my friends in the packing crate of a piano for several days while the soldiers were in town. She was terrified for us."

Olivia paused again before going on, taking a sip of water.

"That was it for my mother. She decided to hire a man to get us to the United States. We left Altar in the middle of the night, without telling anyone, and crossed the border at El Sasabe. It was about 1912, I think."

"My papa used to talk about our crossing the border at El Sasabe, too," Sofía commented. "But we didn't come here until 1918, after the revolution. We came because of the influenza outbreak."

"We both told our stories, Sofía," Alejandro said, "tell us more about your story?"

"No, let's save that for another time," Sofía replied. "It's getting late and we haven't had my birthday cake, yet."

Just then, Antonia came walking through the doorway carrying a beautiful, tall birthday cake on a large silver plate, glowing with lit candles. "I think I heard someone say 'birthday cake'."

"Oh, Antonia! It's magnificent! Gracias, gracias!" Sofía was overjoyed. It had been many years since anyone celebrated her birthday. The rich caramel-colored dulce la leche cake was covered with creamy vanilla frosting, surrounded with fresh berries and topped with many candles. The lovely birthday cake was a fitting finale to a delightful evening.

Antonia set the cake down in the middle of the table. Sofía gave her a quick hug and kissed her on the cheek. "It's beautiful. Thank you."

Then Sofía lightly put her hand on Antonia's arm, a sign she wanted her to stay, and looked over at Olivia. "Is it okay if Antonia stays and has a piece of cake with us?"

Olivia gave her approval. Antonia stood awkwardly, nervously looking down at her hands, as she was a little surprised by the invitation. But once Olivia agreed, she gladly accepted.

Sofía stood over the cake, the warm radiance of the candles lighting up her face as she got ready to blow them out. Pausing for just a moment, she sensed her whole life lay before her. The past had not been kind to her, but she hoped this would be the first of many wonderful experiences in her future. She pulled in a deep breath and blew out all her candles.

CHAPTER 6

THE HEART'S YEARNING

SOFIA ENJOYED HER NEWFOUND FREEDOM from her aunt's tyranny. She was free to leave if she chose to, but for now she was content to stay. She continued working at the restaurant, but she hoped for a life that held so much more. If she was to attain a better life, she knew she needed to improve her English. She asked her cousin for help, and Olivia happily agreed.

Because Sofía hadn't gone back to school once she came to the United States, she was far behind in her education. Olivia spent the next few months trying to help her brush up first on simple mathematics, then she worked with Sofía on reading and writing English. She tried her best, but it was difficult for her and she spoke with a thick accent.

When Sofía thought her English was good enough to explore other opportunities in Phoenix, she decided to look for work outside of Olivia's restaurant and hotel. At first she was afraid Olivia wouldn't understand and think her ungrateful. But Olivia had watched Sofía grow up and understood her wanting some independence.

Sofía found a job in Phoenix at a popular Mexican restaurant just a few blocks from her home. She was hired as a waitress, where she could use both her native Spanish and try using some of the English she had been practicing. The waitresses all wore puffy, white cotton peasant blouses and colorful, full skirts, which complimented their dark hair.

Being both attractive and experienced in waiting on people, Sofía soon became a favorite of the regulars. Discovering she also had a nice singing voice, sometimes she sang along with the Mariachi band that played in the restaurant on the weekends. She loved the attention she received, and she happily worked there for several years.

Though life had improved for Sofía over the past few years, she still felt an emptiness inside. She longed to love and be loved.

When she was a young girl, her heart had been badly broken when her family members died and her father had to send her away. Then her spirit had been beaten down by her cruel aunt for so many years. She hungered for a kind, loving word during those difficult years in her tía's house, or a hug, a warm touch. But none ever came.

It was no wonder that she hardly knew what to do with all the flattery and attention she increasingly received from the restaurant's patrons, especially the men. As she developed into a woman, she became like a moth to the flame.

One young man, in particular, struck her fancy. His name was Enrique Sanchez. He had just turned twenty-six and was very handsome. He stood about five foot ten, with a slender build, and possessed the most beautiful curly black hair and hazel eyes. He began coming to the restaurant regularly, flirting with Sofía and complimenting her beauty and her singing voice. The more often he came, the more overt the flirtations.

He finally asked her to have dinner with him on her night off. At first she was taken by surprise and her first reaction was to tell him no.

She was still a little shy, as she hadn't dated anyone before. Tía Consuela had not allowed it.

But Enrique was persistent, and Tía Consuela was no longer around to forbid it. Sofía finally gave in and accepted Enrique's invitation. She made plans to meet him at a nearby café, called Maggie's, the next evening after work.

Their first date was just for coffee and dessert. Maggie's Café was known in town for its delicious pies.

"Hi, my name's Betty," said their pretty blonde waitress as she flashed a toothy smile. "What can I get for you tonight?"

Sofía and Enrique decided to have a cup of coffee and share a slice of luscious coconut cream pie.

The waitress brought their coffee and pie right away and quickly moved along to wait on the other tables. Sofía thought she was pleasant enough until she noticed Enrique was obviously attracted to her. As the young waitress walked away, he followed her swaying hips with his eyes until Sofía purposely cleared her throat. It broke his stare and brought his attention back to their table.

Sofía wasn't sure what to think of that. She had never dated before. She led a pretty sheltered life, thanks to Tía Consuela. Maybe men are always attracted to beautiful women, she thought to herself. She decided she would let it go for now. After all, this was just their first date. She had no real claim on him.

They shared their rich dessert and had lively, fun conversation. They spoke about their families and where they grew up, him more than her. She felt a connection to him.

One date led to another. Before long they were inseparable. She had not felt cared for in a very long time. There was a warmth that filled the empty hole inside her. She desperately desired the tender touch and affection of another human being.

As their dating progressed, Enrique pressed her for more and more physical intimacy. The more he pressed, the angrier he got when she denied him. She wanted to wait for sex until she was married, as her parents and her priest had taught her. But, reverting to her history of walking on eggshells so as not to bring displeasure, one night, at his apartment, she gave in to him, body and soul.

Week after week, Enrique pressured her to continue having sex with him. Sadly, she felt herself falling farther and farther back into being the weakling she once was at Tía Consuela's hand. She wanted to please Enrique so badly that she would do anything to make him happy. Sofía told herself that Enrique loved her, and this was the only way she could keep him. She began to loathe herself for what she had become.

Two months after she first gave herself to Enrique, Sofía found out that she was pregnant. She was afraid to tell him, afraid he would become angry with her and she would lose him. She agonized over it for weeks, wondering what she should do.

Night after night, week after week, Enrique would attempt to initiate intimacy with her, but she withheld herself from him because of her condition. He became increasingly frustrated with her. He was used to having his way. Unfulfilled, he started to find other ways to occupy his time.

Sitting alone in her room one night, pondering her dilemma, Sofía finally decided she would tell him. She hoped he would do the right thing and marry her – quickly.

She went to work at the restaurant the next evening, keeping an eye out for him if he showed up that night. She was intent on telling him before any more time passed.

The Mariachi band was playing and the music was lively. There was a large crowd that night, every table was full and people were waiting in the lobby. Sofía was very busy waiting on customers, taking orders and filling drinks, but she would make time for him if she saw him that night, she decided.

Since she had been keeping herself from him, he was coming around less and less. She wasn't sure how he would take the news. He had been very agitated with her lately.

About eight o'clock that evening, Enrique appeared in the doorway of the restaurant with a very pretty young blonde on his arm.

He stopped to survey the room, then he led his date over to the bar where they sat on a couple of wooden stools.

Sofía felt the color drain from her face and she felt something like an ice pick pierce her heart. Her knees went weak. Another woman? After she had given her whole self to him, totally and completely? She had given him her virginity and he discarded her like yesterday's newspaper.

This woman seemed familiar to Sofía, but she couldn't place her at first. Trying to hold herself together, she drew in a calming breath and slowly walked over to him, hoping no one could hear her heart beating loudly in her chest. He was talking to his date, smiling at her the way he used to smile at Sofía.

"Enrique," Sofía whispered in his ear, "I need to talk to you. Meet me by the kitchen."

"No, I'm busy. Talk to me some other time," he said, waving her off and returning his attention to his date sitting next to him.

"Enrique!" she insisted in a low but firm tone, "I must talk to you, now!"

"No, I said. Can't you see I'm here with Betty?" flashing his date a quick smile. "You made it clear to me, Sofía, that you don't feel the same way about me as you used to. I'll talk to you some other time. Go away."

In that instant, Sofía recognized the toothy blonde with the swaying hips. It was the waitress from the diner Enrique had taken her to on their first date. She was even more determined to talk to him right then.

"Enrique! I don't want to make a scene, but I *have* to talk to you. It's *important*."

"Okay, okay," he sighed, giving in to her persistence. Turning to his date, he said, "I'll be right back."

"Okay, sugar," Betty replied.

He eased off of his bar stool and reluctantly followed her to the back of the crowded restaurant by the kitchen. She pulled him over to a darkly-lit corner. Looking around to make sure no one could overhear their conversation, Sofía mustered up the courage to look Enrique in the eye.

"What do you want, Sofía?" he asked, irritated that she dragged him away from his date.

"Enrique, I'm pregnant."

"Pregnant?"

"Yes."

"Why are you bothering *me* with this?"

"You are the father, of course."

"No, no, no, no," he said, shaking his head.

"Yes, Enrique, *you* are the father," she said with fear in her voice, afraid of his rejection.

"How do I know that, chica? How do I know you have only been with me?

"You are the only man I've ever been with, Enrique," she told him, with tears filling her eyes to the brim. "I promise you, this is *your* baby. I need your help."

Enrique knew he was the only man she had ever been with. From the first night, he knew she was a virgin. From the way he was squirming, it was obvious he didn't want to be tied down with a baby and a woman he didn't love. He had gotten what he wanted from her and now he just wanted out.

She reached out, her hands trembling, trying to put her arms around his waist, hoping to feel his arms close in around her once more. She wanted him to hold her, to tell her everything would be okay, that he loved her and would take care of her, that he would marry her.

Instead, he firmly took hold of her arms and loosened her grip on his torso, pushing her back a little, trying to distance himself from her and the situation.

"I'm sorry, but this is *your* problem, Sofía. Leave me out of it."

"But, Enrique…"

"I'm warning you. If you try to pin this on me, I'll tell everyone that you've been with lots of men, that you are a whore. I'm outta here."

And with that he turned and walked away from her, took his date by the arm and walked out of the restaurant. Tears began to flow, there was no holding them back – bitter, angry tears. Her heart hurt as she felt it breaking apart. She turned her face to the wall, hoping no one would see her crying. What was she going to do now?

She knew she would never see him or hear from him again. Without his help, she wondered how she could possibly raise this baby alone. Would she have the strength? At least, she thought, she would have someone to love.

CHAPTER 7

OUT OF WEDLOCK

1932, Ruby, Arizona

FOR SO MANY YEARS, Sofía had been a shy, petite girl who always wanted to please. She realized this was what got her into trouble, pregnant and alone. She knew at that moment she could no longer be that girl. She recognized that now she was a woman who would soon be responsible for another life, a tiny baby who would be totally dependent on her.

There was no more room in her life for being shy or weak. If she couldn't reach down deep and find the power to get through this, she and her baby would be in serious trouble.

Beside herself with fear, she felt like she had no one in the world to talk to about her situation. She was too ashamed to tell anyone but Enrique that she was pregnant. She hid her condition for a couple more months under baggy clothing, worrying every day, praying for the strength to raise her child alone.

"What am I going to do?" she asked herself, over and over again. Enrique refused to marry her. She was a pregnant, unmarried woman who barely spoke English. She could work at the restaurant for a few more months, but soon her belly would grow too large and she would be forced to stop working. Once the baby came, she would need to stay home to care for him or her.

As humiliated as she was, she knew before long her condition would be known to everyone who saw her. When her pregnancy became public, the shame and ridicule would be painful. Before others found out, she decided to finally confide in her cousin, Olivia. One afternoon, before she left for the restaurant, she found Olivia sitting in the garden reading.

"Hi, Olivia. I'm leaving for work in a little while. Can we talk?"

"Yes, yes. Sit down." Olivia replied, as she laid her book down on her lap. She looked at Sofía's face and could see something was troubling her. "Is anything wrong?"

"Yes, very wrong, so very wrong. I don't even know where to start. I'm so ashamed, Olivia." The words poured out as she shook her head.

"Calm down, Sofía. Just start at the beginning."

Sofía shared with her cousin what had been going on the past few months with Enrique and how she now found herself expecting Enrique's baby. Olivia was stunned. This was not the young woman she thought she knew. A pregnant, unmarried woman brought considerable shame on her family, especially a family with money and standing in the community. But, she loved her cousin and was filled with pity for her. Olivia resolved to try to help Sofía as best she could.

"Let's move your things into Mama's room," Olivia offered. "Then, when the baby comes you'll have plenty of room for a crib. You can stay with me until the baby is born. After that, we'll see what can be arranged."

Olivia truly loved her cousin like a sister, and she felt sorry for Sofía's plight. But she couldn't help Sofía for the long term. Olivia had been dating Alejandro for more than a year, and they were engaged to be married soon. Alejandro always liked Sofía, but he wanted Olivia to come and live with him in the home he built for them. Consuela's house would be passed down to Olivia's brother, Roberto, so he could marry and raise his family there. When Olivia married, Sofía would be forced to find another home for her baby and herself.

For the next few months, Sofía worked at the restaurant and saved up as much money as she could. She worried every day about where she and her baby would go. "What will become of us?" she wondered.

One afternoon, Sofía arrived at the restaurant to start work and found there was a new waitress the owner had just hired. Her name was Rosa Gonzalez. She was about Sofía's age and also unmarried. She and Sofía became fast friends and spent their free time most days sharing stories of their lives and their hopes for the future.

A few days later, before the dinner crowd began arriving, Sofía and Rosa were cleaning off all the tables and chairs before the rush. They were chatting about their lives and Sofía opened up about her relationship with Enrique. She told Rosa how she met him, how she fell in love with him, and that she now found herself pregnant and alone. She didn't want to burden Rosa, but it felt good to have a friend she could pour her heart out to.

"Enrique was so handsome, Rosa. He flirted with me every time he came to the restaurant. I was flattered. No man had ever given me such compliments, and then he asked me to go out with him. At first I said no because he made me nervous."

"Why would you be nervous?"

"I never went on a date before. What if he didn't like me after we went out?"

"That's silly," Rosa said as she continued wiping down another table.

"I figured he could have any girl he wanted, why would he want me? But he kept asking and asking, so I finally gave in and said yes." Sofía wiped down another chair.

"Sit down, Sofía, I'll finish the rest of the tables. You need to rest your feet before people start coming in for supper."

"All right." She pulled out a clean chair and sat down.

"Tell me more about Enrique."

"We dated for a few weeks, and we had fun together. We were falling in love, or least that's what I thought."

"Guys like that don't fall in love, mi amiga. They make you think they love you, but really, they only want one thing. Telling a girl they love her is just a trick to get them into bed. When it isn't fun anymore, they move on to another girl. I know, I've had my share of that kind of man."

"But he told me he loved me."

"I'm sure he tells all the girls he loves them. That's how he gets them to do what he wants."

"I was so sure he was the one, you know, the one I would spend the rest of my life with. Like Olivia and Alejandro – soul mates. But when I told him I was pregnant and he was the father, he denied it and walked out on me."

"He's just a pendejo. You're better off without him, Sofía."

"You're probably right, but look where I am now – pregnant and alone." She lightly rubbed her protruding belly and a few tears trickled down her cheek. "And he's off to the next girl, probably that girl he brought to the restaurant the last time I saw him."

"What are you going to do when the baby comes?"

"I don't know. I worry about it every day. Olivia is getting married in a few months, so I'm quickly running out of time."

Rosa noticed an older couple coming into the restaurant for dinner, so she handed her damp cloth to Sofía and hurried over to greet them.

"Hello, Señor, Señora," as she nodded to each of them. "Would you like a table for two?"

Sofía got up from the chair and headed to the kitchen to dispose of the cleaning cloth. She was grateful that Rosa was willing to listen to her, but she had no more idea what she was going to do than she did before their chat.

She only had a few more months before the baby would arrive and then a month or two before Olivia's wedding. Sofía could not go on working much longer. Her situation weighed heavily on her mind every day.

The week before Sofía quit her job at the restaurant, she met Rosa's brother, Carlos, and some of his friends. They had come by the restaurant one afternoon, just making a quick stop to say hello to Rosa and hoping to get some free food. Figuring the lunch crowd would have thinned out, they thought maybe Rosa would be able to give them some beans and rice with tortillas that might be left over from lunch.

"Sofía, Sofía! Come over here," Rosa called out to Sofía, who had just come out of the kitchen. "I want you to meet my brother, Carlos Gonzalez."

Sofía padded across the room and said hello. Carlos was polite and returned the greeting.

"Carlos and his friends are on their way to Florida to pick oranges. He's always traveling to one place or another. I'm just happy to have a chance to see my big brother whenever he can stop by."

Sofía thought Carlos seemed nice, even ruggedly handsome. He was not much of a conversationalist, but nice enough. However, in her present condition, she was in no position to think about him any more than that. She thought his work sounded interesting, maybe even a little exciting. He traveled all over the country and saw different places, having the freedom to just pick up and go to some new place.

Hearing him talk about his farm work made her remember back to when she was much younger, when her family first came to the United States. She recalled the time that her family was working as migrant farm laborers and even the children worked in the fields. She remembered they moved a few times from place to place, but when Mama died Papa sent her here to the Phoenix area. That was almost ten years ago. The memories of how hard it really was, moving around to work the fields and orchards, had faded considerably. Now, the nomadic life almost sounded a little romantic.

She and Rosa saw Carlos and his friends off the next morning from Rosa's little house, where she rented a room. They left in an old pickup truck for Florida, and Sofía did not think of them again. She had more important things on her mind. The baby inside her continued to grow and time to give birth was upon her. It was 1932.

Olivia had arranged for a midwife to help with the birth at her home. Sofía's labor was short, her baby was anxious to come into the world. The contractions became increasingly close together and their intensity grew as her labor progressed quickly. She screamed out in pain as she gave the final push.

Before long she was holding her new baby in her arms. It was a girl, a sweet pink baby girl with a few wisps of dark hair on her head. A flood of emotions washed over her in waves – first love, then fear, then excitement, then protectiveness, and more love.

Sofía liked that new baby smell. Holding the baby close to her, she breathed in her sweetness. Bathing her gently, she then wrapped her new daughter in fresh linens that Olivia supplied. Sofía was determined to enjoy every moment of caring for her first baby. This child was an innocent, not responsible for how she came into this world. Sofía intended to lavish on her baby the only thing she had to offer, her love.

She named her tiny daughter Eva Sofía Ramirez. She was committed to doing whatever she had to do to provide for her. Baby Eva was completely and utterly dependent on her mother, and Sofía accepted the challenge, mustering every ounce of courage she possessed. She recognized that this little baby needed her mother to be strong, and Sofía resolved to do whatever she could to never disappoint her daughter.

Olivia did her best to make Sofía and little Eva comfortable in her mother's old bedroom. Roberto brought in a small cradle Olivia had borrowed from a friend. Sofía was very thankful for all the help and the love Olivia and Roberto provided. She decided she would not think of moving out of Olivia's house that day. On that very special day, she would only spend it enjoying her first child.

A few days after Sofía gave birth to Eva, Rosa came to see her. Olivia led her into the parlor where Sofía was caring for her infant, and then excused herself. Sofía and Rosa sat for awhile and visited, while Rosa held the baby and rocked her gently in the hand-carved wooden rocking chair.

"Have you decided what you're going to do now?" Rosa asked quietly, trying not to awaken the baby.

"No. I have no idea. I need money, and I need somewhere to live. Cousin Olivia has been very kind to me, but I can't stay here after she gets married next month. I don't know what I'm going to do."

"I wish I had an answer for you, my friend," Rosa replied, continuing her rocking motion.

They visited for an hour or so, and the time came for Rosa to leave for work. Sofía walked her to the front door and thanked her for coming. Rosa kissed the baby on the head and gave Sofía a quick hug.

"I'll come back in a few days to see you again, Sofía," she said, as she slipped out the door.

Day after day, Sofía tried to think through her situation, but no solution came to her. She knew how to work hard, but it would take more than that. What opportunities would there be for her, a single woman with a baby to care for?

Sofía spent the next few days agonizing about her impending circumstances, trying to come up with an answer. Time was running out and she was feeling desperate. She was rocking little Eva in the rocking chair when there was a light knock at the door. She was home by herself, so she got up slowly from the chair, trying not to wake Eva. With the baby snuggled in her arms, she went to see who was at the door.

"Hi, Sofía. I told you I'd be back in a few days to visit you again." It was Rosa. But she had not come alone. Her brother, Carlos, was with her this time.

"Come in, come in." Sofía said in a quiet but excited voice. She was always happy to see her friend, and now she brought her brother along, too. "Have a seat," she said as she led them into the large, elegant parlor.

Rosa followed her in and took a seat on the sofa, facing the rocking chair. Carlos shuffled into the room after them, his hands stuffed in his pants pockets. He appeared uncomfortable in such luxury. He stiffly sat on the edge of the couch next to his sister.

"You remember my brother, Carlos, don't you? Remember, he was off to Florida with some friends to pick oranges the last time we saw him."

"Oh, yes," Sofía answered, "Carlos. It's nice to see you again. Are you finished with the oranges in Florida?" she asked, trying to make conversation.

"Sí, all done," he said. "I'm just here visiting my sister for a couple of weeks or so. Then I'll be off to California soon with some of my buddies to work in the fields. There's lots of work in California all through the summer – strawberries, tomatoes, onions, garlic, apricots. We'll be working through the end of September, I'm sure. Maybe even into October with the walnuts."

The three of them sat and visited for quite awhile. The sound of voices woke little Eva, but she was content being held by her mother. Carlos told stories of many of the places he had worked and the friends he had made. The work sounded hard, but it seemed to Sofía like an adventurous life. Her memory was obviously dimmed from the time she had to work in the fields as a child.

Sofía listened intently to Carlos's stories. She was attracted to him, and he seemed to return the interest.

"Let me hold the baby," Rosa said, and Sofía carefully passed Eva to her friend. Rosa held her and enjoyed playing with her, but Carlos didn't pay any attention to the baby. Sofía dismissed it as just being a man.

After that day, Rosa and Carlos came to visit Sofía every two or three days, and the relationship between Sofía and Carlos grew with each visit. They enjoyed each other's company, and soon Carlos was taking Sofía out to eat at the restaurants and bars, while Rosa babysat.

Sometimes Carlos would drink too much, becoming belligerent and jealous. Sofía tried to get him to stop drinking so much, but he always told her he worked hard and liked to enjoy himself, that he just got carried away a little. She was so hungry for love and affection that she chose to overlook his drinking.

Sofía's mind was consumed with thoughts about her new relationship with Carlos and her impending circumstances. Her time at Olivia's house was quickly coming to an end, and Carlos's time to leave for the fields and orchards of California was fast approaching.

"Come with me, Sofía," Carlos suggested one night. "You need to work and a place to live. Come with me to California and we'll work together. You can keep the baby near you when you work, and there are houses for the laborers."

"I don't know, Carlos," Sofía answered with apprehension.

"What'll you do if you stay here? Think, mujer, what other choices do you have? Come on, Sofía, come with me."

"I guess there's really nothing to keep me here," she resigned. "I don't have a lot of choices."

"No, you really don't."

"I don't know, Carlos," she said, shaking her head, taking a deep breath and letting out a long sigh.

"Come on," he continued to press.

"California does sound beautiful and exciting," she said, trying hard to convince herself.

"It is," Carlos told her. "And the weather is better, it's not so hot. Not like here in Arizona."

"Hmmm." Sofía took a moment to weigh her options, which were not many. "Okay. I guess I'll go with you," she finally gave in.

She thought going with him to California was the answer to her dilemma, but what she didn't know was that he had left a wife and three children in Mexico. Rosa hadn't mentioned it either. Sofía found out much later that Carlos was looking to start a new life as much as she was. His inviting her along to California turned out to be more for his benefit than for hers.

The morning after Sofía made her decision, she found Olivia in the garden. She told her cousin that she and little Eva would be leaving soon, going to California with Carlos. The news distressed Olivia. She had met Carlos on a few occasions and found him domineering and a bit shady. After he would visit Sofía at the house, she checked the main rooms to make sure nothing was missing. She was not at all sure Sofía was making the right decision, but she couldn't help her anymore. Her cousin was all grown up with a child of her own, and she had to make her own way in the world.

She was sad, too, that Sofía was leaving before her wedding. She loved her like a sister and wanted her to be there. But the group Carlos was traveling with would be heading off to California in a less than a week. If Sofía and Carlos did not go with them, but stayed for the wedding, all the jobs would be filled by the time they got to California.

Within the week, Sofía packed up her things in the large leather suitcase that Olivia gave her, bundled up her baby girl and was on the road to California with Carlos and the other migrant workers. It took three days of driving on hot and dusty roads to reach the Central Valley of California.

The caravan made regular stops together and slept in cheap motels along the way, putting as many people in a room as they could fit. Sofía felt lucky that she and Carlos only had to share their room with baby Eva.

Lying in bed the first night, Sofía wondered if she had made the right decision. It wasn't like she had many options. Baby Eva was fussy and had trouble sleeping, which only added to Sofía's second thoughts. She was heading into the unknown, carrying her innocent child along with her. Only time would tell.

CHAPTER 8

THE FERTILE VALLEY

THE WINDING TWO-LANE HIGHWAY dropped down from the heavily-wooded Santa Cruz Mountains into the lower end of the fertile Central Valley of California. The vista opened up and Sofía and Carlos saw lush, green fields ripe for the picking. The workers they were traveling with had heard about a large farm in Salinas that needed field hands to pick strawberries. By the time they reached the farm, though, most of the jobs were already taken.

Next, they all drove over to a couple of strawberry farms in Watsonville, hoping to get jobs picking. But, again, they were told the farms had already hired all the hands they needed for the season.

The foreman suggested another farm outside of Hollister that was getting ready to harvest their tomatoes and onion fields and would be looking for laborers. There were also some orchards, he said, starting to pick apricots soon. Hollister was about 45 minutes away, so they raced off to hopefully beat out anyone else from taking the jobs first.

Following the foreman's directions, they reached the Williamson's farm and found there were many jobs still available to work in the fields. The Williamson's foreman hired everyone in their group, including Sofía. She planned to keep the baby in a basket by her side and keep moving it as she worked, row by row, shielding her from the sun with a blanket, keeping Eva in her mother's shadow.

The foreman gave them directions to the worker's housing and told them he would meet them there in a little while. It was part of his job to assign them their living quarters and give them keys.

The migrant workers' camp was a couple of miles from the farm, not much more than rows of shacks. The caravan took off and headed to their new home. As Carlos turned from the main road onto the driveway as the foreman directed, Sofía's heart sank. She saw where she and Eva would be living. They were unpainted, well-worn shanties with little porches and a common dirt driveway. She hoped their new home would be better inside.

As the men unloaded their belongings from the trucks, Sofía got out of the cab with Eva in her arms. She walked up to one of the shacks to peer in the window while they waited for the foreman to arrive with their keys. The windows were so dirty it was hard to see in. Hoping by some chance the door had been left unlocked, she tried the knob. It was unlocked.

She pushed the door open and looked inside. It was very sparse with bare plank floors, stained with the bodily fluids of its previous occupants. The pungent odor of urine and sweat was nauseating.

There was little more than a small living room and two cramped bedrooms without closets. Hoping for decent cooking facilities, she found the kitchen area at the back of the house had an old wood stove, a small, dirty sink, and a couple of rickety cabinets. There were no indoor toilets or bathing facilities, those were communal and outside.

Although the living arrangements were not what she was used to in her aunt's fine home in Arizona, it did remind Sofía of her humble beginnings in Mexico, where her mother and father filled their simple dwelling with love. Sofía hoped that she would be able to scrub and clean this place and make a home for Carlos and little Eva. Even though she and Carlos had not married, she was living as his wife and wanted to try to make the best of the situation.

She spent the long, hot days working in the onion fields with her baby by her side in a basket lined with a blanket. Stopping every couple of hours, she would nurse Eva and then place her back in her little basket on her shady side. Sofía tried her best to protect her baby from the heat and dust, which only added to hardship of her work.

After the onions were finished, they worked picking garlic, and then tomatoes. At the end of a long day in the fields, exhausted from the heat and hard work, Sofía had to make supper for Carlos and herself. On top of that, she still had to tend to baby Eva.

One evening, as she was trying to get Eva to go to sleep, she held her and paced around the room with a gentle swaying motion. Carlos had gone to the bar with his co-workers, so she was alone with Eva. It was in quiet times like this that Sofía thought about her life.

Working in the fields was more difficult than she thought it would be. Carlos had made it sound like an adventure when he talked her into joining him. But it wasn't an adventure, it was back-breaking. It was so much harder than she recalled it as a child. Her papa never made her work in the field all day long, not like him and Mama.

Sofía remembered her parents bending over in the fields in Arizona for hours on end, the searing sun on their backs. Starting early in the morning, just as the sun was coming up, they worked until early afternoon. The farm bosses usually let them have a break in the hottest part of the day. Sometimes, though, if not enough rows were completed, they would be expected to come back and put in a few more hours as the late afternoon turned into early evening. The crops had to be harvested before they went bad or a thunderstorm could damage them.

If Papa could see her now, she thought to herself, he would be so disappointed. He had sent her to live with Tía Consuela so she wouldn't have to be a migrant worker, but here she was. She regretted the road she had chosen, she wished she had made other choices. As much as she hated this life, though, what else could she do? That question played over and over in her mind. She needed a place to live and a way to take care of her daughter, she reminded herself.

"Carlos is pretty decent to me and Eva, most of the time," she told herself. Sofía couldn't say she ever loved him, or if he ever loved her. But she had made the decision to go with him, to share his life and his bed. She felt she needed to stay with him just to survive. She often wondered if he only wanted her there to make food for him and satisfy his sexual needs, as well as be an extra pair of hands to work the fields to earn money. They needed each other, but it had nothing to do with love.

Baby Eva was asleep now and Sofía put her down on her little make-shift bed, an old dresser drawer lined with a soft pink blanket Olivia gave her when her daughter was born. She stood over her baby girl for a moment, praying Eva would grow up and have a better life than she did.

"Sweet dreams, mi hija," Sofía said as she walked out of the room and carefully closed the door.

At the end of that first harvest season, Sofía found she was pregnant again. After work one evening, she told Carlos she was expecting another baby in the spring, and he actually seemed happy.

"I want a son," he said. "Girls are not much good in the fields. But a son, a son can work hard and bring in more money. Besides, a son will carry on his father's name."

"I can't make this baby be a boy," Sofía tried to reason. "It's up to God, not me."

"A son," he said again, as if he was giving her a direct order, and walked outside to tell his compadres.

Sofía watched him from the cracked front window. A group of men had gathered and were standing around outside drinking beer, some leaning on the porch posts, when Carlos walked out there. She watched him strut over to them, like a proud rooster. A few moments later, a loud outburst of cheers erupted, along with many of them slapping him on the back to congratulate him.

She wondered if this new baby would help their relationship. Eva was not his baby, and he often let her know it. Maybe having a child of his own would make him a better man. She hoped this baby would be a boy, for her sake and the baby's. Surely that would make him happy and life would be more pleasant, or at least tolerable.

Producing a son for him, though, was not within her power. As she told him, it was up to God. All she could do was pray.

As the summer harvest season came to an end in late August, Carlos and the other migrant workers in their camp decided they should move on to the Imperial Valley. This valley was nestled in the far southeast corner of California, bordering Arizona and Mexico. They had heard there was work there, picking carrots and helping to harvest the sugar beets.

Carlos loaded their things into an old brown truck he purchased for the trip. The rest of the group also packed up their things right away, and they all left Hollister together for the Imperial Valley.

Once again, they found work in the fields and set up housekeeping in another encampment of small, well-worn shanties. Sofía's belly was growing with the new baby, and she would not be able to work much longer. She tried to work a few hours a day in the fields, which would at least make a little more money to help them get through the winter. The rest of her day was taken up cooking, doing laundry and tending to little Eva.

Sofía tried to enjoy that time with Eva. Soon the next baby would be coming, so this time with her daughter alone was precious. She watched Eva learn to pull herself up on furniture and attempt to walk, cheering her on. Sofía would pick her baby girl up and twirl around, singing to her, dancing around the living room with her. It brought back memories of her days singing in the restaurant in Phoenix. For brief periods of the day, she could forget the hardships of her life and get lost in pure joy.

They spent the mild winter there in the encampment in the Imperial Valley and made plans to go to Ventura County, California, in the early spring, after the baby came. Again, there had been word of work there. Eva was walking now, which kept Sofía on her toes. Soon she would have two babies to take care of, in addition to returning to work in the fields.

As the time approached to give birth, Carlos became increasingly anxious. Worrying about another mouth to feed and about Sofía being less productive in the fields, he began to drink more and become angered more easily. He came home late one night from drinking with his friends, obviously drunk. Sofía had already put Eva to sleep and had gone to bed herself.

Carlos was stumbling around in the dark and yelling, "Sofía! Dónde estás? Where are you, Sofía!? Sofía!" He stumbled into the darkened bedroom.

"Shhh…quiet, Carlos. You'll wake the baby."

"I don't care! I don't care about her at all! She's not *my* baby!" he yelled in a drunken slur, trying to keep his balance. This cut Sofía to her core. Her basic maternal instincts made her want to protect her infant daughter from this monster, to scream at him, maybe even cause him physical pain, but she knew it would only make things worse. It took every ounce of strength she had to keep her feelings under control and try to calm him down.

"Carlos, you're drunk. You don't know what you're saying," she said in her best calming voice.

"I know she's not mine. You think I'm stupid?"

Sofía slid out of bed and tried to help him get undressed.

"Here, Carlos, let's get your boots off so you can go to bed," she said, continuing to try to calm him down with a soothing voice.

"That baby in your stomach, is that baby mine?" The alcohol was making him irrational and mean.

"Of course, this baby is yours. Let me help you with your boots."

"How do I know, Sofía? How do I know? Tell me!"

"Carlos, stop!" She knew it was the booze talking, but his words still hurt her deeply.

His calloused right hand quickly clamped around her small neck, and he pulled her face close to his. She could feel his hot breath on her skin and smell the stench of whiskey.

"That baby had better be mine, you whore!" he screamed, as he shoved her hard back onto the bed.

Eva was awakened by all the yelling, and she was crying.

Carlos stumbled back out of the bedroom, and Sofía heard the front door slam. She didn't know where he was going, and she didn't care. Picking Eva up, she tried to comfort her and get her back to sleep. She was glad to have him out of the house. He would find somewhere to sleep it off, and maybe he would be in a better mood in the morning.

Sofía had hoped having another baby, Carlos's baby, would make things better. It only seemed to make things worse. If she could give him a boy, perhaps that would help. If she couldn't, well, she didn't want to think about that.

CHAPTER 9

BROTHERS

IT WAS 1934. SOFIA'S BELLY was growing very large, and she could no longer work in the fields. Her back ached all the time and her feet were usually swollen, but she could not let that keep her from the cooking and laundry, or from caring for her daughter.

One of the other farm worker's wives, Fatima, had experience in assisting with childbirth and agreed to help Sofía when the time came for her to give birth. It was a relief to Sofía that Fatima lived next door and would be there to help her.

Sofía's labor pains started late one morning in early spring. She left Eva playing in a makeshift crib and with great pain walked next door to let Fatima know she felt the baby coming. Fatima immediately helped Sofía back to her own place, where she put Eva down for a nap and tried to soothe the expectant mother. Sofía's water broke and labor quickly came in full force.

Fatima stayed by her side, coaching her, wiping her face with a cool cloth, and finally assisting her with the actual birth. Labor only lasted three hours, but it was intense. The waves of pain grew closer together and more severe, until it was time to push hard and give birth.

"Push, Sofía, push!" Fatima hollered.

Finally, the baby emerged. It was a boy!

Carlos will be happy, Sofía thought to herself. She hoped this would put him in a better mood. His drinking and temper were becoming unbearable. Only a week prior, Carlos had again returned from the bar drunk and irrationally warned her that this baby had better be a son.

"What will you name him?" Fatima asked.

"Eduardo," Sofía replied, as she looked down at the baby boy in her arms. She always liked that name, she thought it sounded strong.

"Eduardo? Hmmm...I like that. It's a good, solid name," Fatima said.

Carlos came home from work later that evening, finding Sofía had given birth. He was thrilled that he had a son – a son that was truly his child. Sofía was right, his temperament did improve, at least for awhile. For the next few months, he drank less and laughed a little more.

Six months later, she found herself pregnant once again. Although Carlos was happy with the first son, the pressure of another mouth to feed drove him to drinking heavily again. The few months of calm that Sofía enjoyed were coming to an end, and she would have to endure his episodes of drunken rage once more.

When Sofía was alone in the house, tending to her two little ones, she thought about the baby that was growing in her belly. This would be her third child, and she was still unmarried. She knew she was generally accepted in the farm worker camps as Carlos's wife, but she privately suffered the shame of it, knowing she was not. At times, she wondered what her mother and father would think of her if they knew how she was living. Then the babies' cries would draw her attention back to the present tasks at hand.

Always trying to find where the next opportunity for employment was, Carlos had gotten confirmation from his fellow workers that there was work to be found in Ventura County. So he packed the family up once more and they traveled there to work the fields of this fertile southern California valley for the season.

They settled once again into the housing provided for the migrant farm workers. It was always poverty-level living conditions, nothing more. Sofía decided she could despair over it or make the best of it. She chose to be as thrifty as she could and provide a good home for her family.

She washed the dingy curtains and scrubbed the wood floors. She cleaned the kitchen sink, counter and shelves as much as possible. To save money on clothes, she washed and mended hand-me-downs from the thrift store in town. Powdered milk and large bags of dried pinto beans and white rice became the basis for their meals. Meat and fresh fruits and vegetables came at a high price, so they were bought sparingly.

Sofía knew her third baby would arrive in just a few months. She got to know some of the other women living in the complex and found one of them had a lot of experience helping to birth babies. Her name was Ysenia. Sofía felt twice blessed to once again have someone close by to help when the time came.

Her water broke a month early and the pains started within a few hours. Not wanting to leave Eva and Eduardo alone, Sofía went to her front door and stepped outside to find someone who could tell Ysenia it was time. She saw another woman she knew walking down the driveway and called out to her to get Ysenia. Within minutes, Ysenia was knocking on Sofía's door.

This time it was a long labor and a difficult delivery. Eventually, the baby's head began to crown and Ysenia gave the order for one more hard push. The baby finally made his way out and gasped his first breath before giving out a good cry. It was another boy. He looked a little small because he was early, but he was healthy.

Ysenia took him and cleaned him up, wrapping him in swaddling. She started to hand the baby to Sofía, but Sofía felt hard cramping. She knew something wasn't right in her body.

"Ysenia!" Sofía cried out in fear. "I feel like I'm still having more labor pains. What's happening?"

Ysenia laid the baby in the cradle. Then she felt Sofía's belly and took one more look between her legs. Another head was crowning.

"Twins!" Ysenia screamed.

"Twins?! Ay, Diós!" was all Sofía could say between the new waves of labor pains. "Ay, Diós!"

Ysenia continued to coach Sofía through the pains and another son was born. Both women were so stunned they were speechless for a few moments.

"What a handsome young man you are," Ysenia said to the second baby boy as she cleaned him up and wrapped him in swaddling, as well. She gave the babies to Sofía, one at a time, to nurse. Sofía was in shock. First her water had broken a month early, and then the surprise of two babies instead of one. With Ysenia's encouragement, she was eventually able to cradle the first son and began to nurse him.

"Are you doing okay, Sofía?" Ysenia asked her. "You look exhausted and you had, well, quite a surprise." Ysenia started cleaning up the rags and bowl.

"I shouldn't have been surprised. I am a twin, and twins do run in my family." Her words were soft and she was getting drowsy. "I just had no reason to think…" She grew very quiet. Ysenia turned back to her and noticed Sofía had fallen asleep. So she took the baby out of his mother's arms and put him down to sleep.

When Carlos returned home from work about an hour after the delivery, Ysenia met him at the door. Carlos was a little startled by her at first, but he knew it meant the new baby had come.

"Sofía went into labor today…" she started to say.

"Is it a boy?" Carlos asked excitedly.

"Well, yes and no," Ysenia answered.

Surprised by her answer, he didn't know what to think.

"What do you mean – yes and no? What kind of foolishness is that?" Carlos sounded irritated by her response.

"What I mean is that you do have another son. In fact, you have two more sons. Twins!"

His eyes got as big as saucers. His heart started to pound. He was excited and terrified at the same time. He felt weak in the knees and grabbed a chair to sit down and catch his breath for a minute. Two more mouths to feed now, he thought to himself. Where will the money come from? He was starting to panic, his mind was racing.

Ysenia watched him for a moment, her brows knitting together in a frown. "Don't you want to see your sons?"

He looked at her blankly. Then he ran his hand over his face as if to wake himself up from a dream and remembered that he had new sons – two more sons! He got up from the chair and rushed into the bedroom to see his new sons. "Ay caramba!" was all he could say, with a look of shock and panic on his face.

They named the boys Arturo and Alfredo. Now they were a family of six. Eva was four by this time and Eduardo was almost two. Sofía had her hands full with all the young ones, taking care of them all by herself. Carlos was no help with the children, he was often at the bar when he was not at work. The burden to feed and raise four children was ever-present. Because of that pressure, the family almost lost little Alfredo.

Carlos was happy about having two more sons, but soon that excitement turned to worry. There were two more children to support, to feed, and to clothe. Work had been leaner than usual, and money was tight, very tight. Over the ensuing months, worry turned to stress, which turned to desperation.

When the twins were about nine months old, Carlos found out that another farm worker in the camp and his wife couldn't have children, and his wife badly wanted a baby. To ease some of the financial pressure, Carlos started thinking maybe he could give her one of his baby boys. When he came home from work one night, during supper, he told Sofía about the childless couple. He suggested to her that they give one of the twins to them.

"We don't have enough money to feed all these kids, Sofía. I think we should give one of the twins to Imelda and David to raise."

"What!?" Sofía was shocked. "Give away one of my babies? No, Carlos. Por favor, no." How could a mother give up one of her own children? This was unthinkable to her.

"Don't ask me to do that, Carlos," she told him, shaking her head, panicking at the thought of it. "I can't do that. No, I can't do that." She resisted the idea. But Carlos pushed hard, strongly insisting, reminding her that he was the head of the house. She got up from the table and tried to walk away. She couldn't listen to any more of this.

"Listen to me, you worthless woman," he growled at her, as he grabbed her hard by her arm. "You *will* do as I say, you hear? We just can't afford to keep all these kids!"

Yanking her arm free, she looked at all her children. The babies couldn't comprehend what their parents were saying, but Eva was old enough to understand. She sat at the table, very still, afraid of her angry father. She had heard him say he wanted to give away one of her brothers. When will he want to give me away? she thought.

Sofía looked at little Eva and felt badly that she had to witness this argument. She could see her daughter was frightened. Why did Carlos have to bring this up in front of the children? she wondered to herself. She dared not say it out loud.

Yes, she knew that finances were extremely tight, and she also knew Carlos would not relent. What she didn't understand, though, was how he could be so cruel to make her give away one of her children – one of *their* children. They obviously didn't mean as much to him as they did to her, she told herself. She could see she was not going to win this fight, because she never did.

She reluctantly gave in, tears streaming down her cheeks. She felt backed into a corner with no way out except to give in. So, she finally agreed to let Imelda raise Alfredo. They would keep Arturo. They didn't choose to keep Arturo over Alfredo for any particular reason, just a flip of a coin.

The next morning, while Alfredo was asleep in her arms, she walked alone to Imelda and David's home, about a half a mile away in another migrant camp. Carlos stayed home with the other children. He had already told David that Sofía would be coming over with the baby.

Sofía knocked on the door and the couple opened it.

"I'm Sofía. Carlos told me you want to have children very badly but you're not able to."

"Yes, that's right," Imelda said. "Come in."

"No, I can't." Sofía needed to leave quickly before she would begin to cry.

She kissed the baby on the forehead and handed him over to Imelda. "This is Alfredo." Sofía's chest was tight as she fought back her tears. "I hope you'll be a good mother and love him and care for him like I would."

"Yes, Sofía, we will," David replied.

Sofía turned and walked away. She cried all the way home.

There was a profound sadness that settled over Sofía because of the loss of her son. She found herself crying several times throughout the day as she thought of Arturo's soft dark hair, his inquisitive brown eyes, his little crooked smile. Little Eva would ask her what was wrong, but Sofía would change the subject and get Eva's attention on something else. Each night she would cry herself to sleep thinking about her lost son.

Carlos saw Sofía's tears every day, and it filled him with guilt. She hardly spoke to him anymore unless she had to. His pride would not let him admit that he had made a mistake. And now Alfredo was gone. He had given his son away, and he couldn't take him back without being humiliated.

A couple of months later, Sofía decided to go and check on Alfredo and see how he was doing. She got a neighbor to come and watch the children while she went for her visit.

She hadn't told Imelda she was coming, she just showed up at her door unannounced. Imelda sheepishly let her in, and Sofía looked around the sparsely-furnished place. It was tidy, but she didn't see a crib or a cradle anywhere.

"Where is Alfredo?" Sofía asked, suspiciously.

"I'll get him," Imelda said. She looked a little embarrassed and quickly left the room. So, Sofía, close on Imelda's heels, followed her to the bedroom. She saw Imelda pull a box out from under the bed and her sweet little baby boy was lying in the box with a blanket under him, sleeping soundly.

He had skinny arms and legs and a bloated belly. She would later find that the baby had rickets, a disease caused by malnourishment. Enraged by what she saw, Sofía angrily pushed Imelda aside and scooped up her son, blanket and all.

"No, no, no, no!" Sofía kept saying, shaking her head. She bundled him up and stormed out of the bedroom. Sofía did not stop to think about what Carlos would have to say about this. She didn't care if money was tight. This was her son, and there was only one thing she could do – she had to rescue him.

She stopped at the front door and turned to look Imelda in the eye. "You will never see this child again, estúpida! Maybe God didn't give you a child of your own for a reason!"

Sofía was fuming mad as she walked back home, carrying her poor sickly son. She knew Carlos would not be happy she brought the baby back home, defying his wishes. But she knew she had to stand her ground on this, no matter what it cost her.

That evening, when Carlos came home from work, he saw that Alfredo was back. His temper started to flare.

"What have you done, woman?!" he shouted.

"I went to see Alfredo today, to see how he was doing," she quickly tried to explain. "I found him in a box under the bed. Under the bed, Carlos!" She showed him what Imelda had done to his son, the skinny arms and legs and bloated belly.

"She was starving him, and who knows what else," Sofía continued. "I couldn't leave him there. I just couldn't."

Carlos was furious. But not at Sofía this time, for a change, he was angry at Imelda and David. Still worried about how he would provide for this child, he agreed Sofía had done the right thing. Somehow they would get by.

* * * * *

Time passed and life continued to be difficult. A couple of years later they returned to Hollister, where they knew work would be plentiful. It was 1939.

After the twins, Carlos and Sofía had another son, Ygnacio. There were now five kids in all - Eva and the four boys. Because the family was growing, they decided to stay put in Hollister for awhile.

Carlos found them a small, old house in town that he rented. It was only slightly better than the shacks they were used to. The house had only one bedroom, where Carlos and Sofía slept. The children shared a room that was originally intended to be used as the living room. It had one big, old brass bed in it and one small wooden dresser. All five children slept in the one bed in the beginning and shared the single dresser.

Eventually, when Eva was about nine, she couldn't stand sharing the bed with her four brothers anymore. So, with only a mat and a small, thread-bare blanket, she made her bed on the floor near the front door.

There was also a long, narrow room that served as a dining area and a rudimentary kitchen at the far end. The kitchen had an old wood stove, a small sink, and one old cabinet with peeling yellow paint. Left by the previous tenants, there was also an old work table for preparing food, very well-worn but still serviceable.

The ramshackle old house had wooden floors with gaps between some of the boards and no rugs to cover them. In the winter or on windy days, the family could feel the cold air coming through the cracks. On the walls was faded, peeling wallpaper and most of the windows had cracked glass and torn screens. For what little rent they were paying, the landlord refused to do any repairs.

Since Eva was the oldest child, she was expected to help care for her younger siblings. She was often feeding them, changing their diapers, and helping Mama with the cooking and household chores. There was a new baby every year or two, so there were lots of dirty diapers to wash.

During the warmer weather, Mama had a tub she filled with soap, water, heated stones and a grate. Another tub was also filled with water for rinsing. In the winter, doing laundry was a lot more challenging. On mild days, it could be done outside. But on very cold days, it would have to be done inside and only those items that were absolutely necessary, like dirty diapers.

Eva and Mama would ring and squeeze out as much water as they could with their hands and hang the laundry on the clothes line to dry. As a child, Eva's hands and arms would become very tired and achy following an afternoon of doing the laundry, not to mention her back. But over the years, she became stronger and eventually was able to keep up with Mama.

Between caring for her younger brothers and working in the fields, there was not much time for Eva to just be a child. Responsibility was thrust on her early, and she often felt like she would never be free of it. Mama needed help with the babies and the housework, and Papa needed her help in the fields. Day after day, year after year, hard work was her constant companion. Sometimes she just wanted to be a child, carefree and happy. She was only seven years old.

Eva's whole young life had been centered around her family and trying the best she could as a child to help them survive. The time had come for her to be able to go to school.

Spanish was the only language Eva had ever spoken. Her mama had learned some English from her cousin, Olivia, but she couldn't use it. Papa wouldn't allow English to be spoken at home. So, Eva didn't learn English until she started school. Mama enrolled her in the first grade at the Catholic school.

To enroll in school, Eva needed to have her birth certificate. Mama had to make a special trip to town, to the county clerk's office, to ask them to order a birth certificate from the county in Arizona where Eva was born. She paid a fee of $1.00 to order it, which she had secretly saved from her grocery allowance. The young woman with auburn hair behind the counter told Sofía it would take a few weeks, and since she had no telephone, she would need to come back and check to see if it had come.

Three weeks later, Sofía again visited the county clerk's office and waited her turn in line. A middle-aged white woman with short wavy dark hair walked up to the counter and asked, "Who's next in line?" Sofía stepped forward and asked if the birth certificate had arrived. She checked the file drawer and pulled out a manila envelope. She handed it to Sofía.

Sofía took it out of the envelope and handed it back to the woman. She asked the clerk, in her broken English, to read it over to make sure it was right.

"Oh, no!" the clerk gasped, pushing her glasses farther up on her nose as she looked intently at the certificate. "This says that Eva was 'stillborn'."

"Stillborn?" Sofia asked, not understanding what that meant.

"That means she was born dead. See, right here." She turned the certificate to face Sofia and pointed at the word.

"No, no, no. No es posible," Sofía argued, shaking her head.

"It says so right here," the clerk said, again pointing to the word 'stillborn.'

"What do we do now?" Sofía asked.

"You'll have to prove it's wrong and pay another fee to get it corrected, Ma'am, and then get another certificate," the clerk told her.

"No, no. No more money." There was no more money she could pay. Maybe no one will notice, she thought.

Mama took Eva's birth certificate back from the woman and left. She then took the certificate to the school's office and got her daughter enrolled. She was right, no one noticed, which was an enormous relief to Sofía. Just the fact that she had an official-looking document with Eva's name on it was enough.

Eva attended the small Catholic school in Hollister with some children from town and a few of the children of other farm workers. Eva felt lucky Mama pushed Papa to allow her to go to school. Not all of the migrant workers allowed their children to go to school, whether public school or Catholic school. Many of them preferred that their children work in the fields and the orchards so the family would have enough money to live on. They kept them out of school as long as possible, moving from farm to farm, until someone noticed and called the authorities.

Because Eva was already seven, she missed kindergarten and went directly into the first grade. The first year of school was very difficult for her. It was hard enough for a seven-year-old to try to learn to read and write, but she also had to learn a new language at the same time. Eva, fortunately, was a bright girl and after a rough beginning eventually caught up and did well.

Her teacher, a nun, from the very beginning expected Eva to stand in front of the class and read "Fun with Dick and Jane" like the other students. When she couldn't read it, the nun would swat her hard with a long pointer and send her back to her seat. Eva didn't even know how to sit at her desk properly, she straddled it. Of course, the other kids laughed at her, and she was embarrassed.

With a great deal of effort on her part, Eva quickly learned to read because she was afraid of the nuns and because she wanted to stop the constant embarrassment. She concentrated on watching the other kids read, and she memorized what they were saying. The words on the pages soon started to make sense. But, because the nuns were so mean and there was a financial cost for attending the Catholic school, Mama decided to take Eva out and enroll her in public school.

Eva's new teacher, Miss Morimoto, was a welcome change from her old teacher. Miss Morimoto did her best to open the minds of her students to all kinds of possibilities by showing them photos of other countries and other people. She talked with them about all the different kinds of jobs available out in the world, encouraging them to think about what they might like to become one day when they grow up.

She knew most of these children came from poor families, many of them farm workers. Without her encouragement to read and learn about life outside of their limited existence, she believed they wouldn't have much of a future.

As time went on, Eva found she loved to read and learn, especially science. She began to see there was a glimmer of hope for her, that she could have a better life than what she had now, she could have more than Mama had. Possibly she could be a teacher or maybe even a nurse. Sofía encouraged Eva to learn all she could, that she could become whatever she set her mind to be.

After school, Eva always came home and changed into her tattered play clothes, then helped her mother with the babies and with supper. They never had much, but they always had food to eat.

Sofía continued to be thrifty and was careful to always buy in bulk. She bought large sacks of flour, rice and beans, as these were staples in their diet. When there was a little extra money, she stocked up on things like canned milk, tomato sauce, spaghetti and macaroni. She also canned rabbit and fruit, when it was available.

Mama even made jerky when Carlos went hunting and brought home an animal he had killed. She would flavor the jerky with spices and place it on the clothesline to dry, covering it with cheesecloth.

At times, they had chickens running free in the yard. Mama would send the older children to catch a chicken for dinner sometimes. Eva and her brothers would chase the chickens around the yard until they wore one of them down and they could catch it. Mama would break its neck and put it in a pot of hot water to make it easier to pluck its feathers.

Sofía could make a piece of steak go a long way, and round steak and gravy was one of the family's favorite dishes, especially when she made hot biscuits from scratch to go with it. Times were tough, and the family didn't eat like people who had money, but Mama always did her best to make sure her family was well fed. There was no sliced white bread or creamy whole milk for the Gonzalez family, but they always had enough food to eat.

As children do, Eva and her siblings found ways to entertain themselves. Sometimes they challenged each other to foot races in the yard or on the street when there was no traffic in the evening. They had marbles to play with and sometimes they played "kick the can" to see whose aluminum can would go the farthest.

Somehow, as they got a little older, they managed to lay their hands on an old bicycle, and they would all take turns riding it. Once, they even built a scooter using two wooden fruit boxes and wheels they had rescued from someone's trash.

When they were younger, they sat on the wooden floor next to their parents' bed and listened to the old radio. The children sat in awe, listening to the adventures of Red Ryder, the Lone Ranger and The Shadow before going to bed. This was their nightly escape from their hard life. Papa was usually gone to town in the evenings, and Mama was busy catching up on housework or tending to a baby. The stories were so exciting to the children that they sometimes carried the adventures to bed with them in their heads, playing them over and over in their minds as they drifted off to sleep.

They were happy when they were playing, as most children are. But once Carlos came home, the mood quickly changed to somber. Neither Mama nor the children ever knew what kind of mood he was in or how he was going to act. They all tried to stay out of his way as much as they could. He only needed the slightest provocation for one of them to receive a slap or a punch, maybe even drawing his ire to use his leather belt or a switch from the nearest tree.

Carlos's punishment of choice was whipping the children with his leather belt or a green switch. A switch was a small branch Carlos made the offending child cut down from a locust tree in their yard for him to use on them. He or she was not allowed to scream or cry, just take the beatings in silence or the punishment would be worse.

Eva counted the days until she could be free of Carlos. She saw children at school every day that did not have to endure the life she and her brothers did. Her father's abuse made her more and more determined to find a way to escape her dire situation and make a better life for herself.

This determination is what sparked hope in her, and that hope helped her get through each difficult day. One day she would be free from that cruel man, she told herself, just like her mother had gotten free from Tía Consuela. But Eva hoped she would not make the same mistakes her mother did that trapped them all in their miserable circumstances.

CHAPTER 10

THE SECRET

THOUGH SOFIA LOVED all her children equally, she knew that Carlos always favored his first-born son, Eduardo. Second to Eduardo, he treated the other boys equally. But he never gave any kind of positive attention whatsoever to Eva. He rarely even spoke to her unless he was ordering her to do something or calling her a fat cow if he thought she was being lazy.

Carlos never accepted Eva as his daughter, and he consistently treated her differently from the other children. He only saw her as another pair of hands to work, which was helpful to him, yet another mouth he had to feed. Sometimes Sofía and Carlos would argue over how he treated Eva, and Carlos would get so angry he would slap or back-hand Sofía. Eva witnessed the arguments and the abuse, but she didn't understand it.

"It's the drink," she told Eva, "that often causes him to take his anger out on me and you children."

"But it's not right, Mama."

"Just do as he asks, mi'ja, and stay out of his way," Mama advised.

They couldn't get through the day or have a peaceful meal without somehow making Carlos mad. Then someone would pay.

Even though they lived in town and had close neighbors, no one ever reported any spousal or child abuse to the authorities. Eva wondered why the teachers ignored the children's bruises and never reported them. Sofía and her children were trapped, without hope.

Then another daughter was born. They named her Lydia. She became the apple of Carlos's eye. She could do no wrong. Eva didn't understand why her papa loved Lydia and not her. One day, when she was twelve years old, she learned why her papa never loved her.

* * * * *

It was a hot, humid Sunday afternoon in the late spring of 1944. Carlos had been drinking out in the backyard, and Eva caught his ire. The back door of their rundown little house quickly creaked open and Eva ran in.

"Mama!" The girl called out in a weak, pained voice.

Mama looked up from her cooking, a baby on her hip, and pulled out a chair for Eva. "What's wrong?"

"Papa. He whipped me again," she cried. Tears from her muffled cries, mingled with dirt, were caked on her cheeks.

"Come, sit." Eva sat down and bent forward. Pulling up the back of Eva's shirt with one hand, Mama surveyed her injuries. "No blood this time, mi'ja, just welts. But I'll get some salve. It'll make it feel better. I think there's some in the bathroom."

Sofía didn't ask what happened, she didn't need to. She already knew. Papa had just whipped the girl again in the backyard with a green switch from their elm tree. Sofía had heard nothing because Carlos warned the girl that if she cried he would beat her harder.

Looking out the cracked kitchen window, Sofía saw Carlos in a dirty T-shirt and work pants sitting on an old tree stump, opening another bottle of beer. The green switch lay on the ground by his feet. It was late afternoon and, from the number of empty bottles on the ground around him, she knew he already had a few.

As Sofía watched him, her face grew red and hot with anger and frustration. She loathed this prison of fear in which he held them all captive, but she was helpless to break free.

She didn't bother to ask her daughter what set him off this time because it didn't matter anymore. Carlos always had plenty of excuses – she didn't move fast enough, she was in his way, she forgot to do something he had ordered her to do, she looked at him the wrong way – the list went on. It never took much to get him started.

"I don't understand, Mama," Eva said as she wiped her eyes with her hands. "Why does he hate me so much?"

Mama turned away from the window and handed her daughter a damp kitchen towel to wipe her face. Then she set the baby down in the old wooden high chair.

Sofía knew the day was coming when she would have to tell Eva the truth about Carlos, but she thought she would have more time. Eva was only twelve. Mama hoped for a few more years, but Eva was asking questions and it could not be put off any longer.

"I didn't want to tell you until you were older, mi'ja, but I guess it's time." Sofía hoped she could spare her innocent young daughter from the truth of her mother's indiscretions.

"Tell me what, Mama?" Eva sat up straight in the chair and her attention was riveted on Sofía's next words.

"I'm so ashamed, niña." Sofía felt heat rising in her face and couldn't look Eva in the eye. She looked down at the floor, then at her hands, wiping them on her worn apron.

"I didn't want you to know, but I suppose it's really better that you do."

"Know what, Mama?" Eva insisted.

"Papa…well…" she paused, wringing her hands, struggling to find the words. "Well, he's not your real father," Mama blurted out, embarrassedly.

"What? What do you mean?" Eva was stunned and trying to understand what her mama was attempting to tell her.

"I was with another man before I met Carlos. His name was Enrique. He was your father, mi'ja. Please forgive me." Sofía's voice was shaking, her eyes swimming with tears.

"Yes, Mama, I forgive you. But I want to know more."

"It's a long story, mi'ja." Sofía just wanted this conversation to be over.

"Tell me, Mama," Eva pressed.

"No, niña, I'll tell you more about it when you're older." Sofía couldn't look at Eva and her words were quick. "But for now, that's all I'm going to say." Then she hurried off to the bathroom to find the salve.

From that day on, Eva never called Carlos her "Papa" again.

Even though she was surprised to learn the man she always thought was her father was not, she was glad that now she understood why he treated her like he did. She realized she had done nothing to cause his hatred and cruelty toward her, and there was nothing she could do to change it.

Although Eva appreciated her mama telling her the truth about Carlos, she knew it meant she would never know her real father. At first she was sad about that, but somehow this new revelation set her free. She no longer felt an obligation to love Carlos simply because he was her father. She no longer desired his love or approval. For her mother's sake, though, she would not disrespect him because she never wanted her mother to be ashamed of her. So, she continued to be an obedient and helpful child.

CHAPTER 11

AN UNFORTUNATE UNION

ON OCCASION, CARLOS ALLOWED Sofía to go into town to do some shopping or go to mass at the Catholic Church. She always tried to take Eva with her, giving them a little time together and showing her daughter there was more in the world than farm work and house work. They usually had to bring the youngest with them, little baby Lydia.

Attending mass gave Sofía a break from the brutality of her life and the constant responsibilities of all the children. She could sit in peace and quiet for awhile, praying and thinking, surrounded by the beauty of the stained glass windows, candlelight and soft music. The baby slept, and Eva sat quietly beside her in the wooden pew.

Being at mass, listening to the priest and the choir, also reminded Sofía that she and Carlos were not legally married, which filled her with guilt and shame. She had been living as Carlos's wife for twelve years now, and they had many children together.

Surely in God's eyes we must be married, she often told herself, trying to justify her marital situation. But, when she went to mass, just being in the sanctuary reminded her that she was not married in the eyes of the Church. And at confession, she was painfully aware that the priest knew she had many children with a man to whom she was not married. Even though Father Marcelo tried to be kind and understanding of her situation, she knew he disapproved of her sin.

After mass, she and her girls went to several stores for their shopping. Sofía was acquainted with some women in the Hispanic community, wives of other farm workers, neighbors, women who also attended mass sometimes, and women who worked in the stores she occasionally shopped in. Many of them knew that she and Carlos were not married, and she could feel their obvious disapproval.

"So many children and they've never married." "Who does she think she's fooling?" "Why won't that man marry that poor woman?"

Many of the women would whisper behind her back or as she walked by. Some were even so bold as to say out loud what they were thinking, as if they were only talking to themselves or to each other, but certainly intended for Sofía to hear. She knew what they meant, and it cut through her like a sharp knife. In her heart she felt that she was Carlos's wife, after all the years they have lived together and the many children they share. But she understood that in the eyes of the Catholic Church and other people who knew them, they were not married.

Occasionally, if Carlos was in one of his rare good moods, Sofía would venture to bring the subject up. Late one Saturday morning, he had just gotten up and wandered over to the dining table. He hadn't gone out drinking the night before because he worked late into the evening and his boss had given him a cash bonus for staying late. Sofía set down before him a good breakfast of chorizo, fried eggs and fresh tortillas. He cleaned the plate and was feeling relaxed and satisfied.

"Carlos, don't you think it's time we get married?" she asked, in as sweet a voice as she could possibly speak.

"What for?" he asked, starting to get irritated. "We've been together a long time, and we have all these kids," he said, motioning with his hand to the children playing on the floor. "I don't know why we need to do that." He always dismissed the idea whenever she brought it up.

"But Carlos, you don't have to face the priest and see what he's thinking. I feel so ashamed in front of him," she said as she poured him another cup of coffee.

"Then don't go to church. You don't *have* to go." Carlos truly wished she would stop going, then maybe she would stop bringing up the subject of marriage.

"And the women in town, they're always whispering behind my back when I'm shopping. Sometimes they just come right out and say things."

"What kind of things?" he asked, as she sat down across the table from him.

"Things like, 'Don't you think it's time you get married, Sofía, with all those children you have? All those illegitimate children?'"

"It's none of their business! We don't need to stand before some stupid priest and say some stupid words so everyone else feels better." He was starting to get angry now. To him, she was already his wife, end of story. Sofía could see it was time to drop the subject, for now.

A few weeks later, Carlos and Sofía were invited over to the modest home of one of Carlos's drinking buddies for a party. There would be plenty of food, drinking and music, Carlos was told. He was looking forward to it, and Sofía was expected to come along.

Carlos waited with excitement for the party so he and his friends could let loose and have a good time, drinking, playing their guitars or bongos, and enjoying the music and singing along. The men in Carlos's circle, mostly other farm workers, lived in a culture of male dominance and a party was one place they could display it.

Sofía, on the other hand, knew it would just be another opportunity to wait on the men. At social gatherings, like this party, the women were expected to stay out of the way unless they were waiting on the men, bringing them another beer or tequila or something to eat.

Sofía never really had close friends, Carlos didn't allow it. But she did have some acquaintances, women she knew in circumstances similar to hers. Some of these women would be at the party, and they would be expected to do their part, as well, and help keep the food and drinking coming. They would also be expected to do the clean up. Like Sofía, the women were often just kept around to do the cooking and cleaning, and to be a warm body in their man's bed. If there was love, it was a bonus.

Eva watched the younger children while the parents went to the party. She made supper for them and then they sat on the floor listening to the radio stories before they went to bed. Mama and Carlos were not expected back until long after they had gone to sleep.

At the party, between serving and cleaning up, Sofía enjoyed listening to the music. It brought back memories of how she used to sing in the restaurant in Phoenix and how so many people had told her then that she had a beautiful voice. This particular evening, without thinking, she joined in on a familiar song some of the men were singing.

She did have a beautiful voice, and it had been so long since she had a chance to sing. She just let the music flow out of her. All eyes were on her and she became the center of attention. The men, on their way to being drunk, all seemed to be very happy to have her join them. All the men except Carlos.

As soon as the song was finished, while everyone else was clapping for more, Carlos came up behind Sofía and grabbed her arm tightly and pulled her out of the house.

Standing on the rickety porch, with only a single bare light bulb illuminating the front yard, he shouted at her, "We have to go *now*, woman!"

"But, Carlos, what's wrong? I was having fun," she tried to explain. "You're hurting my arm."

"You embarrassed me, acting like a whore! You wanted all those men to watch you, to get excited by you!"

"No, Carlos," she begged him, trying to calm him down, trying to pull free from his grip on her arm. "I just love to sing. Please, Carlos, it was nothing. It's just been so long since I had a chance to sing. I was just…"

He grabbed her by the throat and stared her in the eyes. "Sing now, puta! Sing now, you whore!"

She tried to loosen his crushing grip, but he wouldn't let go. She could feel herself losing consciousness. Carlos must have felt her frail body beginning to slump because he finally let go and stepped off the porch. She steadied herself against the porch post and tried to catch her breath, coughing and sputtering.

"You'll never embarrass me like that again, pendeja," he said in a slow, smoldering tone. "Your place is to wait on the men, not to entertain them and get them hot for you." He grabbed hold of her forearm and yanked her down off the porch.

"Carlos, I'm sorry. I'm so sorry. I didn't mean to embarrass you. I was just singing," she tried again to explain.

"Shut up!" he screamed, his anger rising.

"But Carlos…" she started to say as the back of his powerful hand smacked against the side of her fragile face, sending her back against the porch post.

"You're just trying to make me jealous! You make me sick!"

"Get in the truck!" he ordered her with a little shove, then he stomped around to the other side. He got in, slammed the door, and started up the engine.

There was only angry silence on the short drive home in the old green pickup truck. The children had gone to bed and the little house was dark. Carlos grabbed Sofía by the hair and dragged her into their bedroom. He pushed her down on the bed, climbed on top of her, and raped her.

Eva had been asleep on her little mat on the floor by the front door when she was awakened by the sounds of their fighting. She was frozen with fear and tried to make herself as small and as invisible as possible, pretending to still be asleep.

When Carlos was finished with Sofía in the bedroom, he demanded that she go and make him something to eat. It was very late, so she just warmed up some beans and tortillas. He sat down at the table, and she put the plate down in front of him. He looked at it for a moment, picked it up and threw it against the kitchen wall, shattering it with a thunderous crash.

The loud noise made Sofía jump with fear and cover her mouth with her hand to muffle her gasp. She had already been battered and raped that night. What more would he do to her? she worried. Had he awakened the children? Would they have to witness this violence?

Carlos began swearing at Sofía, calling her all kinds of filthy names. He grabbed her by the wrist and hit her in the face with his fist, then he dragged her by the hair out to the backyard where he continued to beat her.

Eva quietly snuck into the bed where her brothers slept to find them awake as well. They could all hear what was going on in the tiny house. They quietly crowded together under the blankets in the big bed, too afraid to come out of it, too afraid Carlos would take his anger out on them, as well.

After awhile, Eva and her brothers heard Carlos come back inside and go to bed. The children lay awake for hours, huddling in the bed, too frightened to go to sleep. Eventually, they heard the back door quietly close, and they knew Mama had come back inside, too.

In the morning, Eva found her mother in the kitchen, making breakfast. Carlos was still in bed sleeping off his drunkenness. Mama was facing the sink, so Eva couldn't see her face at first. But, she noticed the purplish handprint on her upper left arm.

"Mama," she said softly, gently putting her hand on her mother's arm. "Oh, Mama."

"We mustn't speak of this, mi'ja," Sofía replied in a hushed tone as she turned toward Eva. Sofía's eyes were darting around, making sure Carlos was not getting up and coming where he could hear them.

When she turned to look for Carlos, Eva saw her mother's face, the cut lip and the swollen eyes. Eva gasped and quickly put her hand over her mouth to muffle the sound. Then she saw the bruises around her mother's neck where Carlos had attempted to choke the life out of her.

Eva was filled with anger as she took in the full extent of Mama's injuries. Her legs were bruised and Eva assumed Mama likely had bruises on her abdomen, as well.

Eva thought back to the feelings of terror she had felt the night before, as she lay on her mat and listened while most of the beating happened. She wanted to scream at the top of her lungs, to call Carlos every foul name she could think of. But she knew she dare not make a sound or she would run the risk of waking him, like poking an angry bull.

Eva wanted to pummel his face with her little fists, but she knew she couldn't. She wanted to hate him for what he had done to her mother, to all of them, but Mama said it would only poison her heart and he would win. So, all she could do was give Mama a long, gentle hug and quietly weep with her.

Carlos eventually woke up and stumbled out of the bedroom and went into the little kitchen. He sat down at the table, rubbing his rough, cracked hand over his face and then through his greasy, disheveled hair. He looked around, wondering where Sofía was and if there was anything for him to eat.

It was Sunday morning and the children were outside playing. Sofía had been watching them and came back inside to see if he was up yet.

"Sofía, bring me something to eat!" he ordered as he saw her come in.

She knew he would be up soon, so she had a warm beef burrito and fried potatoes waiting for him. She quietly walked over and gently set the plate down on the table in front of him, not saying a word, trying not to upset him in any way.

He looked up at Sofía and saw what he had done to her. His eyes got wide, and he was speechless for just a moment. He was fighting off a hangover, but his blurry memory came flooding back and he remembered what he done to her in his drunken rage the night before.

"Sofía, I'm sorry… so sorry." He sounded apologetic, remorseful. "I didn't know what I was doing. You just made me so angry, so jealous. With the way you were showing off, and the tequila, I just lost control," he went on, trying to shift the blame.

The words tumbled out of his mouth as if he was trying to sound like he was sorry. Maybe he was, a little. Sofía was not sure she believed him. His violent outbursts were getting worse, especially when he drank. But this was the first time he actually seemed like just maybe he was sorry afterward. She didn't know what to say, so she said nothing and looked away.

Carlos stood up and put his arms around her. She flinched. She didn't want him to touch her. It gave her a sick feeling in the pit of her stomach.

He seemed to feel some shame for what he had done to her – not necessarily because he felt he did something wrong, but more because he knew others would see her and know how badly he had beaten her. They would know the kind of man he really was.

"How can I make this up to you, Sofía? Tell me."

Tears filled her eyes and no words would come. She buried her face in her hands and cried.

"I know, Sofía, I know how I can make it up to you. You've been talking about wanting to get married. So…let's get married. Will that make it up to you?"

Yes, she had been asking him for some time to marry her, to make her a respectable woman. But after what he had done to her last night, the thought of it made her stomach turn. Her knees went weak and she grabbed a chair and sat down.

She was not sure she wanted to marry this man she did not love and who clearly did not love her. But what other life could she have? They already had six children together. There was no leaving. At least, if they were married, she could hold her head up at mass and around the community. So she reluctantly agreed.

They made plans to have a small ceremony at the Catholic Church with just the children and a handful of his friends and their wives.

Carlos and Sofía were married about a month later. By then, her bruises and cuts were healed – at least the ones on the outside.

CHAPTER 12

WAR AND PEACE

IN 1941, WORLD WAR II BEGAN. Eva was nine years old. Her family heard of the bombing at Pearl Harbor, but it didn't mean much to them. It seemed so far away from California and had little impact on their meager lives and their sleepy little town of Hollister.

One thing that did change, though, was that they received ration books. The government issued a ration book to every man, woman and child. Carlos and Sofía had six children at the time, so they received eight books. The government told the people they were free to continue buying food staples as they wanted, but the little stamps in the ration books allowed them to buy certain "restricted" things, like sugar, coffee, cigarettes and gasoline. The citizens were informed that these goods were rationed so there would be plenty of these items for the soldiers fighting in the war.

Sofía didn't know it at the time, but one of those soldiers was her little brother, Marcelo. Years later she found out that her younger brother, whom she had not seen since she left her family in Arizona when she was twelve, had changed his last name and joined the United States Army at the beginning of the war. He was fighting the war in France in defense of the United States when he was badly wounded and later died in an army hospital in France.

There was one particular thing that was rationed during the war which did affect Sofía's family – shoes. They were allowed two pair of shoes a year. This was fine for the adults, whose shoe size doesn't change. But if the children outgrew their shoes before it was time to use another stamp, they passed the outgrown shoes along to a younger child and went barefoot, hoping someone would eventually pass their shoes on to them.

Going barefoot was very uncomfortable for the children, even painful sometimes. The rundown little house the Gonzalez family lived in had no lawn or concrete, only dirt all around their house. There were many times the children would cut their feet on glass or metal, which at times got infected.

It was important they kept shoes on their feet as long as possible. If they wore out the soles of their shoes before they outgrew them, they stuffed cardboard in the bottoms if the outsides were still in decent condition. This helped them to keep shoes on their feet a little longer.

When Eva was about eleven or twelve years old, near the end of the war, the Christmas season was approaching. There were never any presents from Santa for Eva or her brothers and sister, like the other kids at school received, because Carlos couldn't find work in the winter.

But there was one particular Christmas that they did have a tree. Eva's school gave the "classroom trees" to needy families, and that year her family got one. The decorations had all been stripped off first, but at least the school workers did leave the tinsel on. So, Eva and her brothers happily added decorations they made from paper and colored macaroni.

Another Christmas, Eva and her family received surprise gifts from firemen and strangers. Late one night, right before Christmas, a big red fire truck stopped in front of their house. The family had already gone to bed. There was a sharp knock at their front door.

The door was close to where Eva slept on her little mat on the floor, and the knocking woke her up. Mama and Carlos came out of their room and the boys sat up in their big old brass bed.

Eva opened the door and was surprised by a tall, muscular fireman wearing his uniform. He had a big box of books in his arms.

"Merry Christmas, little lady," he said. "Can we come in?"

Eva was speechless. She looked at Mama, who nodded yes. Eva looked back at the fireman and nodded to him. She backed up out of the way and let him by. Then another fireman brought in a large box of used toys right behind him. They set their boxes down and went out for another load.

"We'll be right back," the first fireman told Carlos and Sofía in a deep voice. The kids were quietly watching with wide eyes. This time the firemen brought in a couple of boxes of food.

"Gracias, gracias," Mama kept saying. Carlos just watched in disbelief. That year the Gonzalez family had a good Christmas.

A few years later, shortly after the war, a service club in Hollister started a new Christmas tradition for the town. Every December, on a Saturday before Christmas, the club arranged for all the children in town to go to the movies for free. Eva and the older brothers were allowed to go.

The movie theater showed westerns and cartoons to entertain the kids. It was a very special time, children of all kinds sitting side by side in the darkened theater, laughing and enjoying themselves. That day, there was no skin color, there were no rich kids or poor kids. They were just kids enjoying a fun afternoon at the movies.

After the movies and cartoons were over, volunteers stood at the doors and handed each child a bag filled with hard candy, unshelled walnuts, an orange and an apple. Eva and her brothers always appreciated those gifts and took them home to share with the younger children and with Mama.

Eva was twelve when the war ended. It was 1944. She was in the sixth grade, and her younger brothers attended the same elementary school as she did. They learned how cruel children can be to one another. Too often students were rude and unkind to them, calling them all sorts of demeaning names and making fun of them because they were poor Mexicans who wore hand-me-down clothes and tattered shoe. Over the years, as Eva's brothers got older, though, they stuck together and then no one dared to pick on them.

The next year, Eva went to junior high school. The morning of her first day of school, she got up early to get ready for school and catch the bus. Mama had made her a slip from a used flour sack and bought her two new dresses and a pair of shoes for school. Sofía was good at squirreling away money if there was any extra.

"The bus will be here soon, Mama. I need to take a lunch with me," Eva reminded her.

"Don't worry, niña, I'm taking care of it." Mama packed her a lunch made of two tortillas from breakfast that she smeared with cold refried beans left over from dinner the night before. She rolled them up like burritos, wrapped them in a cloth and tied a string around them. That was lunch.

On the first day at her junior high, Eva was both nervous and excited for a new school. She didn't know what to expect. When she walked into class, she immediately felt out of place. Most of her classmates were from middle-class white families. They wore crisp, new clothes and brought their lunches in brown paper bags or brightly-colored metal lunch boxes with pictures on them. But not her.

She was a poor Latina among a classroom of more affluent white students. She spoke with an accent, her skin was darker, and her clothes were not nearly as nice as theirs. Because of these differences, she sensed them staring at her, heard them whispering as she passed by them. She would hear them giggling behind her back and assumed they were laughing at her. As if being beaten down by Carlos at home was not enough, she had to fight against being seen as worthless at school, too.

Eva was a little surprised there were no other Mexican children in her class. Her mama told her she thought it was probably because most of the Mexican families made their kids work the fields with them after the fifth or sixth grade. They needed the income and didn't think their children needed any more education.

But, having her children get as much education as possible was important to Sofía. She knew it was their only way out of their poverty. She pushed hard to get Carlos to let the children stay in school, at her peril sometimes, and Eva appreciated it.

When class was dismissed for lunch that first day, Eva watched the girls in pretty pastel sweaters with shiny black patent-leather shoes sit at tables outside with their friends. She watched as they took their sandwiches out of their lunchboxes, their neatly-made sandwiches on sliced white bread with layers of delicious-looking meats and cheeses, slathered with creamy white mayonnaise in the middle and crisp green lettuce leaves.

She looked down at her cloth-covered cold bean burritos and felt ashamed. She didn't dare let anyone see. She slyly inched her way over to a large bush on the perimeter of the lunch area, looked around to make sure no one saw her, and quickly crouched down on the other side of the bush to eat her lunch in secret. She felt small and poor. After that, during lunchtime, she walked to nearby Piedmont Park to eat lunch alone.

Eva had been having lunch alone for a couple of weeks when a boy in her class noticed her walking off by herself. He followed her.

"Eva!" he called out, when he had almost caught up with her. She spun around in surprise at hearing someone calling her name.

"Alex?" She recognized him from her class, with his dark wavy hair and chestnut brown eyes.

"Where you goin'?"

"Um…I was walking to the park to eat lunch."

"Can I come with you?" he asked.

"I guess so."

They reached the park bench where Eva usually ate her lunch and sat down. Eva didn't really want to show Alex her cloth-covered burritos, but she had no way of hiding them now. He opened his crumpled brown paper bag and pulled out a peanut butter and jelly sandwich on white bread and an orange.

"What do you got?" he asked.

"Just some bean burritos," Eva replied, trying to hide her embarrassment.

"I'll swap you half of my sandwich for one of your burritos."

"You want a cold bean burrito?"

"Sure. I like Mexican food."

"Why?"

" 'Cause I'm one-fourth Mexican," he said proudly. "My dad's mom is Mexican. I don't get to see my grandma much, she lives in Arizona. But when we do visit her, she makes fresh tortillas and tamales and all kinds of good stuff."

"Okay, then. Here you go." Eva handed Alex one of her burritos and took half of his sandwich. "I've never eaten sliced white bread before," she remarked. "It tastes…well…fluffy."

"Fluffy, huh?" Alex chuckled.

"Yeah, fluffy. Don't laugh."

"Sorry. I just never heard that before. I guess it's a girl thing."

"So you're part Mexican?"

"Yep," Alex answered, with his mouth full of burrito.

"What else are you?" Eva asked.

He swallowed before he answered her. "Mostly Italian, with a smidge of Irish," he replied with a big grin on his face, proud of his heritage.

"Do you want to come and have lunch here again tomorrow?" Eva asked.

"No, I better not. My friends'll miss me and start askin' questions. Then they'll make fun of me for havin' lunch with a girl."

"I get it," Eva said, feeling a little disappointed. She thought maybe she had been too forward, pushed too hard too fast. But she was just so anxious to have a friend.

"I'm not makin' any promises," Alex told her, "but, I wouldn't mind doin' this again sometime. Just not tomorrow." Then he took another bite of his burrito.

They sat on the bench for awhile and enjoyed their lunches, talking about school and a little more about their families. Eva was careful not to share very much about hers.

After school, Eva rode the bus home in silent contemplation. She stared out the window all the way home, pondering her future, seeing possibilities dancing around in her head. She felt a strong yearning deep inside to find a way to escape this wretched life. She had seen a better life, the life that the other girls in her class were living. She just knew there had to a better life out there for her, too. Hope began welling up within her – hope and determination.

I'm sure I don't have to live this terrible life my mama has, she told herself. I'm just sure I don't. When I grow up, I'm going to have a good job and a good life. If those other girls can do it, I can do it, too.

The school bus came to a squeaky stop in front of her little old house, and the bus driver pushed the lever to open the doors. Eva quickly got off the bus and ran up to her shabby front door. She pushed it open and was ready to get to work. She changed out of her school clothes and put on her old, worn work clothes. It was time to take care of the babies and help Mama start supper. Life for her was still the same on the outside, but today she got a glimpse of a better life and things changed for her on the inside.

Over the next few years, that seed of hope took root in Eva's heart and began to grow. She worked hard on her schoolwork and did well in her classes. Alex continued to meet her at the park for the occasional lunch swap until Alex moved away. His father took a job in another town. Eva was heartbroken to lose her friend. She hoped he would write to her, but he never did.

Eva's junior high years would be over in a couple of months, and she looked forward to going to high school. Her bus drove past Hollister High every day on the way home. As she stared out the window at the school each day, she dreamed of the possibilities that lay before her once she graduated from it.

When she finished junior high, there was only one more summer of farm work standing between her and starting school at Hollister High. Or so she thought.

* * * * *

As Eva's brothers got older, near junior high age, and were able to work full days, Carlos moved the family to the farm labor camps for the summers. The camps were near Tres Pinos, about fifteen or so miles outside of Hollister. The shacks at these labor camps were just one large room and a small area for cooking and serving meals, no refrigerator and no stove. Cooking was done on a camp stove, and there was a sink and a small work table for preparing the meals. The place had virtually no furniture except a beat-up little dresser. There was no table to eat at and no chairs to sit on, only rough wooden boxes to rest on at meal time.

Carlos always brought a mattress for himself and Sofía to sleep on, and he brought bedding for the rest of the family to sleep on the floor. The make-shift showers and restrooms were in a communal building at one corner of the camp, which made it pretty inconvenient for everyone when they wanted to shower after a long, hot day working in the fields and orchards.

The Gonzalez family stayed all summer at the labor camps, usually working in the fields first, then picking prunes and ending with picking walnuts in the fall. Eva and her siblings were always at least two weeks late returning to school. They tried hard to catch up with their classes, but it was tough.

Eva looked forward to getting through the summer and entering high school. It was the summer of her fifteen birthday. It was 1947.

At supper one evening in late July, with the family sitting around on the wooden crates, she was talking to her brother, Eduardo, about what classes she was hoping to take in high school when they returned to Hollister.

"Forget it. You're not going to high school," Carlos said, very matter-of-factly. This was the first Eva had heard of this.

"What do you mean? I *have* to go," she pleaded. Her heart was set on it. She knew her future depended on it.

"You've had enough school, muchacha. We need you in the fields. You need to help support this family!" Carlos answered in his usual gruff manner. His face was now wrinkled and weathered from the years he spent drinking and working in the sun, and his hair was beginning to gray.

"No, I *need* to go to school," Eva implored him.

"Silencio! That's enough! I said no!" he yelled as he leaned forward and raised the back of his calloused hand to her as a warning to stop pressing the issue.

Eva sat in stony silence during the rest of the meal and helped Mama clean the dishes when they were finished. She just *had* to go to high school, she told herself.

With just an eighth-grade education, she knew she would never escape this cycle of poverty. Eva was determined to find a way to go to high school. Summer would be over soon, so she didn't have much time.

On a sweltering Saturday afternoon near the end of August, after picking prunes from early morning, she and her brothers were given a break during the hottest part of the day. She took that opportunity to walk a mile or so from their camp to the tiny grocery store on a dusty country road.

She had taken a little white envelope from her mother's well-worn chest of drawers and a scrap of brown paper torn from an old bag. She scrawled a short note on the paper that said, "Please help me go to high school. My father Carlos says I have been to school enough, but I want to go to high school. I live at 57 Tres Pinos Rd., Tres Pinos – Eva Gonzalez."

She folded the paper and gently laid it in the envelope. She licked the flap of the envelope with hope and anticipation and wrote her return address on it. She didn't know where to send the envelope, so she simply wrote "School Superintendent, Hollister, California."

Eva had been clutching a shiny copper penny in her sweaty hand to pay for the stamp. She opened her hand and looked at the penny for a moment, remembering back to when she had found it and how she had a strange sensation deep inside that this penny could someday change her future.

A month or so before, she had gone to town for cooking supplies with Mama. The penny had been lying on the sidewalk. Eva noticed several young white girls, about nine or ten years old, in crisply-ironed summer dresses step right over the shiny copper coin.

What's a penny to them? she thought. It seemed to her that they got whatever they wanted. Why would they ever stoop down to pick up an insignificant penny? They probably get a big allowance, she thought to herself. Once they were past, Eva stepped in and quickly scooped it up. She felt that one day she would need it. As it turned out, this was the day.

She walked up to the small counter, crowded with displays of cigarettes, candies and an old cash register. The elderly, gray-haired storekeeper had seen this petite teenager in the store a handful of times, usually with a younger brother or sister on her hip. He had gentle blue eyes and always treated her kindly, often wondering what kind of future this bright young girl would have in this poor farming community. Leaning on the counter and peering over his wire-rimmed glasses, he looked at her inquisitively.

"Can I help you, señorita?"

She held out her hand and displayed the precious coin that she hoped could change her life.

"One stamp, señor, por favor. I mean, please."

He handed her the stamp as she requested. She licked it with excitement and affixed it carefully to her envelope. She walked over to the mailbox in the front corner of the little store, closed her eyes, whispered a quick prayer, and dropped it in the box. It was in God's hands now.

Early one evening, almost two weeks later, a large black sedan pulled up near their row of shacks, and two men in black suits and hats got out of the car. A large man emerged from the driver's side and then a tall, thin man got out of the passenger side. Eva heard the car pull up from inside the shack. She quickly tiptoed across the room and peeked out the corner of the window from behind the dingy curtains.

Five or six young children in tattered hand-me-downs were playing out front. They stopped their play and stared in awe at the shiny new car and the looming white men in black suits. This was a sight these little Mexican children were not used to seeing.

"Do you know where we can find Carlos Gonzalez?" the tall man asked the children. The children spoke some English, because they were learning it in school, and some of them recognized the name. One boy pointed up the dirt driveway.

Carlos was standing with a few of the other field workers, drinking beer and talking. He turned toward the children when he heard his name. He knew enough English to know the men in suits were asking for him.

Carlos sheepishly walked toward the two white men, afraid he was in trouble for mistreating his children. The men looked to him like they could be from social services.

"I'm Carlos Gonzalez."

"Mr. Gonzalez," the big man said sternly, "I have been notified that your daughter, Eva, did not start high school last week. You, Mr. Gonzalez," pointing a large, fat finger at Carlos, "could get in a lot of trouble if she doesn't get herself to school on Monday morning. Comprende? Do you understand?"

"Sí, but I didn't know," Carlos feigned, shrugging his shoulders, acting innocent. "I make sure she is there." He was glad that was all they wanted.

"See that you do, Mr. Gonzalez. We don't want to have to come back here again."

And with that, the two men in black suits climbed back into their car and slowly drove away, leaving a trailing cloud of dust. Eva's heart leapt in her chest as she turned away from the window and tried to take in the enormity of what she had just heard.

"Gracias a Diós!" is all she could say quietly to herself. She wanted to shout it out loud, at the top of her lungs. But, for fear of what would happen, she kept this exciting turn of events to herself.

Eva's future had been changed.

CHAPTER 13

A MEAN TRICK

IT WAS SUMMER, 1948. There was a lot of work to be done in the fields, picking tomatoes, harvesting onions, and picking apricots in the orchard. Carlos had decided to move the family to the farm camp near Tres Pinos for more than just the summer. He had found a farmer to hire him on his large farm to work full time, and he gave them another rundown, old house to live in. At least, this one was a little larger than the last.

Carlos thought moving the family to the farm was a great idea because then it would be easy to have the older kids help him work the farm on the weekends and school breaks, not just the summers. This meant the children would be working more, would be isolated, and they would have to ride the school bus from Tres Pinos to Hollister when school resumed in the fall.

It was August, which was an especially hot part of the summer. Eva had just turned sixteen. She and some of the older brothers had worked hard all week in the fields. Carlos told them he would take them to the movie theater in Hollister on Saturday because they had worked so hard and brought a good week's pay into the house.

"Really? Are you really going to take them to the movies, Carlos?" Mama asked.

Mama was surprised by the offer, but she was glad to see her older children would have a break from the work for awhile. She wanted them to simply be happy kids, if only for a few hours.

"I said I was, didn't I?" Carlos replied, acting irritated that she dared to question him.

Eva and her brothers spent the morning getting ready and looking forward to going to town for some fun. It wasn't often they were allowed to spend the family's hard-earned money on such "foolishness", as Carlos would say. Of course, he never described his drinking as "foolishness", but he thought there was no need for the kids to spend money on anything fun. However, for some unknown reason, he offered to reward them for their hard work.

The movies started at noon on Saturday, and they would be showing some news reels and cartoons before the double feature. Eva and the boys excitedly looked forward to this day off.

About eleven o'clock on Saturday morning, they piled into Carlos's pickup truck, with Eva and Carlos in the cab and the five brothers in the back. Mama stayed home to watch the younger children. It was about half an hour's ride to Hollister from Tres Pinos.

On the outskirts of Hollister was an old bar called "Johnny's." This was one of Carlos's favorite hangouts after a long week in the fields. Unexpectedly, instead of driving past the bar, Carlos pulled over to the side of the road. The kids were surprised that he stopped here since the plan was to get to the movie theater before the show started. That's what Papa had promised them.

"No, we can't stop here," Eva said. "We'll be late for the show."

"Don't tell me what to do, girl," he growled. "I'll be back in a few minutes," he said as he climbed out of the truck.

"You boys stay here, and I'll be right back. I'm just going in to get a beer, and then we'll go to the movies." And with that he ducked into the darkened bar.

Eva stepped out of the vehicle and leaned on the side of the truck bed. She was mad, but she didn't want to show it.

"He'll be right back," she told her brothers. "He said it would just be a few minutes." She tried to assure them, even though she wasn't sure herself that he would be. Carlos wasn't known for having only one beer.

Eva and the boys tried to wait patiently, but time passed slowly in the afternoon heat. It had been almost an hour since he had gone into the bar, and they were all becoming irritated and impatient. It was getting hotter as time went on, and they were afraid they would miss the beginning of the movie.

"I'm gonna go and see if he's almost done," Eduardo offered.

"No, I'll go in," Eva said. "I'm the oldest. Maybe he'll listen to me."

She tried her best to muster up the courage to go into the bar. She was a sixteen-year-old girl going in to confront a mean and likely already-drunk man. She had to be strong and try to get him to do what was right. He had promised her and the boys the movies as a reward, but now it seemed he would rather drink away the money and the afternoon.

"Papa?" she called out as she entered the dark bar. Her eyes had not quite adjusted yet from the bright summer sunshine outside. Slowly she could make out the figures at the bar and found her father half-way down. She hadn't called him "Papa" since she learned he was not her real father. But she thought, for this purpose, maybe it would soften him up.

"Papa? Isn't it time to go now?" she asked in a low, soft voice, but received no response.

"Papa?" she said with a little more volume and force. "I think it's time we go now."

Her eyes adjusted to the dim light just in time to see the back of his hand and then feel the sting of it on the side of her face.

"I'll go when I'm good and ready! You don't tell me what to do!" he snapped.

"But Papa, you promised," she said quietly as she turned to go.

He grabbed her by her hair. "Don't talk back to me, muchacha," he yelled and then pushed her away.

Tears started to fill her eyes, her cheek still stinging, but she was determined not to let her brothers see her cry. She took a deep breath, wiped her eyes, and held her head up high as she walked through the doorway out into the bright sunlight.

Eva didn't want to share what just happened with her brothers. She tried to put up a facade and keep her emotions under control. Though she was furious, she decided to let Carlos get away with it this time, but she told herself she would never let a man hit her again. Not ever.

"Is he coming?" Eduardo asked. "It's really getting hot out here. My shirt is starting to stick to me."

"Yeah. And the movie has probably started already," Arturo added, as he shoved his hands in his pockets and kicked the dirt.

"I know, guys. I'm sorry, but he's drinking in there, and I don't think he's coming out for a long time. I'm so sorry."

The boys were angry and disappointed. How could their father do this to them? They had worked so hard, and he'd promised to take them to the movies as a reward. Now this. Drinking away the day and the money they worked so hard to earn. Not caring about them, only about his drinking.

"I'm gonna go in and make him come out!" Eduardo declared. "We can't let him do this to us."

Eva knew Eduardo would feel the wrath of their father even more fiercely. Eduardo would likely come out with a black eye or worse, she feared. Even if he was Carlos's favorite, the alcohol would blur any distinction between the children. Carlos was an angry man who, on rare occasion, would show a glimmer of kindness. But he didn't have enough goodness in him to see a good deed through.

"No, Eduardo. Please. He's been drinking for more than an hour, now. You know when he drinks it makes him even meaner than usual." Eva was trying to protect her brother.

Eduardo noticed the rosy handprint on the side of Eva's face and knew what she meant. He had seen that and much worse on their mother when she tried to stand up to him, and he understood what Eva was telling him. They all had experienced it to some extent.

"Then I'll go," little Mateo exclaimed. "I'm not afraid."

"Eva's right, little brother, all we can do now is wait. The picture show will have to be put off to another day," Eduardo reluctantly admitted, kicking the old truck's back tire as sweat trickled down his back.

So, Eva and the boys waited in the heat until after five o'clock when Carlos finally stumbled out of the bar. She and her brothers were hot, thirsty and extremely disappointed.

Eva was afraid to let Carlos drive them home in his drunken condition. Even though the boys were very angry with Carlos, somehow they were able to talk him into riding in the back of the truck with them, where he promptly passed out. Eva would have to drive. She didn't have a driver's license, but she was the oldest and had some experience driving around the farms.

One of the boys dug the keys out of Carlos's pocket and handed them to Eva. She wiped the beads of sweat from her forehead with her hand and slid into the driver's seat. She nervously started the engine, slipped it into gear and slowly drove the pickup back to their home in Tres Pinos so her brothers would be safe.

The boys pulled their father out of the back of the truck and helped him stumble to the house. Mama met them at the door. Her children all looked drenched and exasperated.

"What happened?" she asked.

"Do you really have to ask that, Mama?" Eva replied as she pushed past her, with an expression of disgust on her face. Taking one look at Carlos, Sofía knew exactly what had happened.

"Supper will be ready soon," Mama called out after them. Eva and the boys went to change out of their good clothes and try to find something else to do to take their minds off of this frustration.

Carlos was passed out on his bed. Without him at supper, Sofía thought, perhaps they could have a peaceful meal.

She stood over him, staring at him, wishing she could hurt him as much as he had hurt her children. But what good would it do, she thought, it would only come back on her in spades. So she did the only thing she could, she walked away and went to tend to the young ones and finish making supper. Maybe one day, she hoped, he would get what he had coming to him.

CHAPTER 14

A PIVOTAL MOMENT

LIFE WENT ON AS USUAL for Eva. Not much changed except her age. Every day that she grew older was a day she grew closer to escaping her miserable life. Working in the fields and orchards all summer long and into the fall, riding the bus from Tres Pinos to school in Hollister with some of her brothers, tending to the younger brothers and sisters, and dealing with Carlos's abuse – that was her life. There were nine children now. It was 1949.

While the older children were at school, Sofía savored the time she could spend with the younger ones, the babies. Between mending torn clothes, changing diapers, doing laundry, cooking and cleaning, she looked for opportunities to have one-on-one time with each of them, to rock them to sleep in her arms and sing softly to them. She danced around the room with them when they woke up from their naps. These were the parts of her day that helped to keep her from losing her mind.

Soon her sanity would be tested. She had not told Carlos yet, or anyone else, that she was pregnant again with her tenth child. Though she loved each of her children very much, she truly hoped this one would be the last.

The labor and birthing process of so many children had taken its toll of wear and tear on her petite body, not to mention the financial stress each child added. Combine that with the years of working in the fields and the ongoing violence she suffered at Carlos's hand, she found herself at the very outer limit of what she could endure.

Years ago, when Sofía was a young girl, she pictured her life so much differently. When she gave birth to Eva, she placed her own wishes and dreams on her daughter, hoping Eva would have the life Sofía realized she would never have for herself. But now, with the miserable life they now shared, she wondered if her dreams for Eva would ever be possible.

On the bus ride home from school each day, Eva often gazed out the window and thought about her life. She daydreamed about becoming a nurse, helping people and making a good living, being someone others had respect for. Thinking back about how she almost didn't get to go to high school, she was glad for the opportunity to continue her studies and to work toward a better future.

She also dreamed of having a husband that loved her and treated her like a queen. She saw some of the fathers of other students in her class, as well as men who worked at the market and shops. They seemed to be kind and hardworking, not like her stepfather. The kids in her classes seemed happy and well cared for, so she assumed they must have good, loving parents at home. That's the life she wanted.

Eva didn't really see herself having any children, though, because she had been feeding, diapering and caring for babies for as long as she could remember. She just wanted to focus on her own happiness and the adoring husband she hoped to have someday.

Conditions at the Gonzalez home were not getting any better as time went on. Carlos drank more and became more and more abusive, not only to Sofía, but to all the children. Eva felt she could no longer take the violence that defined her home life.

Guilt weighed heavily on Eva. She believed that she was the cause of much of Carlos's abuse of her mother because he so intensely resented her. She was a constant reminder of Sofía's life before him, that Eva was another man's child, and he had to support her even though she was not his own.

Eva was seventeen, and a junior in high school. She had a close friend at school, named Rosie, that she spent a lot of time with. Carlos and Sofía knew Rosie's parents, so when Eva asked to spend the weekend at her house, Mama let her. Carlos didn't argue about it, at least not in front of Eva.

More and more, Eva started spending weekends at Rosie's house and going to school with her on Monday mornings. It was such a relief to be away from her own home, away from Carlos. The girls listened to the radio, worked on homework together and just talked for hours. She didn't want to spoil their fun together by telling Rosie about her awful life, she only wanted to enjoy her respite.

But Carlos couldn't just let Eva have her freedom from him. He began accusing her of staying out all weekend so she could go out with boys, inferring she was sleeping around with boys in town. He told Sofía that several friends of his told him they had seen Eva on a street corner in town getting into cars, like she was a prostitute. He even told Eva to her face that she was a puta, a tramp.

One weekend, when she was staying over at Rosie's house, Eva shared with her some of the things that happened at home. The girls were sitting on the bed talking about all kinds of stuff, and Eva started opening up. She hadn't planned to open up about her family's dirty secrets, but fear and a pool of emotions were always bubbling just below the surface. Before long, it all came spilling out.

"You don't know how lucky you are, Rosie."

Rosie had a confused look on her face.

"I wish I could live in a home like yours," Eva told her.

"What do you mean?"

"Your papa and mama don't fight," Eva said.

"Sometimes they do. They'll argue sometimes until one of them gives in. Usually Papa."

"No, Rosie, I mean really fight. Does your papa hit your mother?" Eva asked.

"No, never. They just yell at each other."

"The old man, my stepfather, he hits my mama all the time," Eva shared, with tears glistening in her eyes. She paused, not sure she should continue, but the words kept coming out anyway.

"Sometimes he hits her really hard with his fists. He hits the rest of us kids, too, with his hands or belts or switches from the tree."

"Oh, Eva," Rosie said, as she put her arm around her friend. "I didn't know."

"He even told my mama that I stay the weekends in town with you so I can stand on street corners picking up guys. The old man said his friends saw me. He has such a dirty mind!"

"What? Are you kidding? Oh, Eva." Rosie couldn't believe what her friend had to go through. This was the first time Eva told anyone about her life at home.

"He's just a dirty old man."

"Oh, Eva… Oh, Eva," Rosie was so stunned by what Eva was telling her that that was all she could find to say.

"There's something else. I've never told anyone this before, except my mama. But once, when Mama wasn't home, I was in the kitchen cooking at the stove. He came up behind me and stood really close. I could feel his breath. I was so scared. Then he put his hand up under my blouse."

"Oh, no," Rosie gasped.

"Yes. I just reacted and pulled away from him really fast. I was so scared."

"Then what?"

"He just started laughing and walked away, like it was some big joke."

"Did you tell your mama?"

"Yes. She told me not to be alone with him again. I think she knew it could be worse next time."

"Did your mama say anything to him?"

"No, I'm sure she didn't. He would have gotten mad that I told her," Eva said. "When the old man gets mad at me, he usually takes it out on my mama." Eva's voice was quivering. She tried to stop the tears, not wanting to look weak in front of her friend.

There was a long pause. Rosie didn't know what to say.

"I don't like telling people about what happens at home," Eva said, reaching for a tissue on the little table next to the bed. She was clearly embarrassed, but she was also relieved to have finally told someone. The tears started to flow and run down her cheeks. Rosie cried with her and did her best to comfort her.

"You can't tell anyone, Rosie. It'll only make it worse. Promise me," Eva implored her.

"You *need* to tell somebody. There must be someone who can help," Rosie tried to reason. But Eva was afraid. Eventually she had to go back home.

The next day was Monday, and Eva went to school with Rosie. She thought more about what Rosie said, about her needing to tell someone what was happening at home. Eva desperately wanted to get away from Carlos and stop the nightmare her family was living, but she was afraid.

After mulling it over in her mind all day, she ran into Rosie after school by the lockers. She told her she'd been thinking all day about what she should do. Rosie continued to encourage Eva to go to the authorities to report the abuse. Eva was finally convinced that was what she needed to do and left right away for the Sheriff's Department.

Stepping into the two-story white stucco building that housed the county offices, she followed the signs directing her to the Sheriff's Office. She found the right door and peeked in. Seeing a middle-aged man in a tan sheriff's uniform sitting at a desk, she nervously walked up to the counter and caught his attention. He strolled over to the counter, and Eva timidly introduced herself.

She then proceeded to tell the sheriff her story. He acted like he was listening to her, so she thought she would finally get some help. But he didn't believe her. He thought she was making it up, just another teenager wanting to get away from home.

She begged him to help her. But all he did was insist that she go back home. His unwillingness to help made her so angry. She couldn't figure out why he wouldn't help her.

While she was talking to the officer, a county nurse that Eva knew walked by. The nurse worked for the social services department and had come to their house to check on Sofia after she gave birth at home to some of the younger children. Her name was Naomi Walker.

She stopped to say hello to Eva when she saw her through the doorway. Eva explained to Nurse Walker what was happening and how she was trying to get this sheriff to help her.

"Sheriff, this girl is telling you the truth. I've been to her house. I've seen how her father treats her mother and the children. You have to help them." Nurse Walker was sure her corroboration would get things moving. Sadly, she was wrong.

"Like I told this girl, Ma'am, there's nothing I can do. I'm sorry," the sheriff said. "Just go on home to your people, girl."

"Her people?" the nurse asked. "What do mean by that?"

"Oh, you know, the wet-backs. I'm not going to get in the middle of their goings-on."

"Sheriff, this girl needs your help."

"I can't do anything for her, sorry." Eva and Miss Walker could both see he wasn't going to help any Mexicans, or "wet-backs", as he put it.

"You're disgraceful, Sheriff." Nurse Walker blushed with embarrassment by his obvious prejudice.

"Eva, come out here with me," she said as she led Eva out into the hallway, closing the door after them.

"I'm going to give you my telephone number. You call me next time you have a problem at home. Maybe I can come up with something." She took a piece of paper out of her purse, wrote her number on it and handed it to Eva. Miss Walker didn't know how she could help, but she couldn't walk away from this girl without giving her some kind of hope.

Rather than being defeated by the sheriff and his unwillingness to help, just knowing Nurse Walker was on her side made Eva all the more resolved to find a way out. What she didn't know was how soon she would need to take Miss Walker up on her offer.

Late in December, just a few days before Christmas, when she was still seventeen, something happened that Eva would never forget. It was a moment that altered the course of her life.

Because of the family's bleak financial situation, none of the children expected anything in the way of gifts. But they did hope they would at least get a Christmas tree they could decorate with some homemade ornaments and strings of popcorn. Last Christmas, Carlos took them up into the hills to chop one down and hauled it home, strapped to the top of his truck. That way they could have a tree for free.

This December, Carlos had gone with a few other men to do some work in southern California. Since there was no harvesting in the winter, Carlos's cousin had asked him to come down and help him on a commercial construction site as a laborer for a few weeks. There was plenty of work, he said, and told him to bring some of the other farm workers if they wanted work, too. This would bring in a little more money to help them make it through the winter. He told Sofía he would be back by Christmas.

By December 24th, Carlos had not come home. It was Christmas Eve, and they had not gotten a tree yet. Eva didn't want to disappoint her brothers and sister, so she decided she would get the family a tree. She found Carlos's axe in the shed and took a few of the older brothers with her. She drove Carlos's truck into the hills where they had gone the year before to get a Christmas tree.

They hiked in the woods and inspected quite a few trees until they finally decided on the best one. She and the boys took turns hacking at the tree until it eventually fell. They loaded it in the truck and drove back home.

Carlos and the other men returned while Eva and the boys were out finding a tree. Carlos was waiting for them. They excitedly came into the house, the boys dragging the tree in behind them, Eva carrying the axe, all wanting Mama to see the beautiful tree they brought. They froze in their tracks when they saw Carlos standing there next to Mama, a gnarled scowl on his face.

How could they know Carlos would be furious that they took his axe and his truck without his permission? His breath and slurred speech told them he had been drinking with the other workers before coming home, as usual. This always made him angry and irrational.

"Who told you it was okay to take my axe and my truck? Huh? Who told you?!"

"Carlos, it's Christmas Eve..." Sofía started to say. Her words were cut short by the back of his hand hard across her mouth.

"Shut up, woman!" Carlos screamed.

The children's eyes darted over to Mama. Her lip was bleeding and a few tears started to fall. She mustered what courage she could and tried once again to stand up to Carlos.

"No, Carlos. It's Christmas Eve and the children deserve a tree," Sofía said in a quiet, even tone.

"I told you to shut up!" Carlos balled up his fist and struck Sofía in the face, knocking her to the floor.

The boys were shocked by what their father was doing, but Eva was filled with raged. She had had enough. The next few moments seemed like she was moving in slow motion in her mind. She still held the sharp axe in her hands. Driven by the instinct to protect her mother, she swung the axe over her head and started to lunge at Carlos. She was going to kill that devil once and for all.

But the oldest son, Eduardo, caught sight of Eva out of the corner of his eye and quickly grabbed her arms to stop her. If it hadn't been for Eduardo's quick action, Eva surely would have killed Carlos that day.

Carlos never saw the axe coming and did not realize Eduardo had just saved his life. The other boys ran to Mama's aid as Carlos stomped off to the bedroom to sleep off his drunkenness.

That was a defining moment. Eva knew in that instant she had to leave home or the next time she certainly would kill him.

She waited until after Christmas to tell her mother that she needed to move out soon, and that she would start looking for another place to live. Sofía was sad to think of her daughter leaving, her first child, her oldest daughter. She hugged Eva for a long time, remembering the first day she was placed in her arms as a tiny baby.

"I remember, mi'ja, when you were just a baby. You were so little, so sweet." Sofía's eyes were tearing up.

"Mama, don't cry."

"I would hold you and rock you. I had such great hopes and dreams for you, Eva. I'm sorry things turned out the way they did. I'm sorry I ever met your father, Enrique."

"Mama, don't say that."

"I'm even more sorry I ever met Carlos." Sofía's tears were streaming down her face. "You should have a better life than this, mi'ja."

"I love you, Mama." Eva put her arms around her mother and let her cry.

Sofía hated the idea of Eva's leaving, but she knew it was probably for the best. She could go out on her own and find her own way in the world.

She began pondering how she would be able to make it on her own. Where would she go? How would she support herself? Where could she find a part-time job? Who could help her? She had to finish high school. Then she thought of Nurse Walker and her offer to help.

The first day of school after Christmas vacation, Eva went to see Miss Walker at the county social services office as soon as school was out for the day. Eva told her what had happened on Christmas Eve and that she really needed to move out of there. Miss Walker had been thinking about Eva since she ran into her at the Sheriff's office and had already decided she would be willing to take her in if it came to that.

So when Eva came to her that day, she quickly agreed that Eva she could come to live with her, if it was okay with her mother. Eva went home and talked it over with Mama. Because they had already talked earlier about Eva moving out, she easily got her mother's permission. Eva could see that it hurt her mother deeply, but Mama gathered the courage to accept her leaving, agreeing it was likely the best thing for her. It came as no surprise that Carlos was happy to see her go.

Eva moved her things to Miss Walker's home and quickly settled in. She felt as free as a bird. This was a new feeling for her and she relished it.

What she didn't know at the time was that Sofía was pregnant again. Eva felt terrible when she found out, as if she was abandoning her mother when she really needed her. If she had known Mama was expecting another baby, she probably wouldn't have left home until after she graduated from high school, as difficult as that would have been.

But she didn't know until the baby was about to be born. Eva had been gone for several months and Carlos forbade Sofía to have contact with her. As her due date approached, Sofía convinced Carlos that she needed Eva's help at the house with the other children while she was gone to the hospital for the birth.

Sofía asked her daughter if she would come and stay with the younger children while she was in the hospital having the baby. With some trepidation, Eva agreed to go back to her old home. She knew she would have to keep her distance from Carlos, but Mama needed her help. So, she went back home to care for the kids for almost a week, cooking, changing diapers and doing laundry. During the entire time she was at the house, Carlos never looked at her or spoke to her once.

Eva lived with Nurse Walker until after she graduated from high school. She was a good friend to her, almost like a second mother. Naomi Walker had never married and never had any children, so she treated Eva like the daughter she always wanted. This hard-working teenager talked about becoming a nurse, too, and she knew Eva was bright enough to accomplish that, if she set her mind to it.

Having lived alone for many years, Naomi was happy for the company and for someone to help her fill the emptiness in her house and in her life. She hoped that rescuing Eva from her abusive home life would help to give her a better future. Only time would tell.

CHAPTER 15

A NEW LIFE FOR EVA

IT WAS 1950. Eva began her senior year at Hollister High School and worked hard on her studies. Living with Miss Walker was such a dramatic improvement over her old life. She had her own bedroom for the first time in her life and considerably more freedom. She became more outgoing and began making more friends. Naomi taught her to appreciate music and art and encouraged her to do her best in school. She also helped Eva find part-time jobs babysitting and cleaning her friends' houses. School was challenging and work was hard, but she was determined to do well at both.

Eva blossomed into a pretty, petite young lady, barely five feet tall. She had matured early and had the curvy figure of a woman. She was often taunted by the teenage boys at school because she was a full-figured Latina with ample breasts. Walking home from school one day, she was accosted by a couple of white boys teasing her about her bosom.

"Nice bag of groceries you have there," said a tall, gangly boy with dirty blond hair, referring to her holding her books across her full chest as she walked.

"Mind if I squeeze your melons?" His scruffy brown-haired friend hollered, grabbing at her.

Eva was mortified. The two boys were talking loud enough that other students leaving school could hear them. All she wanted to do was get away from them, but they wouldn't get out of her way. She would step one way, they would be there. She would step another, they would be there, their barbs and insults becoming increasingly explicit. They had her cornered.

The last thing she wanted was for them to witness her embarrassment, her weakness. She could feel tears bubbling to the surface, but she would not give them the satisfaction. Eva was strong that way. She stood still for a few seconds as they circled her with insults and tried grabbing at her.

Reaching her boiling point, she planted her feet, slammed her books to the ground and the next one that stepped in front of her felt the full fury of her small but strong fist in their face. Standing only five feet tall did not stop her from what she had to do. She had years of contending with her brothers, years of wringing out laundry and years of doing field work that brought strength to her when she needed it.

The nasty blond bully was the unlucky hooligan to step in front of her first. She punched him so hard in the face that she broke his nose and bright red blood began gushing out.

"My nose! My nose! You broke my nose!" He cried like a little girl, holding his hand up to his nose, trying to stop the flow.

By that time, other students had gathered around and saw what had happened. They burst out laughing and cheering at what this diminutive girl had done to defend herself from these bullies.

"You're in big trouble, girl! I'm gonna tell the principal," he warned. "Oh, man, you broke my nose!"

"Go ahead," Eva shot back, "I *want* you to go get him and bring him out here. I have something to tell him myself. I'll wait right here for you." Eva had found her courage and wasn't going to let them bully her again.

"He won't believe you. You're just a 'spic'!" the boy yelled.

"I've been called worse," she replied, as if it meant nothing to her, but still those words stung.

A parent had seen the crowd gathering, and he rushed over and stepped in.

"Anyone see what happened?" he asked, looking from face to face in the crowd.

Five or six students called out that they saw what happened and would be happy to tell the principal. These two boys were known bullies, often picking on other students and getting away with it. Eva's courage inspired them to speak up for her. The two troublemakers knew they were beaten and turned and slinked away.

Eva picked her books up off the ground and started to walk away. One of the girls in the crowd, a pretty redhead with sparkling blue eyes, walked up alongside of her. This girl was also a senior and had seen Eva in one of her classes.

"Hi. My name's Margaret. You were really brave today," she said. "I don't think I could've done what you did."

Eva stopped and turned toward her, a little surprised. She had seen this girl around school, but Margaret had never spoken to her.

"Thanks. I don't know where that came from," Eva responded. "They just wouldn't let me leave, and I couldn't take it anymore. Something just came over me. I guess fighting with my brothers all these years really came in handy."

"How many brothers do you have?"

"Seven."

"Wow, what a big family! I only have one brother," Margaret told her.

Not knowing what else to talk about, they stood there for a second or two in awkward silence, both trying to think of something else to say.

"Hey, my friend, Donna, and I are going to a USO dance this Saturday night. It's at Fort Ord, by Monterey. Would you like to come with us?" Margaret asked.

"I don't know," Eva hesitated. "I've never been to a USO dance." The truth was that she had never been to a dance of any kind before.

"Oh, it's lots of fun. All those army guys, so cute in their uniforms. Really dreamy, you know. Tell me you'll go with us. It'll be a kick."

"Okay," Eva agreed. It sounded like fun, but what would she wear? She didn't exactly own any party dresses.

She hoped she hadn't made a mistake agreeing to go with these girls, but maybe it would be good to try something new. And it might be nice to meet some nice young men. She hadn't dated at all. She was trying to concentrate on her studies and save whatever money she made at the various jobs she worked in her spare time.

That evening she told Miss Walker about what happened at school with the two teenage boys. Naomi was furious at the boys, but she was very proud of how Eva had stood up for herself. She was also pleased that some of the other students were willing to stand up and support her. Naomi could see Eva was becoming a strong and confident young woman and was glad she was able to help her escape the life she had left behind in Tres Pinos. She wished Eva's mother could see how much her daughter was blossoming. Hopefully, someday she would.

Then, Eva told Miss Walker about her new friend, Margaret, and how she had invited her to go to a USO dance with her and her friend, Donna, whom Eva had not met yet. She was glad to see Eva was starting to make more friends. It wasn't very common in their town for the white kids to socialize with the Mexican kids. This was a good sign, she thought.

Eva looked troubled. "What's wrong?" Naomi asked.

"I don't know how to dance."

"Oh, don't you worry. I can teach you. We have a few days. We can start this evening," Naomi offered.

"That would be great, but even if I learn how to dance, I don't have anything to wear to it. There's nothing in my closet that says 'party dress'." She had a little money saved from her babysitting and house cleaning jobs, but didn't really want to spend any of it. She liked knowing she had that money in her savings account in case of an emergency.

"Well," Naomi said excitedly, "why don't we see if I have anything in my closet that you could wear. I have a few dresses I can't seem to squeeze into anymore, but I keep them around because I keep hoping someday I will. Come on, let's go see."

Eva's countenance lit up and a big smile spread across her face. Naomi put an arm around Eva's shoulder and off they went to her bedroom to see what they could find.

Naomi had been a single woman for many years, a spinster some would say, because she never married. During World War II, she had been an army nurse. She'd fallen in love with an army officer named James, and he asked her to marry him. He had taken her out to dinner and dancing at a popular night club and proposed to her over glasses of sparkling champagne. That evening, she had worn a beautiful sapphire blue dress with rhinestone buttons, and James had told her she was the most beautiful woman in the world. He popped the question and she gladly said yes.

That was the last time they went dancing. A couple of months later, James was killed in the war. That beautiful dress was never worn again.

Naomi pulled the stunning blue dress out of her closet and lovingly looked it over. She gently ran her hand over the glittering buttons, remembering how in love she had been and how beautiful she felt the last time she had worn it. Naomi unzipped it and handed it to her.

"Try this dress on. Let's see how it looks."

Eva carefully tried it on. She didn't know the story behind the amazing blue dress, but she could imagine it held sentimental value to Miss Walker by the way she looked at it and tenderly caressed it.

For a moment, Eva was speechless as she caught the first glimpse of herself in the full-length mirror. She never thought she could look so attractive, but the dress was stunning on her and accentuated her curves. She twirled around like a model on a runway, keeping one eye on her image in the mirror.

"What do you think?" Eva asked. "Isn't it perfect?"

"Gorgeous! Absolutely gorgeous! It's a little long, but other than that, it looks gorgeous on you, dear. Take it off and let me hem it for you," Miss Walker offered. "It won't take long."

Eva didn't really want to take it off. She loved the feeling it gave her. She thought she looked sophisticated and grown up. She thought she looked like someone with a bright future.

CHAPTER 16

FIRST LOVE

SATURDAY EVENING CAME, and Eva looked stunning in the beautiful blue dress. Margaret and Donna picked her up at Miss Walker's house in Margaret's father's nearly-new Chevrolet sedan. All gussied up for a night out, the girls chatted and giggled the hour-or-so drive to the USO in Monterey. The main topic of conversation: men.

They pulled the car into the USO parking lot and quickly made their way inside. Standing in the doorway, they looked like something straight out of a Hollywood movie. Three beautiful young women in eye-catching dresses – one hot redhead, one sexy blonde and one exotic brunette. Heads turned all over the room and all eyes were focused on the three of them.

"That's one great entrance, girls," Donna said, full of confidence and allure.

Stepping into the dance hall, they were greeted by many eager young men in uniform, hoping for a chance to dance with each of the girls. Eva and her friends spent the next couple of hours dancing with one young soldier after another.

Toward the end of the evening, Eva found herself dancing with a young man stationed at Fort Ord. His name was Richard. He had piercing blue eyes fringed with dark eyelashes. His thick brown hair was neatly clipped, and he had a friendly smile that made her feel warm all over. They were drawn to each other like magnets, and they danced the remaining few songs only with each other.

The first number they danced to was a slow song, "Mona Lisa" by Nat King Cole. Richard gently took Eva's right hand in his left hand and put his right hand on the small of her back, drawing her toward him a bit. Their eyes met for an instant and then Eva looked away, too shy to maintain the gaze. Neither knowing what to say, they danced without talking for a few minutes. The song ended and they stopped, let go of each other and stood there for a moment in uncomfortable silence.

Right away the next song began. This one was faster, and Richard led Eva around the dance floor. She wasn't an experienced dancer, like he was, but he led her in such a way that it was easy for her to follow. She was glad, though, when the song was over that the band went back to playing another slow one. This time, Eva felt more comfortable and at ease with Richard, and they were able to have some easy conversation.

"Are you from 'round here?" Richard asked her.

"Well, about an hour from here, from a little town called Hollister," she answered.

"Did you grow up there?" he asked.

"No. I've been in Hollister since I was about five. What about you, where are you from?" she asked him, changing the subject.

"I grew up in Wisconsin. It's a long story. It wasn't good. I don't want to spoil this evenin'. We'll save that story for the next time we're together."

"The next time? How do you know there'll be a next time?" she asked in a flirtatious way. The dazzling blue dress was somehow giving her a new boldness.

"I'd like to come visit ya in Hollister sometime, if that's okay."

"Maybe," she said, playing a little hard to get. "Let me think about it."

They finished their dance and the band announced that was all for the night. Margaret and Donna were collecting their coats and purses, getting ready to head back to Hollister.

"Eva, at least gimme your phone number." Richard said. "I'd like to call ya tomorrow."

"I don't know, I barely know you," she answered.

"I wanna see you again. I'm leavin' Fort Ord next week for a few days of trainin' at Camp Pendleton. I'd like to come see ya before I have to go."

She didn't want to seem too eager. But, after the third time he asked, she eventually gave him her phone number. No boy had ever asked for her phone number before. She wondered what Miss Walker would think.

Richard phoned her the next afternoon, and they made plans to go on a picnic Sunday at noon in Bolado Park, a few miles outside of town. Miss Walker was pleased Eva was going on a picnic with a soldier, rather than out to the movies or some other dark place. She knew Eva was inexperienced with men. An afternoon picnic seemed safe.

Eva packed a delicious lunch in one of Miss Walker's large picnic baskets, and she even loaned Eva an old blanket to put down on the grass. Richard stopped by the house and introduced himself to Miss Walker. He picked up the heavy basket, and Eva carried the blanket out to the car.

Richard had come to pick her up in his buddy's black Ford sedan. He helped Eva into the car and put the basket in the back seat. Then he slid into his seat and started the car. Naomi waved to them as they drove away, hoping this soldier boy would be a gentleman.

It was early spring and the afternoon was sunny with a gentle breeze, perfect for their picnic. They arrived at the park and quickly found a nice spot near a large oak tree to spread out the blanket and the food. They sat and talked for hours, learning about each other, feeling the mutual attraction.

"Tell me about yourself, Richard. I don't even know your last name."

"It's Falkenberg."

"Well, Richard Falkenberg, tell me about yourself and your family."

"Okay. Well, let's see. My father was from Germany and my mother was from England. I don't know exactly when they came here to the U.S., sometime before I was born. My father had family in Wisconsin, so that's where they settled down. I never knew my father 'cause he died when I was a baby. My mom got married again after a few years, and my stepdad moved in with us. We got along okay. Then, my mom died when I was twelve. That was really an awful time."

"I'm sorry, Richard. I've never had anyone close to me die. It must've been terrible."

"It was. What made it worse was that I had to be raised by my stepfather – there wasn't anyone else, I guess. He was okay to me when my mom was alive, but after she died he resented having to be stuck with me, not being his own blood and all. Then came the new wife, that made things worse. My stepdad remarried, moved that woman into our house. And the woman brought her two no-good sons with her. They made my life hell. I was still just a boy, and I really missed my mom. My new stepbrothers were hellions, always doin' bad things. But all they had to do was blame stuff on me and I got beat for it. My stepdad never believed me, so he beat me a lot."

"That sounds horrible," Eva said, empathizing with what he had gone through.

"It was bad, real bad. So, when I was seventeen, I ran away and joined the army, hopin' it would be better than stickin' around that miserable place. But enough about my life, tell me about you."

Eva could relate to Richard and his life story. She was well acquainted with an abusive stepfather. But at least she had her mother.

"I'm living with Miss Walker now, but I have seven brothers and two sisters. I'm the oldest. I don't get to see my mama very often. Like you, I have a mean stepfather, too. He beat my brothers and me. But what I really couldn't take anymore was his beating my mama."

"How come you're livin' with Miss Walker?" Richard asked.

"Well…because one day the old man was hitting my mama and I just snapped. I took an axe and almost killed him with it. I would have, too, if one of my brothers hadn't stopped me. I knew right then that it was time to get out, or next time I would kill him for sure."

Richard could see he wasn't the only one with a tough past. He found Eva strong and interesting. She had a beautiful smile and made him feel like she cared about him. It had been a long time since he felt like anyone cared about him. He was thoroughly enjoying her company.

As she was talking, he reached out and put his hand on hers, and she felt a tingle go up her arm. Stopping for a just moment, her mind went blank. She forgot what she was saying until he picked up the rest of the sentence.

They continued talking and sharing back and forth about the details of their lives. Time passed quickly and the sun was beginning to set, signaling it was time to go home. They packed up their blanket and picnic basket and headed to the car. He slipped his arm around her shoulder and she felt a warmth flood her body. This was a new sensation for her, and she decided she liked it.

Their easy conversation continued on the drive back to Hollister. Richard helped Eva out of the car and carried the basket to the front door. She knew Miss Walker would be waiting for her inside, eager to hear about her afternoon. But she paused at the door and turned to face Richard.

"I had a wonderful time today," she told him.

"So did I. Do you think we could do it again sometime?"

"What did you have in mind?" she asked.

"How 'bout a movie next Saturday night?"

"Sounds like fun." She nervously looked down at the blanket draped over her arm.

Richard stroked her cheek with his finger and she felt a chill down her spine. He bent down and kissed her softly on the lips. Their first kiss – her first kiss. She looked up at him and gave him a sweet little smile. He looked into her hopeful eyes for an instant and then turned and stepped off the porch with a grin.

"I'll phone you this week, Eva," he called to her as he walked to the car. She felt the lingering warmth of his lips on hers. She waved at him as he drove away, then turned and floated into the house.

Their bond quickly grew and deepened over the next few months. Richard came to visit her as often as he could, called her when he couldn't. When he wasn't able to borrow a buddy's car, he would take the Greyhound Bus and then walk the mile and a half to her house.

Richard's commanding officer called him to his office one day and told him he had new orders for him. He was going to be shipped out to Korea. After leaving his C.O.'s office, Richard went directly to a payphone on base and called Eva. He told her he was being sent to Korea soon and would be gone for the next six months.

The news was so unexpected it made her stomach twist. A cloud of sadness enveloped her and she had to sit down because she felt her knees weaken. She was falling in love with him and now he was going to be gone for a long time.

"Give me a minute, Richard, I feel sick."

"I'm sorry, Eva. I didn't wanna have to tell you, but they didn't give me much time. I love being with you. Please understand, it wasn't my choice."

"I know, I know." Tears began to flow, and she was glad Richard couldn't see her.

They made plans to go out to dinner one last time before he shipped out the next morning. He picked her up early that evening, and they drove to Pinky's, a popular diner in town. The restaurant was busy, but Richard had called ahead and reserved a booth for them.

Sitting across the table from each other, they held hands and made small talk. Neither one wanted to talk about his leaving in the morning.

The attractive blonde waitress came and took their orders, giving Richard a wink as she left. The waitress didn't think Eva saw it, but she did. Eva wondered to herself why she would do that. Just a flirt, she thought and dismissed it. When the food came, another waitress brought it because they were so busy. Just helping out, she said.

They ate their dinner, hardly tasting it, just making small talk. Their minds were on his leaving, but they tried to avoid the subject by talking about anything else. They could avoid it no longer. Once they were through eating their dinner, the conversation came around to Richard's departing in the morning.

Richard took Eva's hand in his and looked at her face. He wasn't going to see it again for a long time and he wanted to remember her eyes, her smile, her hair. She studied his face and wondered what he was thinking. He wanted to tell her how much he was going to miss her, but the words were difficult to say.

"These last few months with you have been terrific, Eva. I can't believe I'm leaving tomorrow, and I won't see you for at least six months. It's going to be hard…really hard."

"I feel the same way. It'll be torture, Richard. I won't see you until after I graduate. It'll be like an eternity." She hung her head and was starting to softly cry. Picking up her napkin, she dabbed her eyes. "I'm sorry for being so …"

"I love you, Eva," Richard interrupted.

This surprised Eva. She looked up at him, through her tears. It wasn't just that they hadn't been going out that long, for she was having those feelings, as well. It was that she couldn't ever remember anyone in her entire life saying those words to her. She knew her mother loved her, but she couldn't recall hearing those words actually being said out loud.

"I love you, too," she blurted out in response, before she could think about it too much.

"I wanna marry you when I come back from Korea. Will you wait for me?" he asked.

"Oh, Richard!" she said, "It's only been a few months. Are you really sure?"

"Yeah, I'm sure. Will you marry me?"

"Yes, yes, yes!"

He leaned over the table and kissed her firmly on the mouth. She was dizzy with excitement, and Richard seemed pleased with himself.

They got up to leave and started toward the door. Passing by the pretty blonde waitress, Eva again noticed she winked at Richard. I'm sure she thinks he's handsome, she's just flirting with him, Eva thought to herself. He's my man, she told herself confidently, and he's going to be my husband.

Richard stopped at the cashier's counter and paid the bill, then held the door open for Eva to walk out of the diner first. She took his arm as they walked down the street to the car, his buddy's black Ford sedan. He opened the car door for her, and she turned and gave him a warm passionate kiss before getting in.

She cuddled up next to him as he drove her home, and he put his arm around her. She felt safe and loved in that moment, a feeling she had never felt before. She wanted that feeling to last forever.

There was no ring yet, only a promise. The next six months would pass quickly, she assured herself. She would keep busy finishing her senior year at school, saving her money and planning her wedding. When he returned from Korea, she kept reminding herself, they would start their wonderful new life together as man and wife.

CHAPTER 17

WEDDING BELLS

AS EVA EXPECTED, the next six months were a whirlwind of activities. She and Richard wrote letters back and forth, and she updated him on the wedding plans and the money she was saving. Working a part-time job as a nursing assistant, Eva put every penny aside for the wedding and their future together. She wrote to Richard every week and got at least one letter each month from him. Girls, she told herself, are a lot better at writing letters, I guess.

While making all the wedding arrangements, Eva finished her senior year and was preparing to graduate from Hollister High. It was 1951.One day, at the end of a long day at school, Eva was coming out of the front doors of the main building. Her arms were full of books and she had wedding plans on her mind.

"Hey, Eva!" The male voice sounded familiar. She spun around to see a tall, good-looking young man with wavy dark-hair coming through the doors behind her.

"Alex?" She was surprised to see him. They had been friends in junior high, but then his family moved away. She missed their lunches in the park. She missed him.

"Who'd you think it was?" He grinned at her. He had grown about a foot and was quite handsome.

"Well, I don't know. I haven't seen or heard from you in over three years."

"Yeah, you're right. My voice has changed since then."

"What are you doing here?" she asked.

"What? No 'welcome back', no 'happy to see you'?"

"Okay, okay. Welcome back, Alex, I'm so happy to see you." She hoped he picked up the sarcasm in her voice.

"That's better." A big smile spread across his face.

"So, why are you here?" she asked again.

"My family just moved back. I was in the office enrolling. I'm starting classes tomorrow. Surprise!"

"That's great. I'm glad to have you back." She didn't want to tell him she was heartbroken when he left, that he was the only bright spot in her life. She had had a secret crush on him in junior high, but she was sure he didn't return the feelings.

"If you're not doing anything tonight, why don't we get together. You can catch me up on all the town gossip."

"Well, I don't know." She didn't know why, but she hesitated to tell him she was engaged.

"Oh, come on. It's Friday night. Unless you already have a date."

"No, I don't have a date tonight. But, well…I'm engaged."

"Oh." His countenance fell. "I'm sorry, I didn't know. Congratulations, Eva." He looked disappointed, like a little boy who just had his bike taken away.

"Thank you." She stood there awkwardly, not knowing what else to say.

"I guess I'll see you in class then. Talk to you later." Alex felt awkward, too, and he walked off quickly.

"That was uncomfortable," Eva said to herself, making a quick exit in the other direction.

Eva finished out the school year and only spoke briefly to Alex on a few occasions. Even though at one time she had a big crush on him, she couldn't think of him like that anymore. She tried to block him out of her mind, reminding herself she was committed to marrying Richard. They would both be graduating soon and pursuing separate paths in life. Her life would be with Richard.

* * * * *

Occasionally, Eva ran into her mother at the market in town or on the street, and they would hug and talk for just a few minutes. Sofía could never stop for very long to chat, though; she always needed to get back home before too long.

It was during one of those brief visits that Eva told her mother about her graduation day and implored her to please come. She said she would try, but it wouldn't be easy.

Over the next few weeks, Mama was often on Eva's mind. It was one of the most important days in her life, and she sincerely wanted her mother to be there. She wasn't sure Carlos would let Mama and her brothers and sisters come to the graduation because he hated Eva so much.

But, it turned out to be a wonderful day. Mama was able to come and share that special day with her. Unfortunately, she had to come alone. Carlos eventually gave in to Sofía's pleading, but he had forbidden Eva's brothers and sisters from coming.

Lydia, Eva's little sister, babysat the two youngest so their mother would be free to attend. Eva was overjoyed to see Mama that day. Not just because it was her graduation day, but also because, since moving out at sixteen, she hadn't seen much of her family at all. Carlos absolutely would not allow it.

Sofía was so happy to be there for Eva on this special day. She was so proud of her daughter, the first in her family to graduate from high school. She could see how much Eva had grown up, how happy and confident she looked. Her hair was cut into a stylish bob and she spoke with more confidence and directness than Sofía had remembered.

After the ceremony, Eva was able to spend a little time with Mama before Carlos would be expecting her home. Mama brought Eva up to date on each of the children, purposely avoiding any talk about Carlos and the misery he continued to inflict on them. She didn't want to taint this wonderful day. Before Sofía had to rush off, Eva took the opportunity to tell her that she was engaged and would be getting married soon.

"Married? That's wonderful, mi'ja. I'm so happy for you." What else could she say? Sofía wondered to herself. She hoped Eva was making the right decision, she was so young, not quite nineteen. Sofía knew so well the suffering and despair that came from marrying the wrong man.

"Thank you, Mama," Eva said as her mother gave her a long, warm hug.

"Tell me about your young man. What's he like? Where's he from? What does he look like?" Mama had so many questions. She had come to this ceremony today so delighted to see Eva graduate from high school. She didn't expect to find out she was getting married, too.

Eva went on to tell her mother about Richard and his life in Wisconsin, and that he was in the army. She described his blue eyes and thick brown hair.

"Blue eyes? You mean he's white?" Sofía asked.

"Well, yes, Mama."

"We've never had a gringo in our family. And he doesn't care you're Mexican? He knows about your family? That we work in the fields?"

"He knows, Mama. He doesn't care. He loves me. I hope you'll come to my wedding."

"Oh, Eva." Mama shook her head. She dreaded the thought of having to ask Carlos for permission again, but she knew this was important. It would take some begging, some bribing, maybe even some fighting.

"I want to be there, I just don't know if I can. We'll see. I have to go." She needed to get back home before Carlos started getting mad that she was gone too long. Eva pleaded with her mother to find a way to come to the wedding.

"I love you, Eva," she said, her eyes glistening with tears. "I'm really happy for you."

Sofía didn't know when she would be able to see her daughter again. She hoped Carlos would let her go to the wedding. She knew it would be another battle.

"I love you, too, Mama. I really hope you can come."

"I'll try to be there," she said. "I promise, I'll try." She turned and walked away, not wanting Eva to see the tears beginning to form. She was happy for her daughter. She hoped Eva would find love with a good man and have the kind of life she had wanted for herself, but never found.

Sofía's thoughts were filled with Eva and her future as she walked home. She wanted to be at the wedding with all her heart – her first child to marry. But would Carlos let her? That she didn't know. And with Eva marrying a white man, a "gringo," Carlos would certainly not be pleased and would make sure she knew it. She just wanted her daughter to marry someone who would love her, take care of her, and treat her well.

She had two months to figure out a way to attend her daughter's wedding. It wouldn't be easy.

* * * * *

Naomi was a huge help in planning the wedding and overseeing the event. It wasn't going to be anything large or fancy, but she wanted it to be special for Eva.

She loaned her wedding gown to her, the one she had bought for her own wedding day before her fiancée was killed. As her wedding gift to the bride and groom, she offered to pay for the wedding cake, which Eva gladly accepted.

Eva asked her friend, Margaret, to be her maid of honor and Richard chose an army buddy, Gary, to be his best man. Margaret planned to wear a lovely deep green dress she already owned and Richard and the best man would be wearing their dress uniforms.

Miss Walker's little red brick Presbyterian Church provided the minister, the organist, the reception hall, and all the furnishings and tableware for the reception as part of the charge for renting the church. Eva covered the punch and all the decorations of the church and the hall out of her remaining savings. Her plans were coming together and everything was going well.

She made out her guest list, which was quite short, as she didn't have many friends and didn't even know if her mother or siblings could come. Miss Walker invited a few of her friends to fill in the church, people that Eva had met or had worked for.

Eva wondered if she should invite Alex. They had been friends in junior high, but then he moved away. Since coming back to Hollister, things had been awkward between them, but they still talked briefly once in awhile. With so few friends to her credit, she counted Alex among them. Given that she had to order a minimum of fifty invitations from the printer, she had plenty of extras. She decided to send one to Alex, not expecting that he would come.

Richard was finally back from Korea two weeks before the wedding and called Eva from Fort Ord a couple of times a week. The day before the wedding, he came to Hollister to see her and brought his best man with him.

They were going out on the town in Monterey that evening for a bachelor's party, the night before the big day. Richard promised Eva he would be at the church by noon the next day, in plenty of time for the wedding. Eva didn't know they were going out with the pretty blonde waitress from Pinky's and her friend – one last fling before tying the knot. Eva also didn't know he had been out with her before.

She woke up early that Saturday morning – it was her wedding day. The sun was shining, and she expected it to be a perfect day. She thought of Mama and hoped she was coming. Her mother had always been the most important person in her life, the person who encouraged her to get an education and make something of herself, the person who protected her when she could, even to her own detriment. Eva would be enormously disappointed if her mother couldn't be there on this most special day.

Miss Walker was already up and had breakfast waiting for her, all her favorites – pancakes, eggs sunny side up, sausages, fresh-squeezed orange juice and coffee. This would be the last day they would be having breakfast together, and Naomi wanted to savor it. Unfortunately, Eva couldn't eat a bite because of her nerves. Naomi could tell Eva's mind was on something other than eating – Richard and the wedding.

Naomi had met Richard several times early on in their courtship. She thought he seemed like a nice-enough fellow. He was nice looking and polite, and always seemed to treat Eva well. But, she knew Eva had had her heart set on going to nursing school, so she wasn't sure how that was going to work out now. It was Eva's choice, after all, not hers. Naomi just wanted to be there to support her and make this day a happy one.

After breakfast, they loaded the wedding gown and all the decorations in Miss Walker's station wagon and went to the little church to decorate it and the reception hall. The decorations were not lavish, but with some flowers and candles, the cozy sanctuary would be lovely.

There would be plenty of time for Eva to get dressed in her wedding gown after the decorating was done. Miss Walker would even have time to help her with her hair. Both Eva and Naomi were giddy with excitement.

The wedding was scheduled for two o'clock in the afternoon, so having Richard and the best man there by noon would allow ample time for everything to be ready for ceremony to begin on time. But twelve noon came and went. Eva started to get a little panicked.

Miss Walker helped her with her hair and tried to keep her calm, reassuring her that there was plenty of time. "They must be running a little late, that's all," she told Eva.

One o'clock rolled around and the groom and best man still had not shown up. Margaret arrived already dressed and looking pretty. She went to the bride's room in the back of the church to see if there was anything she could help with.

Margaret tapped lightly on the door, then stepped inside. Eva was seated in front of the mirror, and turned when the door opened. Eva smiled at her, glad to see her friend. Naomi was standing behind Eva with a comb in her hand and smiled, too, when she saw Margaret come in.

"I just wanted to see if there were any last minute things that I could do for you," Margaret offered.

"Richard and Gary aren't here yet," Eva told Margaret, her smile turning to a frown. "Where could they be?"

"I'm sure they'll be here any minute. Don't you worry, Eva. I will find 'em." She turned quickly and walked toward the door. "I'll be back soon," and she was gone.

Margaret stepped out of the back door of the small church, closest to where she parked her car, and saw Richard and Gary getting out of a late-model black sedan. A voluptuous blonde woman was behind the wheel of the car. Gary grabbed their uniforms out of the back seat while Richard walked around to the driver's side, leaned in and gave the woman a long, passionate kiss.

Then the men casually walked around to the front church entrance like innocent choir boys. Neither man had seen Margaret watching them. They thought they had pulled off their wild night undetected.

Margaret quietly slipped back inside through the back door. She felt sick, not sure what to do next. Her good friend was about to marry a man she just saw kissing another woman – on their wedding day.

Richard and Gary had been in Monterey for his bachelor's party, and it appeared to Margaret that Richard had spent the night with this blonde. Her head was spinning. She leaned against the wall to steady herself. Should she tell Eva what she saw? Save her from a bad marriage? Or should she keep quiet and hope it meant nothing?

Miss Walker caught sight of Richard and Gary coming in the church doors, and she quickly made her way over to them.

"Richard, you're late," Naomi scolded.

"I know, sorry."

"We don't have much time. You boys follow me and I'll show you where to change."

She escorted them to the groom's room to change into their dress uniforms. Then she stopped briefly at the bride's room to let Eva know they had finally arrived.

"Richard and Gary are here, and I put them in the groom's room to get dressed," Miss Walker informed her. Eva's nerves began to calm down. "I'm going to go back to the sanctuary to see to some last minute details. Do you need anything?"

"Just my mother."

Besides fretting about where Richard was, Eva was also worried that Mama might not make it. She badly wanted her mother to share in her special day, but she knew it could be dangerous for her.

"I'll keep an eye out for her. You just relax. This is your big day." Miss Walker left and headed for the foyer. She saw Sofía come through the front doors and went over and greeted her with a big smile. Sofía was happy to see Miss Walker, too, and told her how much she appreciated the help she had given Eva.

"Let me take you to the bride's room so you can see your daughter. She's back there getting ready," Naomi told her. Sofía's eyes lit up with delight.

Miss Walker knocked on the door and waited for a reply.

"Come in," Eva said.

Miss Walker walked in first, and then Sofía came in behind her. When Eva saw her mama, she jumped out of her chair and ran over to her mother, throwing her arms around her.

"Oh, Mama! I'm so happy you're here, I'm so happy you're here! I didn't know if you would make it." They embraced for a long time, both trying not to cry, then finally released.

"You need to get your wedding dress on, mi'ja."

"Help me with it, Mama."

Sofía helped Eva into her wedding gown and fastened her veil on her head.

"You look beautiful, Eva!" Sofía could no longer contain her emotions and started to cry.

"Oh, Mama, no." Eva reached for a tissue and handed it to her mother.

"I'm so happy, mi'ja." Sofía wiped her eyes.

"I don't mean to interrupt, but it's almost time, Eva," Miss Walker advised. "We really should get your mother to her seat."

"I'd better go," Sofía said, giving Eva one more quick hug before she followed Miss Walker out of the room. She stopped in the doorway and turned back momentarily for one more glimpse of her daughter in her wedding dress. Eva looked so lovely, so grown up. Sofía whispered a prayer over her and closed the door.

Naomi escorted Sofía down the aisle to sit on the front row, in the place reserved for the mother of the bride.

"Here, Mrs. Gonzalez. This is your seat," she said as she motioned toward it with her hand.

"Gracias." Sofía proudly sat down in her place of honor. Naomi took the seat next to her.

"I'm so glad you were able to come today. How did you manage it?" Naomi asked, knowing from Eva that Carlos would probably forbid it.

"I told my husband weeks ago about Eva's wedding. I asked him if the niños and I could come. At first he said no, he wouldn't let me or the niños come. But, this was too important to just let that be the end of it. I just kept asking as often as I could. I guess I just wore him down."

From what Eva had shared about her stepfather and his temper, Naomi knew what a risk Sofía had taken to keep asking Carlos for permission to come. Somehow she had convinced Carlos to at least let her come by herself, after all it was her daughter's wedding. But he remained adamant that none of the children could go.

Most of their sons were in junior high and high school by that time, but the boys refused to defy their father. They had learned what a high price they would pay if they disobeyed him. So Sofía was content to come alone.

After Margaret came back inside from the parking lot, she wanted to go to the bride's room to stay with Eva until the wedding started, but she had not yet decided what she should do about Richard. She wrestled with whether or not to tell Eva what she just saw. Should she tell her and ruin her wedding day? Maybe ruin her happiness for life? Or maybe by telling Eva she would keep her from marrying an unfaithful man? But, on the other hand, she thought to herself, should she simply keep quiet because maybe it was just the remains of an out-of-control bachelor party and it's over? She went back and forth, back and forth in her mind.

"Eva loves him," Margaret told herself. "They will be married today, and then they'll be living on the base, far away from here. I can't imagine how he'll ever see that woman again." She decided she would not tell Eva.

She went to the bride's room and stayed with Eva until it was time for the ceremony to start. After a little while, Naomi came in and told them it was time to begin, then went back to her seat. Richard was already standing at the front of the sanctuary with the minister and the organist was in place.

Margaret walked with Eva to the foyer and found Gary already there, waiting to walk down the aisle with the maid of honor. The organist started to play. Margaret, with a small bouquet of yellow flowers in one hand, put her other hand through Gary's arm. They slowly marched down the aisle, turning as they took their places at the front.

Eva took her position in the back and waited for the music to change. She had no father or brothers there to walk her down the aisle, as most girls do. She was left to walk down the aisle alone.

Holding her modest display of white roses and carnations with both hands, she nervously waited for her cue. The organist began to play the wedding march, and the minister gave the hand signal for everyone to rise. The guests instinctively turned to watch the bride entering. Alex was seated on the aisle, but Eva didn't notice. Her eyes were focused on her groom. She stepped into the sanctuary and slowly proceeded to the front. A big smile spread across Richard's face when he saw Eva, and it made her whole body tingle.

Sofía and Naomi had a front-row view of the nuptials, and they generously shared a box of tissue. Their girl was getting married.

The minister began his discourse, and Richard and Eva exchanged their vows. Margaret's stomach was churning as she stood next to Eva, and she began to sweat. She knew what was coming.

"If anyone knows any reason why these two should not be joined together, speak now or forever hold your peace," the minister recited.

Margaret chose to say nothing. She hoped she was doing the right thing.

CHAPTER 18

HOPE FOR SOFÍA

THE YEAR WAS 1957. Eva had been gone from her family for years, traveling from army base to army base, following Richard as the military moved him around the country. Her return to her hometown in California was bittersweet. She was returning to her family, but she was also coming back to a place that held painful memories.

Eva wasn't sure how she would feel coming home to Hollister because so many things in her life had changed. She was a different person than the naïve young bride who left. Now she was married, living the lonely life of a military wife, with children of her own. She was raising her children mostly by herself – a son and a daughter. This was not the life she had dreamed of as a teenager, but this was the life she had, and she was determined to make it work.

The first person she wanted to see was her mother, Sofía. But she was afraid of running into her stepfather. Visiting her mother would be tricky. If she timed it just right, hopefully Carlos would be out working, and she would have some time alone with Mama.

As soon as Eva arrived in town, she checked her family into a small motel on the edge of Hollister. The faded blue paint was peeling and weeds were growing up through the old, cracked asphalt in the parking lot. A sign blinked "VACANT" with an irregular beat. The motel was in desperate need of repairs, but the price was right.

Early that afternoon, she drove out to the farm worker shanties in her old green Ford station wagon with the children in the back seat. Rory was four years old and Angie was three. Eva told them that they were going to meet their Grandma Sofía and that she wanted them to be on their best behavior.

As the car approached the rickety old house, Eva felt the familiarity of it. She saw the same cluster of rundown shacks in which she had spent so many difficult years. The sight of them brought back a flood of painful memories. Her back stiffened and her stomach tensed. There were a handful of pleasant memories in this place, with her mama and her siblings, but they were few and far between.

Eva pulled the car up in front of the familiar front porch and helped the children out. She hadn't seen her mother in more than six years, and this would be the first time Sofía would see her grandchildren. Eva thought this would be a wonderful surprise for her poor mother.

She couldn't call Sofía to tell her she was coming because her mother didn't have a phone. Eva feared that if she sent her mama a letter, Carlos would find it. And if he knew Eva had contacted her mother, he might take his hatred of Eva out on Sofía yet again.

Eva had received a couple of letters over the years from one of her brothers. Her oldest brother, Eduardo, had gotten married a couple of years ago and asked Miss Walker for his sister's address. He figured Eva would keep in touch with Miss Walker, and he was right. He wanted to let her know he was getting married and how the family was doing.

In his letters, Eduardo told Eva that Carlos's drinking and his violent abuse against their mother had not diminished, maybe even grown worse. Reading this made Eva distraught. There was nothing she could do to help her mother because she was so far away. She hoped this trip would change that.

With her children in tow, Eva nervously rapped on the door a few times. The door slowly opened and Sofía peered around it. Suspicion gave way to delight, and she opened the door wider. A broad smile spread across her face, and she threw her arms around her daughter. She hugged her hard and didn't want to let go. Finally, she released her embrace and took a small step back.

Eva was astonished at how much her mother had aged, appearing as worn out as her tattered and faded house dress. She had not expected to see the wrinkles and graying hair. Trying not to let her mother see her surprise, Eva put a smile on her face and kept her voice cheerful.

Sofía was happy to see the two little children hiding behind their mother's full skirt, shyly peeking around it.

"Are these my grandchildren?" Sofía asked excitedly, as they would be her first.

"Yes, Mama, this is Rory," pulling him out from behind her, "and this is Angelina," pulling her out from the other side of her skirt. "We call her Angie for short."

Sofía scooped her granddaughter up in her arms and kissed her gently on the cheek. With her other hand, she affectionately stroked Rory's soft brown hair.

"Qué bonita!" she exclaimed. She was surprised by Angie's fair skin, dark blonde hair and blue-green eyes. Then she remembered that Eva's husband was white. Not that that fact was something she should forget, but she had not seen Eva in years, and time and her traumatic life had faded her memory of the wedding.

"Oh, come in, come in," she said to Eva, leading her grandson by the hand while still holding her granddaughter in her arm. Eva noticed the large dark bruise on the side of her mother's face near her eye, but she didn't want to say anything about it. Obviously, nothing had changed.

They all stepped into the weathered shack, and another wave of memories rushed at Eva. It had been nine years since she had set foot in this place, but all of a sudden the emotions came flooding back like it was yesterday. She half expected to see Carlos walk into the room, but caught herself. A shiver ran up her spine and she tried to shake off the feeling.

Nothing had really changed. Not the worn-out furniture or the smell of Mama's beans and tortillas. The oppressive atmosphere of poverty and despair still weighed heavily in this place. Not even the pungent stench of fear had diminished one bit.

Grandma Sofía offered the children something to eat, but Eva had brought some of their favorite crackers and toys to keep them occupied. The children were busy on the bare wood floor getting their toys out of the beige canvas bag Eva had brought and sharing the crackers.

Eva tried to keep her mind focused on reconnecting with her mother, hoping she could give her mama some time to get to know her grandchildren. She did her best to keep the conversation cheerful and light about Richard and the children, but Mama looked worried. She noticed her mother kept watching the little plastic clock on the wall. Eva tried to ignore the distraction and continued with her story.

She filled her mother in on what her life had been like since she married Richard. They initially moved to Fort Lewis in Tacoma, Washington, where Rory was born.

"Then we moved to LaCrosse, Wisconsin, after Angie was born," Eva went on to say. "That's where Richard's relatives are."

Because Eva didn't want to burden Mama with the sordid details, she left out the parts about Richard going ahead of her to LaCrosse to try to find work. His enlistment in the army was up shortly after Rory was born, and she had unexpectedly gotten pregnant again right away. Richard moved the family to Salt Lake City, Utah, to go to a special trade school, but that didn't work out for him. So he figured he could find work where his family lived in Wisconsin.

He told Eva he was going to be staying with his Aunt Gertie and left her address and phone number. He promised Eva he would be back for the baby's birth. Then they could all move to Wisconsin with him. But he was never at his aunt's house when Eva called him. She left messages with the aunt, but not one time did he ever call her back. She sent him a letter, still no response.

Eva waited in Salt Lake City. She was almost out of money, and the baby was due any day. She had made friends with a neighbor lady, a nice woman in her forties named Lucy who stayed home all day. Her husband, Jim, had a decent job and didn't want her to work. Lucy and Jim couldn't have children, and they loved playing with Rory. She offered to watch the little boy when the time came for her to go to the hospital.

When Eva's contractions began one afternoon, she took Rory to Lucy's apartment and called for a cab from there. With no insurance or money to pay for the delivery, Eva had already decided to throw herself on the mercy of the Mormon Hospital a few blocks away. She knew they wouldn't turn her away, and she was right.

They checked her in, took her in a wheelchair to a room and got her situated in bed. The room was sterile and quiet. She shared the room with two other mothers who recently gave birth who were asleep from exhaustion. An older nurse with graying hair came in and out, checking on Eva's progress. For a fleeting moment, watching the nurse, Eva wondered what her life might have been like if she had pursued a nursing career instead of marrying Richard.

When her contractions increased dramatically, she was wheeled on a gurney to the delivery room. Even with nurses and doctor buzzing around her, she felt lonely and abandoned. She wanted her husband to be there, but he wasn't. Even though she called often and left messages for him, Richard did not come. She gave birth to her daughter all alone.

A few days later, Eva and her baby girl checked out of the hospital and went home. Lucy enjoyed her time with little Rory and offered to keep him for a few more days to help out. She knew Eva would have a difficult time with a newborn and an eleven-month-old baby, and Lucy loved playing mom. Eva gratefully accepted her offer, but she went to check on her son every afternoon.

Day after day, Eva waited for word from Richard, a returned phone call or a letter. But she didn't hear anything from him. It had been weeks since she left messages informing him that he now had a daughter.

Having no idea where her husband was, Eva was getting more concerned by the day. She was stuck in Salt Lake City with two babies and her money was running out. By this time, Angie was four weeks old and Rory was twelve months. Richard missed his son's first birthday and his daughter's birth. Eva was angry and desperate. She marched down to the Red Cross office in town and asked them for money to buy a bus ticket to go to LaCrosse and find him.

With both infants, Eva took the Greyhound Bus and reached LaCrosse after several long days on the road. Fortunately, there were kind strangers along the way that were willing to help her with feedings and diaper changes. Some of the passengers offered to rock one of the babies while Eva tended to the other. When they arrived in LaCrosse, it was a warm summer evening in June. The year was 1954.

The bus was traveling on the road that passed in front of Richard's aunt's small farm. The driver pulled over and stopped to let them out near the little brick single-story house. He retrieved Eva's suitcase from the storage area of the bus and set it off the road for her. She walked with her children up the dirt driveway to the front door, which set about twenty yards off the road. Eva knocked and waited. She hoped Richard was home.

His aunt answered the door and was surprised to see Eva and the babies. Unfortunately, Richard wasn't there, and his aunt didn't know when he'd be back.

Aunt Gertie was a pleasantly plump German woman in her early fifties and seemed embarrassed by Richard's actions. Color rose in her cheeks, and she apologized profusely. She had taken countless phone messages that Richard obviously had not returned. Now here they were, face to face, and there was nothing helpful she could tell his wife.

"He just said he was going out, wherever that is. He didn't say when he'd be back, never does," Gertie said. "But you come on in, now."

Standing on the porch, Eva had her newborn daughter in one arm and little Rory by the hand. He was already walking. They squeezed through the doorway, past Gertie, who was holding the screen door open for them.

"Just look at those sweet babies," she commented as they went by her. "I'll go get your suitcase, dear. Okay? Okay."

Gertie brought the suitcase in and put it down in Richard's room. It was past supper time and she figured Eva must be hungry. She waddled into the kitchen and made a big plate of meats and cheeses, along with flaky crackers on the side.

She came back into the living room and set the platter down on the coffee table. "I'm sure you must be famished, honey."

"I am kind of hungry," Eva replied.

"You go ahead and dig in, okay? Okay." Aunt Gertie took the sleeping baby from Eva's arms so she was free to eat. Rory was fast asleep on the sofa next to her.

They made polite conversation and waited and waited for Richard. It had been almost four hours. Darn that Richard, Gertie thought to herself. The situation grew more awkward with each passing minute, but Gertie did her best to make them all comfortable. She tried to keep up the conversation and provide them with food and drink.

"It's getting late, sweetie. Let me go make up a place for the babies to sleep, okay? Okay." Gertie handed baby Angie back to Eva, then wandered off down the hallway.

She went in the spare bedroom and made up a sleeping area for both the babies on one of the beds by rolling blankets and towels around the area so they wouldn't roll off. Then she came out with a pillow and blanket for Eva to use while she waited for Richard on the sofa.

"Unless there's somethin' else you need, honey, I'm goin' to bed. Okay? Okay."

"Well, there is one thing. I need to warm some milk in a bottle for the baby. She'll be waking up soon. Do you mind if I use your kitchen?" Eva asked.

"Oh, you betcha. Go on ahead and use anything you like." Aunt Gertie shuffled off to bed.

Eva warmed a bottle and held her baby while she drank. She paced the room with her little daughter in her arms until she fell back asleep. Then she put her down to sleep on the bed with Rory.

Finally, about one-thirty in the morning, Richard stumbled into the house. Eva had been asleep on the sofa and woke to the noise. He smelled like a brewery and cigarettes. There was no doubt where he had been. She was furious. She had two questions – "where did you get money to buy beer and who were you drinking with?"

After fighting and arguing and crying for quite awhile, Eva decided to forgive him for not keeping in touch with her, for not being there for Angie's birth, for going out drinking with what little money he had. She reluctantly agreed to stay in LaCrosse for the foreseeable future. With two babies and no money, she knew she didn't have much choice.

Richard told her hadn't been able to find steady work and was too embarrassed to let her know. The truth was, according to Aunt Gertie, he had secured two different jobs but had been fired from both. Eva suspected as much.

So, the next day she asked Aunt Gertie if she would watch the babies for a few hours so she could go into town and look for work. Gertie happily agreed and wished her luck.

Within a couple of hours Eva was able to find jobs for both of them at a poultry processing plant. Aunt Gertie consented to watching the babies while they worked so they could save up enough money to move out on their own. Richard didn't last two weeks at the poultry plant before he got fired. So, Eva demanded he re-enlist in the army, which he did.

This was not a story Eva wanted to share with her mother. So, leaving out all the messy particulars, she continued on with telling Sofía about their move to an army base in Newport News, Virginia. Eva gave only the surface details of her many moves over the past six years and how she was kept busy setting up her houses and having babies.

"But now, Mama, we live in Seaside where Richard is stationed at Fort Ord again. That's where I met Richard at a USO dance, remember?" Eva was happy she was close enough now to see her family again.

"I hope that means I'll be able to see you and the niños again." Sofía knew Carlos would not like having Eva at the house, but maybe she could sneak by, like today, or they could meet somewhere in town.

"Yes, at least for awhile."

Sofía's countenance fell and she looked sad. "What do you mean 'for awhile'?"

"Well, Richard's been reassigned to a base in Germany, and he'll be leaving soon. The kids and I are going to follow him a few months after he ships out," Eva told her. "We're really excited to go to Europe. But don't worry, Mama, the kids and I will be here for a few more months."

Eva wanted her mother to believe she was happy. The truth was that she found out, over the years, that her husband had a wandering eye. From time to time, he would be attracted to other women, and she would have to rein him in. But she didn't want to burden her mother with that, so she kept those details to herself and only spoke positively about her life with Richard. Eva knew Mama had enough to deal with in her own life.

Sofía filled her daughter in on what was happening with the younger children who were still at home. Hector had just started high school, and Miguel and Christina were in elementary school. They weren't home from school yet, but the bus, Mama said, would be bringing them home in another half hour or so.

They continued to visit for a little while, but Eva couldn't help but notice that Sofía kept looking at the clock and keeping close track of the time. She seemed agitated and fearful. After they had visited for a few more minutes, Sofía told Eva that she should go because the niños would be home from school soon and then Carlos would be coming home from work.

Sofía walked over to the window and peeked out to make sure Carlos was not out there. Fortunately he wasn't there, but Eva could see real fear starting to rise up in her mama. Sofía's eyes were darting around like a scared rabbit, her shoulders tensed. It broke Eva's heart to see her mother this way, what the years of abuse had done to her.

"Mama? Are you all right?"

"I didn't want to tell you this, but I'm more afraid of Carlos than I've ever been." Eva saw the terror on her mother's face.

"Why?"

"A few nights ago, he came home very drunk. I heard him staggering around the house, slamming cupboard doors, looking for more liquor. But he couldn't find it." Sofía put her hand on her chest. "I tried to lie very still so he'd think I was asleep. But he came into the bedroom and put a knife to my throat, accusing me of hiding his whiskey." Her hand moved from her chest to her neck, and a tear trickled down her cheek. "I've never been so frightened."

"Oh, Mama," was all Eva could say, as she put her arm around her mother's shoulders.

"I'm afraid he's going to kill me." Sofía's voice was shaking. She looked out the window one more time. "I didn't want to tell you, mi'ja, but I'm so scared."

"I'm going to get you out of this horrible place, Mama," Eva promised her. But she knew that right now she had to leave before the school bus dropped her brothers and sister off.

"Don't worry, Mama, I'll be back," Eva said in a low voice, not wanting her children to overhear. She stepped in close to Mama and whispered to her. "I hate to see you still having to live this way. You deserve better than this, you deserve to be happy. That man is no good, Mama, no good. He'll never change. I got away from here – you can, too."

"No, I can't leave, mi'ja. I want to, but where would I go? How would I live? No, at least here I have a place to live and food to eat. And what about the your brothers and sister?"

"I'll figure it out. You deserve better, Mama – *you do*. Hector, Miguel and Christina, they deserve a better life, too. I don't know what to do yet, but I'm going to do something to get you out of here, and them, too."

"Come on, Rory, Angie – time to go. We'll see Grandma again soon." She tried to keep an upbeat tone to her voice and a smile on her face so she didn't upset her children. Eva quickly gathered up the snacks and toys and put them in the bag and led the kids to the door. She turned and gave her mother a long hug.

Eva felt compassion mixed with anger stirring up inside her. She was determined to find a way to rescue her mama, to rescue them all. After all the years of cruelty, Sofía did not have the strength left to break away, but Eva definitely did.

"I'll be back, Mama. Don't worry. We'll figure it out. I promise."

Sofía's eyes brightened a little at the possibility there might be a way out for her. After all these years of torment and abuse, she smiled at the thought that it was her daughter who gave her hope. Sofía thought back to the day she gave birth to Eva and how she knew her young daughter would do great things. She never dreamed Eva would be her savior.

The thought of escaping was both exciting and scary at the same time. Sofía wasn't sure if she should dare to hope, if she should allow herself to dream of being free, of leaving this wretched life behind. Disappointment would be crushing.

Sofía knew she couldn't risk telling her children about Eva. They might accidentally let it slip and Carlos would find out. He would never let them leave. More than likely he would explode with anger and kill her in a fit of rage.

But, Eva had escaped, she reminded herself. Maybe Eva could save them, too…maybe.

CHAPTER 19

THE RESCUE

THE NEXT PERSON EVA WANTED to see was her sister, Lydia. The following morning she got Rory and Angie up early, and they drove out to her sister's house in San Juan Bautista, a rural mission town just outside of Hollister. Lydia was eighteen and recently married. She had married Manuel Montoya about six months before she graduated from high school. Manuel worked on a local farm for several years and was moved up to supervising the laborers.

Eva had sent Lydia a letter a few weeks before, telling her that she and the children were coming for a visit. As they drove up, Lydia came rushing out of her old mission-style house, excited to see them. They had not seen each other in almost eight years. As soon as Eva stepped out of the car, Lydia's arms were around her sister's neck with a tight, warm squeeze.

"Oh, I have missed you!" Lydia said.

"Look who I brought to see their Tía Lydia!" Eva opened the door to the back seat, and Rory and Angie climbed out of the car.

"These must be your children! Oh, qué bonito!"

"Yes, this is Rory and Angie."

"Well, I'm so glad you're here. I got your letters, but I'm glad you're finally here in person. Come, come, let's go in the house." Lydia spread her arms out and corralled them all like a mother hen gathering her chicks. They all stepped into the weathered white stucco house.

Everyone made themselves comfortable around the kitchen table. Lydia brought out some cookies and milk for the children and coffee for Eva and herself. The sisters chatted for awhile about Eva's drive from Seaside, Lydia's job, and what Manuel was up to.

The children quickly finished their snacks and were getting restless. Eva set their big canvas bag on the floor in the living room so they could occupy themselves with the books and small toys while she and her sister continued to talk.

"I went to see Mama yesterday," Eva told Lydia, as she stirred sugar into her coffee. She looked over at the children to make sure they were out of earshot. Keeping her voice low, she continued. "Looks like nothing has changed. She had a black eye. The old man is still beating her, isn't he?"

"Yeah," Lydia replied flatly, confirming what Eva already knew.

"It tears me up inside, knowing what he's doing to her. She looked like a scared little rabbit."

"I know," Lydia agreed. "But I don't know what we can do about it. Papa gets so angry, especially when he's drinking. You should've seen him last Thanksgiving."

"What happened?"

"It was terrible," Lydia said, thinking back to that day.

"Tell me."

"It was Thanksgiving Day and Mama told all of us we would be eating about three o'clock. She was cooking a big turkey. Papa told her he was going out for awhile and he'd be back for dinner."

"Was he?"

"No. We were all ready to eat, but he was still gone, so we waited. Mama tried to keep the turkey and everything warm, but it was almost five o'clock and he still wasn't back. The turkey was drying out and everyone was getting really hungry, so Mama said we should go ahead and eat."

"I bet the old man didn't like that," Eva said.

"Oh, he was furious. He came back about seven-thirty, and of course, we already ate. He was drunk, stumbling around and shouting at Mama that we should've waited for him. He took what was left of the turkey and threw it out in the dirt. Then he started cursing and beating Mama. Ygnacio and Mateo tried to stop him, especially Mateo."

"I hate that man!" Eva said, shaking her head. The kids turned and looked at her with big eyes, wondering what was happening. "Don't worry, kids," she said to them in a calmer voice, "it was nothing. Go back to your toys."

Eva realized she needed to watch the tone of her voice with the children nearby.

"Then what happened?" she asked Lydia quietly.

"Papa kicked Mateo out of the house, said he wasn't going to have him getting in the middle of his business. He was only sixteen, and he had nowhere to go. So, Eduardo and Belia let him stay with them."

"Who's there to protect her now?" Eva asked.

"Nobody, really. The others are too young."

Lydia was not the black sheep of the family, like Eva was, so she had regular contact with Mama and checked in on her as often as she could. They both lived outside of Hollister, with Tres Pinos being about fifteen miles to the east and San Juan Bautista about ten miles to the west. With her job, a husband to take care of and the twenty-five-mile distance between them, it was hard to see Sofía very often. But, she did whenever she could.

"I promised Mama yesterday that I would do all I could to help her get away from the old man," Eva told Lydia. "Did you know he held a knife to her throat a few weeks ago?"

"Ay, Diós mio! No, I didn't know. I mean, I knew things were bad, but I had no idea."

"I'm afraid he'll kill her next time if we don't do something."

"But what can we do?" Lydia asked.

"I've been thinking about it since I left her. I think the first thing we need to do is find her a job, something where she can live on her own and take care of herself and the younger kids. Do you have any ideas?"

Lydia thought for a moment. "You know, I've been working at one of the canneries in Hollister since Manuel and I got married. I wonder if they would hire Mama, too. Tomato season is starting soon, so I know they'll be hiring more people. I could ask."

"And if we could find her a place to live... Oh, Lydia, I think we can do this." Eva's confidence was growing.

"I don't know, but I'm willing to help." Lydia said. "What do you think we should do?"

"I'll go back into town and see if I can find a little house for her to rent. I've got some money saved up, so I can put down a deposit. Maybe even pay the first month's rent for her. Do you think you could watch Rory and Angie for me for a few hours?"

"Sure, sure. They'll be fine here with me. Take your time. Do what you have to do. Don't worry about the kids, I can take care of them."

"Thanks, Lydia. I'll be back as soon as I can."

Bending down, Eva kissed her children good-bye as they played on the floor. She gave her sister a quick hug, picked up her purse and was out the door. She was a woman on a mission, determined that she was going to rescue her mother and her siblings.

As Eva drove back to Hollister, her mind raced with different ideas to explore – where to go, who to talk to, what to say. She kept seeing Mama's face popping up in her thoughts, the big black bruise near her temple, her eyes full of fear. The vision only made her more resolute in her mission. She would find a house today for her mother and her brothers and sister and nothing would stand in her way.

She drove up and down the residential streets of Hollister, searching for "For Rent" signs in yards, with no luck. Stopping at a corner grocery store to pick up a newspaper, she scanned the classified ads for "Homes for Rent," looking for homes that were $100 a month or less. There were only two, and the ads gave the addresses. Driving by the first one, she saw it was in poor condition. That would not do.

So she decided to go on to the second one. She drove her car up in front of the house, next to the picket fence, and looked it over. She got out of the car and walked around the property. It was a decent-looking house on a hill with white painted clapboard siding that could use some sprucing up, she decided. The little house had a good-sized covered porch in front and a screened-in back porch for doing the laundry.

There was also a small two-room cottage in the back, off of the alley, that was included in the rent. The ad called it a "cottage", but it actually looked more like a very rustic cabin with its well-worn, dark-stained wood exterior. Eva thought it would be perfect. With Richard leaving for Germany in a few weeks, she and her kids could stay in the cottage and help Mama pay the rent for a few months before they left to join him.

Eva called the phone number in the ad and made arrangements to meet the owner of the property later that afternoon. She sat on the porch and waited for him to arrive. This house, she thought, could make rescuing Mama and the children possible. Adding to that the bonus of the cottage for herself and her children, she felt giddy with excitement. This was it. It had to be.

She stood up as soon as she saw a car pull up in front of the house and a kind-looking old man got out. He was short with small wire-rimmed glasses, a round tummy and thinning, gray hair.

"Eva?"

"Yes, are you Mr. Jonas?"

"Yep, that's me. Here, let's go inside and take a look around." He stuck the key in the lock and jiggled the knob to get it to open. "These gal-darn old houses, looks like something else I need to fix." He pushed the door open and let her go in first.

He waited in the living room as Eva quickly walked from room to room.

"Can we go down to the cottage and take a look at it, too?" She wanted to make sure it would work for them.

"Sure, ma'am. Right through here." He led her to the back porch and down the stairs. The yard sloped downward, toward the cottage and to the back alley.

He slipped another key into the lock and opened the door for her. Eva stepped inside and looked around. There was a living area and a bedroom, which was all she would need.

"Will this work?" Mr. Jonas asked.

"Yes, I'll take it!" she announced enthusiastically. "Are those my keys?"

"Not so fast," he cautioned. "I'll need to have you fill out this application and make sure you can pay the rent each month."

"I can pay it, sir. My husband is a soldier in the army," she told him proudly. "He's stationed in Germany, and the government pays us like clockwork. And my mother will be living with us, and she'll pay her part from her job."

"And where does your mother work?"

"I believe she'll be working at one of the canneries," she replied. "They're processing tomatoes this time of year, I think."

"Ya' know, I was in the army, too, when I was a younger man," he said. "I had a much better physique in those days," he noted, as he patted his protruding belly. "You seem like a nice young woman, and I like to help out fellow soldiers when I can. If you can pay the deposit and first month's rent, the house is yours."

Eva filled out the rental agreement, signed it, and handed over a hundred and fifty dollars in cash that she had saved up. She felt very proud of herself for having done this for her mother. It was Eva's name on the lease, not her mother's, but she was sure it would all work out. It had to.

Being a bit lead-footed, she drove back to San Juan Bautista exhilarated and excited for what lay ahead. She couldn't wait to pick up her children and tell Lydia the first step to helping their mother escape had been accomplished.

The next step, Eva thought, would be to get Sofía a job, hopefully at one of the canneries in town. She had just told their new landlord she believed Mama would be working at one of the canneries, and she didn't want to be a liar. With a place to live and a job to support herself and her younger children, Mama could finally be out from under Carlos's control.

Eva drove up in front of her sister's house and turned the engine off. She was barely out of the car before Rory and Angie came running out, Lydia trailing behind. Eva crouched down and spread her arms out wide. The kids eagerly ran into them and gave her hugs.

"I hope they've been good for you, Lydia," Eva said as she stood up.

"We've been having a great time, haven't we, kids?" The children nodded and laughed. "Come in, Eva, and tell me what happened today." Eva had been gone for several hours, and Lydia was anxious to hear. Eva and the kids followed her into the house.

"I'm sorry I've been gone so long, but I did find Mama a house." Eva was bursting to tell her all about it. She eagerly described the house and the cottage and how perfect it was. Then she gave Lydia a detailed narration of how she got the landlord to let her rent the house.

"What about furniture?" Lydia asked.

"Oh, no. I hadn't thought of that."

Eva couldn't believe she hadn't thought about furniture for Mama's house. She was certain Sofía could not take any of the furnishings with her when she left. It was up to Eva and Lydia to find the necessary pieces for her. Lydia told her sister about a church in Hollister that had a thrift store ministry, she thought it was on 5th Street, just off of Main. Eva said it sounded like the perfect place to look.

Lydia had to work the next few days at the cannery, so she wasn't able to babysit the kids while her sister went furniture hunting. Eva took them with her while she visited the thrift store. She hoped the store could provide her with the beds, sofa and dinette set she needed for the family at a price she could afford.

Eva parked the car in front of the thrift store and took Rory and Angie inside with her.

"Don't touch anything," she warned her little children. "Stay close to me, and don't touch anything," she repeated for emphasis. She couldn't afford to spend money on something that accidentally got broken.

"Hi, there! Can I help you?" a woman called out from behind the big brass cash register. The thrift store was run by a sweet, elderly woman named Alice, with short, white curly hair, rosy cheeks, and a round, full figure.

"Yes, I want to talk to someone about some furniture."

"Oh, what sweet little kids. They're real cuties!" Alice was enamored by the children and came out from behind the counter. "Do you think your mommy would let you have a sucker?"

The children both nodded fervently.

"Okay, but just one," Eva said.

Alice plucked a couple of suckers out of the jar on the counter and peeled the wrappers off. She handed one to each of them.

"What do you say?" Eva asked her children.

"Thank you," they told Alice, in unison.

While the children enjoyed their candy, Eva discreetly explained to Alice the abusive circumstances that Sofía and her brothers and sister were living in. She went on to tell Alice how she felt responsible to rescue her mother and her siblings from this dangerous situation. Alice's big, soft heart was touched by Eva's love for her family, and she was eager to help.

She took Eva and the kids to the rear of the store and introduced them to her husband, George, who was working in the back shop repairing some of the donations, getting them ready to put out in the store. He was sitting at his workbench with a hammer in his hand, repairing a drawer from a used dresser.

George was tall and thin with his gray hair worn in a short crew cut. With dark horn-rimmed glasses, he wore a pair of old weathered jeans and a red plaid flannel shirt. He turned and stood up when he heard their footsteps.

"George, dear, this is Eva and her children. Can you show her where some of the larger items are kept, please?

"Sure, honey pie," he said to Alice, trying to get a rise out of her. He winked at her, then he turned his attention to helping Eva. "Right this way, ma'am. I have some nice things you might be interested in right over here."

George led the way. Immediately, Eva caught sight of a dinette set that would be just right for the family.

"You're in good hands now, Eva. You go on ahead and keep shopping. I'll just take these little cuties to the toy section and let them play. I'm sure we can find something they'll like," Alice offered.

She led Angie and Rory to an area stocked with used toys near the checkout counter. Then, while keeping an eye on them, Alice made a few phone calls to members of her church and rounded up more of the furnishings she knew they'd need.

Once Eva had examined all the larger pieces of furniture she could use, she walked up to the front of the store to talk with Alice. Together they made of list of the things she needed, including the ones Alice had made phone calls about.

"How much will all of this come to?" Eva asked, looking in her purse to see how much cash she had left.

"Under the circumstances, let's just say it's our gift to your mother. We're happy we can help out."

"But, but, I…" Eva couldn't find the words to thank her.

"Just give me the address," Alice interrupted, "and I'll have George and his buddies deliver all the things to you tomorrow. Will that be soon enough?"

"Tomorrow? Really?" Eva was astounded and extremely grateful. "Thank you so much! God bless you, Alice!" she said, wiping her tears, giving Alice a big hug. She was overwhelmed by how much this woman and her husband cared about people they had never met.

Eva wrote the address down for Alice and agreed to meet George and his friends at the house the next day at noon. She still couldn't believe how much these people were going out of their way for total strangers – locating all the things they needed and then delivering them for nothing on top of that. She was completely amazed.

The next morning, while Lydia watched Rory and Angie once more, Eva drove out to Tres Pinos. She remembered Mama saying that Carlos left early for work, around seven o'clock in the morning. Then, about thirty minutes later the school bus usually came to pick up the children. She knew she had a very slim window of opportunity.

If Eva timed it just right, she figured she could arrive at her mother's house right after Carlos left and before the school bus came. Sofía had no way of knowing what day her daughter would come back for them, but each day she hoped *this* would be the day. Because there was no safe means of letting her know, Sofía knew Eva would just have to show up when she had things worked out.

Eva parked her car off to the side of the main road and watched for the truckload of workers to drive out of the encampment. She kept her head down so no one would see her as the truck passed by. Carlos would not know her car.

Once Eva was certain Carlos had left, she pulled onto the dirt driveway and drove to the little shacks. She parked her car, looked around and approached the door. Knocking with eagerness, she was anxious to give her mother the good news.

Mama opened the door slightly and peered out. A big smile spread across her face when she saw it was Eva. She swung the door open wide to let her in. Sofía hoped this meant Eva had good news for her.

Eva's brothers and sister were surprised to see a visitor so early in the morning. They excitedly started asking Mama questions, one after another. "Who is this woman?" "Why is she here?" "Why's she here so early in the morning?"

Mama thought she'd better explain to them who Eva was. They hadn't seen their big sister in eight years. Once she introduced Eva to them, they were all so surprised and excited that they started firing off another round of questions.

When Eva married and left the area, Hector was seven, Miguel was only two, and Christina was just a little baby. Miguel and Christina didn't really even know Eva, but they had heard about her from Mama and Lydia, as well as the older brothers. Even Hector didn't really remember his older sister very well. Though he was seven when she married, he was only five when she moved out of the house. After that, she was forbidden contact with her siblings.

Once the excitement died down a little, Mama tried to get the kids busy doing something else so she and Eva could talk. She pulled her eldest daughter over to the couch and they sat down. If Eva had good news for her, she felt there would be plenty of time for them to get reacquainted.

"Go back in the kitchen and finish your breakfast, muchachos," Mama said, "the school bus will be here soon."

Eva did have good news for her mother, news that would change their lives.

"I've found a house for you, Mama, for you and the kids," Eva told her quietly, trying to keep her own excitement in check.

Mama was overjoyed. She had barely even let herself hope. Tears began to flow, and she could hardly contain herself. She grabbed the corner of her apron and wiped her eyes.

"Could it be true?" she wondered. "Could she finally be free?" She took hold of Eva and hugged her for a long time. "Oh, Eva... Oh, Eva..." was all she could say.

Finally, Mama released her grasp and stood up quickly. All of a sudden she realized she needed to keep the children from getting on the school bus. She was afraid to tell them the truth of what was happening just yet, fearful they would be too afraid of Carlos to go with her. So, she told the kids they were not going to school that day. Instead, she told them, they were going on a special trip with her and Eva.

"We're going on an adventure," Eva explained, trying to make it sound fun.

"I'm letting you have a day off from school because your big sister is in town," Mama told them. "We're going to have a fun day!"

The kids looked at each other, not sure what to think of that. It didn't sound like Mama. But any day they didn't have to go to school was a good day, they decided.

When the school bus drove up, Sofía ran out and told the driver to go on, the kids were all sick today and she was keeping them home from school. Then, she and Eva set about shoving all of their clothes in cotton flour sacks she had saved to make some play clothes for Christina. Now these sacks had a much more important use.

Eva picked up the bags of clothes, and the few other belongings they had, and loaded them into the trunk of her car.

"All right, now. Everyone in the car!" Eva ordered, and they all climbed in. She drove down the driveway, kicking up dust, watching the shacks slowly shrink in her rear-view mirror.

Sofía turned around and watched the row of old houses fade from view behind her. She had escaped, and now she was free.

As Eva turned onto the main road, Sofía saw the last of what felt like a prison camp in which she had spent so many years. With that camp gone from view, she began to feel the tension releasing from her body. The fear that had held her hostage for all those years was beginning to dissipate. She knew it would take time to truly be free of it, but it felt so good to experience that gripping fear slipping away.

Drawing in a long, deep breath, Sofía let out a huge sigh of relief. She and Eva exchanged smiles. Then, she turned back around in her seat and faced forward, concentrating on what was before her, never to look back again.

As Eva drove, she thought about Carlos, and she was sure he would be angry when he found them gone. She wondered if he would come looking for them. Certainly he would be mad that Sofía had left, but not because he loved her. His anger would be, instead, because he would now have no one to wash his clothes and cook his meals. He would have no one to warm his bed or be his punching bag. Carlos would also be furious that Sofía took his children from him.

"Where are we going, Eva?" Mama asked. Eva had promised to find them a place to live, but Sofía had no idea where it was or what is was going to be like.

"We're going to Park Hill, just up the hill from Main Street. I found a house big enough for all of you. And the price was right. It's not a beautiful house, but it will be a lot better than where you came from."

"What are you talking about, Eva?" Hector asked. "I thought we were going on an adventure."

"We are, little brother. A big adventure. You're moving to a new house."

"What?!" The kids looked confused and fearful of what Papa would say.

"Don't worry, everything will be fine. You'll see." Eva explained to her brothers and sister that they were going to live in a new home with Mama, and they wouldn't have to be afraid of their father anymore.

The children all looked at each other for a few moments, stunned by what Eva had just told them. It took some convincing by Eva that they were safe and did not need to worry. It took several minutes for them to process what she said, then Hector spoke up first.

"Where are we gonna sleep?" he asked.

"I'm hungry," little Christina piped in.

"We're almost there, muchachos." Eva said. "Look, there!" as she pointed up the street. "See the big truck that's backing up to that house? That's it! They're bringing the furniture."

Sofía had been so focused on getting safely away from Carlos that she really hadn't thought about beds and tables and sofas. Her eyes grew wide, and she was speechless. The children, too, were looking at the truck, their mouths dropping open. "Where did all that stuff come from?" Miguel asked.

"You'll see, you'll see," Eva answered.

She parked the car across the street and the kids jumped out and ran to the house. Eva and Sofía made their way across the street, as well, and over to the men getting out of the moving truck.

"Mama, this is George," Eva said, as she introduced Sofía to one of their benefactors.

George introduced the other two men that had come to help him unload all the furniture and carry it into the house. Sofía was overcome with gratitude and wanted to know what she could do to help. The men told her they would take care of everything. But the boys wanted to pitch in, so they let Hector and Miguel help by carrying the smaller items, like the dining chairs.

Eva unlocked the door and swung it wide open. Little Christina was the first inside and made herself at home, marveling at her good fortune. Sofía was still stunned and amazed, standing out in the yard watching the men unload. It was all used furniture, but to her it was beautiful.

As they carried the furnishings in, Eva and Christina directed the men to which rooms they wanted them to put the items in. There was even an old brass bed delivered for the cottage, along with a small dresser and sofa, for the times Eva and her kids would come to visit.

She walked back out into the front yard and stood with her mother watching the men bring in the last of the furnishings. Eva put her arm around Sofía and gave her a little hug.

"Eva?" a young man's voice yelled from the yard next door.

Eva turned around to see who was calling her name.

"Alex? What are *you* doing here?"

"Is that any way to greet an old friend?" he asked, as he hopped the low white picket fence that separated the two yards and walked over to Eva and her mother.

"I'm just so surprised to see you." She hadn't seen him since he hugged her and congratulated her at her wedding reception.

"It just so happens I live next door," Alex replied, a little smile spreading across his lips.

"Mama, this is Alex," Eva said, introducing them. "He and I went to school together. Alex, this is my mother, Sofía Gonzalez."

"It's very nice to meet you, Mrs. Gonzalez."

"Thank you," Sofía replied softly, not very comfortable with social graces.

"And where's your husband?" Alex asked, looking down at the wedding ring still on Eva's finger.

"He's at Ford Ord right now," she said. "And I have two children now."

"Where are they?" Alex asked.

"They're with my sister. She's keeping them from being under foot during the move. They'll be here later, for dinner."

"I'd love to meet them."

"Why don't you come by later and eat with us?" Eva offered, trying to be polite.

"No, no. I'm sure you'll all be tired from the move today."

"Oh, we haven't been doing much but watching the men haul the furniture into the house. I just point to where I want them to set things down," Eva explained. "Once we get the beds made up, we just need to unpack the dishes and silverware and wash them. There's not really much for us to do."

"What about making dinner? I don't want you to have to cook for another person."

"Oh, my sister, Lydia, is bringing the food. So there. You have no more excuses." Eva said with a grin.

"Are you sure there'll be enough?" Alex said, not wanting to impose.

"Yes, we're sure," Sofía assured him, feeling more comfortable with him. "Please, come."

"Well, I do love Mexican food. And I would like to get to know my new neighbors."

"It's settled, then," Eva said.

"So, tell me, which one of you is moving in?" Alex inquired.

"My mother is, along with two of my little brothers and my little sister," Eva offered.

"Good to know. Well, I'll get out of your hair and let you finish up here. Be back about six?"

"Yes, that would be good," Eva answered as Alex began to walk away.

She turned her attention back to her mama, placing an arm around her shoulders again. They watched the last bit of furnishings being unloaded, confident her little sister, Christina, would tell them where to put the last of the items.

Eva was still overwhelmed by Alice's and George's kindness and generosity to her mother. The women thanked the men over and over again until they were finally unloaded and gone.

Lydia and Manuel brought Rory and Angie to the house that evening, along with dinner for the whole family. Lydia had spent the afternoon making tamales and refried beans. Eva washed the donated dishes and silverware and Christina stacked them on the table.

There was a firm knock at the door. Sofía jumped, and her eyes instantly got wide. Eva could see Mama thought it might be Carlos coming for her.

"That must be Alex, Mama, it's all right," Eva said, as she walked toward the door, trying to calm her mother down.

Eva thought, just for a fleeting moment, that it might be Carlos, too. But she pushed that thought out of her head and opened the door. She was relieved when she saw it was Alex.

"Come on in, you're just in time."

Eva led Alex into the kitchen where everyone had gathered. She introduce him to Lydia and Manuel first, and then to Hector, Miguel and Christina.

"And these are my children, Angie and Rory."

Alex crouched down and put one knee on the floor, so he would be at their eye level. "Hello, Angie and Rory. It's very nice to meet you." The children smiled back at him, unsure of who he was.

"Are you gonna live here, too, mister?" Rory asked him.

"No, I live next door. I'm just visiting."

"Okay," Rory said.

"Let's eat!" Lydia ordered, as she placed a platter of steaming tamales on the table next to the pot of refried beans and tall stack of warm tortillas. "Everyone grab a dish."

Alex took his place in line and Eva watched him load up his plate. She remembered the first time she met him, when they first had lunch in the park together in junior high. He had told her then how much he liked Mexican food. She was glad to find out he lived next door to her mother. Knowing she had a nice, strong young man for her neighbor made Eva feel like Mama would be more secure.

When everyone was finished eating, Sofía started collecting the dirty dishes.

"Mama, no. You sit down and take it easy. We'll clean up," Lydia told her.

"I don't need to take it easy. I haven't done anything all day but watch other people work. And I'm too excited to just sit. Let me do this, please. I want to wash my new dishes in my new kitchen!"

"Okay, but you have to let us help," Eva said.

"All right." Mama knew they were going to help her whether she wanted them to or not. Even Alex picked up a few plates from the kids, along with his own, and handed them to her at the sink. Eva, who was drying, stood next to Mama.

"Thank you for inviting me, Mrs. Gonzalez. The food was delicious and I really enjoyed myself here. I think it's time for me to go, I have to work tonight."

"Alex, please call me Sofía. I'm glad you came."

"I'll walk you out," Eva offered, handing her drying cloth to Lydia.

Eva walked him out the front door and they paused on the porch. She was glad to reconnect with her old friend.

"You said you have to work tonight?"

"Yeah."

"What do you do?" Eva asked.

"I'm a police officer."

"That makes me feel safer, for my mother, I mean."

"For your mother? Why is that?" His eyebrows furrowed and he listened intently.

"It's a long story. But let's just say I rescued my mother today from a very bad situation, and I hope my stepfather doesn't come looking for her."

"I'd like to hear the long story."

"Not tonight. Sometime I'll explain it to you, just not tonight. It's been a long day."

"Are you staying here, too?" He wondered what her situation was.

"Just for a couple of months. Then I have to go back home to Seaside."

"Where your husband is stationed?"

"Yes, temporarily. He's being transferred to Germany soon. We'll be joining him later, after he goes through his training and arranges for the family housing. Then I'll go back to Seaside to pack things up for the move."

"Well, if you'll be around for a couple of months, I guess I'll see you a few more times."

"Yes, I guess you will. We can talk more then. I better let you get to work."

"Eva," he paused, looking into her warm brown eyes, "don't worry about your mom. I'll keep an eye out for her." Then, he stepped off the porch and went home.

Eva turned and stepped back inside the house, returning to the kitchen to finish helping with the dishes.

"Alex seems like a nice guy," Lydia said to Eva, picking up the last dish to dry. "I don't remember you talking about him before."

"That's because I never did. You were just a little kid when I knew him in junior high. I had a secret crush on him. But then his family moved away, and I forgot all about him. Then, he moved back our senior year, but by then I was engaged to Richard."

"Hmmm. He's pretty cute."

"Lydia, I'm married…and so are you, by the way."

"Doesn't mean he isn't cute," Lydia said. "I wonder what he does for a living."

"He's a policeman."

"Really?"

"Yes." Eva lowered her voice and looked around to make sure their mother was not within earshot. "I asked him to keep an eye out for Mama. You know, in case the old man shows up."

"You don't think Papa would do that, do you?" Lydia asked with a hushed tone, leaning in toward her sister.

"You never know – he might."

The sisters realized their older brothers had no idea of the rescue efforts yet, but it was getting late and Lydia and Manuel wanted to head home soon. Eva and Lydia agreed they would fill their brothers in the next day, before Carlos tried to turn them against Mama for leaving him. But for tonight, Eva decided, they would just enjoy the peace and quiet.

With mama and her siblings settled in their new home, Eva hoped they would all enjoy a restful sleep. She knew this would be Sofía's first good night's sleep in over twenty-five years.

* * * * *

The next step in Eva's plan was to help her mother find a job. It was now Mama's responsibility to support herself and her three growing children, a responsibility she was happy to take on. It would take more money than she could earn by herself in the beginning, though, but somehow they would make it work.

For the first few months, Eva could help a little with the rent. Then, she would need to go back home to Seaside and get ready for their move to Germany. Hector was thirteen now, maybe he could get a part-time job after school to help out, she thought.

Eva took Mama to the employment office at several different canneries so she could submit an application. There weren't a lot of choices for an unskilled worker like Sofía, so they were really counting on one of the canneries in Hollister hiring her. Lydia had put in a good word for her mother at the cannery where she worked, and it seemed to do the trick. They hired Sofía to work on the line processing tomatoes. It was physically demanding work, but she was used to hard work. Nothing was going to keep her from her freedom ever again.

Sofía and her children had been enjoying their new house for a few weeks, as well as their new, peaceful life. Without warning, that peace was shattered when Carlos showed up drunk. He had heard from one of their sons that Sofía was working at a certain cannery, and he eventually worked her address out of him.

Carlos had been out drinking that Saturday night and decided he would go to Sofía's house and show her she couldn't just leave him whenever she wanted. He was going to teach her a lesson.

About ten o'clock that night he parked his old truck out in front of her house and started beating on the front door and hollering. Sofía and the children were getting ready for bed when they heard the commotion. They all rushed to the living room, but Mama told them not to open the door. Instead, she phoned Alex to see if he had gone to work yet.

"Hello," Alex said.

"Alex, this is Sofía. My husband is beating on the door and we're really afraid!"

"I'll be right there. Call the police station and tell them I said to send another officer."

Alex was already dressed for work and grabbed his pistol. He shot out of his front door and ran over to Sofía's. He attempted to get Carlos' attention, hoping to subdue him without incident.

"Mr. Gonzalez! This is the police! Step away from the door!"

Carlos paid no attention. He continued to pound on the door and scream at Sofía. Alex repeated himself as he slowly walked up behind Carlos. He reached for Carlos' wrist to try to handcuff him, but Carlos spun around and swung at the officer. Alex ducked and then punched Carlos in the face, sending him flying back against the door. Carlos swung again, missing Alex, the momentum sending him stumbling forward. He hit his head on the porch post and knocked himself out momentarily.

Alex took that opportunity to handcuff him. He pulled Carlos up on his feet as the second policeman drove up. Practically dragging Carlos to the car, Alex told the other officer to take him to the station and book him for drunk driving, disturbing the peace and assaulting an officer. He'd be there shortly to finish the paperwork.

After Carlos was gone, Alex went to the door and knocked lightly, calling out Sofía's name.

"Sofía, it's Alex. Carlos is gone. Can you open the door?"

She opened the door, standing in her night clothes with her children. They looked terrified, the children huddling together around their mother, their eyes misty and wide.

"Sofía, Carlos is on his way to jail. He won't be bothering you anymore tonight. You're all safe. Hopefully he learned his lesson and won't ever be back."

"Thank you, Alex," Sofía said, with tears filling her eyes. She gave him a big hug and thanked him again.

The next morning, Sofía told Eva what had happened the night before. She and her children had slept through it in the little cottage behind the house. So grateful for what Alex had done, Eva wanted to show her appreciation in some way.

That afternoon, she decided to bake a chocolate fudge layer cake for Alex, and she took it over to him to thank him for what he had done for her mother and the children. She knocked on the door, but there was no answer. So she went around to the side detached garage to see if he was there.

"Alex!" she called out.

He slid out from under his 1954 Chevy coupe, where he was "tinkering," he said. He was covered in grease, wearing an old white T-shirt and jeans that accentuated his trim, muscular physique.

"Oh, I'm sorry," Eva said, a little flustered at how masculine he looked. "I didn't want to bother you. You look busy."

"Not too busy. What do you have there?"

"I just wanted to say thank you for what you did for my mama last night. So, I made you this chocolate fudge cake." Eva held it out to him and he happily took it from her. "I remembered that chocolate was your favorite."

"A chocolate fudge cake, huh?" he said, looking down at it with one eyebrow dipped for emphasis. "I hope you're a good cook."

"Oh, Alex." She knew he was just teasing her. "You're such a good friend. I don't know what would have happened if you hadn't been there to protect my family last night."

"Well, you are very welcome, Eva. Anytime. I'm here to protect and serve. Now, let's go inside and have a piece of that fudge cake. It looks delicious."

"Oh, I better not. It wouldn't be seemly. Remember, I'm married."

"Sorry, I forgot for just a moment." A sharp pang of disappointment surprised him. "Well, I appreciate the cake, and I'll enjoy every single bite of it."

"I'd better get back to the house and see what my kids are up to. Talk to you later."

Eva walked away and went back into Grandma Sofía's house. Alex watched her until she disappeared through the doorway, thinking back to the pretty young girl he knew in junior high. He recalled how he had a crush on her back then, but he was too shy to ever tell her. Then his family moved away. But he never forgot about her.

When he moved back to Hollister during their senior year in high school, he hoped to rekindle his relationship with her again. But when he first connected with her, he learned she had just gotten engaged. A few months later he watched her get married. After that, he put her out of his mind, thinking he would never see her again.

Now she had come back into his life, but she was married with children. He knew he would have to keep his distance so old feelings didn't resurface. Eva would be gone in a few weeks, so it shouldn't be too hard to control himself until then, he thought.

CHAPTER 20

A MARRIAGE SHATTERED

ONCE EVA KNEW HER MOTHER and siblings were well settled in their new home and their new lives, she returned to Seaside to get ready for their move to Germany. Besides having a lot of packing to do, she had two preschoolers under foot. Richard was scheduled to return from Germany soon to help with the move.

He arrived at Fort Ord, as planned, and they started packing things up and making phone calls to arrange appointments for the vaccinations that Eva and the kids required. His plan was to take his family to stay with Lydia and her husband for a few weeks until it was time for them to follow him to Germany. Sofía's cottage was available, but there was more room at Lydia's house. While Richard was there, the cottage would get a little cramped trying to sleep the four of them.

During their stay in San Juan Bautista, Eva and the children would get the numerous rounds of immunization shots they needed in order to travel overseas. This was a lot to go through in preparation for the big move to Europe. Eva prayed it would all be worth it.

When the time came, Richard drove his family to Lydia and Manuel's place in their black and white Ford station wagon. He was able to stay with them for a few days before he shipped out.

When it was time to go, he planned to take a Greyhound Bus back to Fort Ord and would leave for Europe soon after. The time came and Eva and the children drove Richard to the bus station, wanting to send him off with hugs and kisses. He crouched down and hugged both the children at once, then kissed them both on their heads. When he hastily kissed Eva good-bye and boarded the bus, she couldn't help but feel a bit disappointed by the lack of passion between them, knowing it would be months before they would see each other again.

On the drive back to Lydia's place, Eva couldn't seem to shake that feeling. Peering in the rear view mirror at her children in the back seat, she tried to think positive thoughts of her family's new life in Germany. She had endured Richard's infidelities and his employment ups and downs. With his military promotion to sergeant at the base in Europe, she looked forward to him having a stable job and better income. Eva also hoped Richard would finally settle down and be the husband she always wanted - someone to love her and be committed to her, and only her.

One afternoon, a couple of weeks after Richard left, Eva and the kids climbed into the car for a drive to Hollister to visit Grandma Sofía. They had planned to visit all day with Grandma and then spend the night in the cottage so they could have their last round of immunization shots the next morning.

Eva woke up early, thinking about what she had to do that day. She let the children sleep a little longer while she got herself ready and laid out their clothes.

"Get up, get up, sleepy heads." Eva pulled their covers back. "It's time to get up and have some breakfast!"

She dressed each of the children, then they climbed the back stairs to Grandma's house for the eggs, chorizo and fried potatoes. After breakfast, they all piled into the station wagon and went to the doctor's office to get the last of their shots, with a promise of ice cream cones afterward as a reward for their bravery.

With a few sniffles and tears, they were all glad to be finished with their immunizations and leaving the doctor's office. Eva and the kids stopped for ice cream, as promised, before driving back to San Juan Bautista. She was proud of how well her children took their shots. They had been painful, but the family couldn't be together again without them.

It was a crisp, sunny fall day, and the drive through the country was relaxing. The leaves were turning an entire array of golds and oranges, with some starting to drop to the ground. Looking into the rearview mirror, Eva noticed the kids had nodded off in the back seat. As Eva's car pulled up in front of the old stucco house, Lydia saw them from her kitchen window and went to the door to greet them.

"Rory, Angie, wake up! We're here," Eva announced to her children. She hopped out of the car and opened the door to the back seat. The combination of the cool air filling the car and Eva's belly tickles brought both kids out of their nap. They giggled and climbed out of the station wagon as Tía Lydia came to the front door. She called to them from the doorway.

"Come inside, you guys, it's cold out there. Lunch'll be ready in a little while. Let's get something warm to drink. Brrrr, it's cold," she said, rubbing her hands together.

Once inside, they gathered around the old chrome and turquoise melamine kitchen table – hot chocolate for the little ones and coffee for the grownups. The warm beverages were comforting on such a chilly autumn day.

Rory and Angie quickly finished their hot chocolate and were ready to play. Lydia and Eva chatted as the kids went outside to play on the old swing set that was left there by the previous tenants. Eva kept an eye on them from the kitchen window near the dining table.

As they sat chatting, Lydia remembered a couple of pieces of mail for her sister that she had tucked into her sweater pocket when she went out to the mailbox earlier that morning. She pulled out the envelopes and gave them to Eva.

"Oh, Lydia, look! A letter from Richard!"

"Open it!"

Eva hurriedly opened it, anxious to find words saying he couldn't wait for them all to join him in Germany. Lydia watched her sister's face with anticipation. She was surprised to see her expression fall, sadness washed over Eva's face and tears filled her eyes. Eva laid her head down on her arm that was resting on the table and began to sob.

"What's wrong?" Lydia asked, baffled by Eva's response to the letter. "What is it?"

Eva couldn't stop crying but limply handed the letter to her sister. The words stood out on the paper as if they were written in neon lights. *"I've met someone else here in Germany, and I think I'm in love with her."*

Lydia was furious. It was all she could do to contain herself, knowing she needed to console her big sister at that moment. She was glad the children were playing outside, giving Eva a chance to let her tears pour out. Lydia pulled her chair close to Eva and put her arm around her. She stroked Eva's hair and patted her back gently.

"I am so sorry," Lydia said softly.

Eva tried to pull herself together. She walked over to the sink and got a glass of cold water.

"What a jerk! What an absolute jerk!" Lydia declared. "What's the matter with him? You're just too good for him. That's all there is to it – you're just too darn good for him!"

"When I think back over all the second chances I gave him," Eva said, shaking her head, "it just makes me sick."

"What do you mean?"

"Time and again I overlooked the women, the drinking, and the spending."

"Are you saying there were other women?" Lydia couldn't believe what she was hearing. Eva had never told her about any other women, any other infidelities.

"Last year, while Richard was stationed at Fort Ord, I almost left him." Eva paused and stared out the window, thinking back to that time.

"It was our sixth wedding anniversary and the couple next door, the Freemans, offered to babysit the kids so we could go out to celebrate. Richard was supposed to be home by six-thirty. I took the kids next door at six o'clock and went back to our apartment to finish getting ready. I'd been saving a little money out of each paycheck and hid it away. It would pay for our celebration that evening, and I planned to surprise Richard with it when he got home."

"What happened?" Lydia asked.

"By seven-thirty he still wasn't home. So I thought I should go next door to tell the Freemans they probably wouldn't need to babysit anymore. They talked me into staying at their apartment with them and watching television until Richard came home. So, I left him a note on our front door telling him to come next door to get me."

"Did he come and get you?"

"No. About an hour later I thought I heard the front door to our apartment close and muffled voices talking and laughing in the distance. I left the Freemans and went to our apartment but no one was there. The note was off the door, and I could smell Richard's cologne. I ran to the window and looked out at the street in time to see him putting a pretty blonde woman into our car, and then they drove away. I went to see if my little stash of money was safe in my underwear drawer, but it was gone. Richard must've known I had hidden it there. He didn't get home until about one o'clock in the morning."

"What did you do then?"

"I confronted him about not coming home to take me out to celebrate our anniversary, about the blonde woman and the missing money. We had a big fight. Of course, he denied it all. Said he had to work, and I must've seen someone else that looked like him. Did he think I was that stupid?"

"Oh, Eva, I'm so sorry," Lydia said, trying to comfort her.

"Oh, no. It gets worse. I asked him about the missing money. He said someone must have stolen it, or I misplaced it. My head was spinning. 'How could this be happening?' I asked myself over and over. Even though I knew what he said wasn't the truth, I wanted it to be the truth. I needed it to be the truth."

"What do you mean you needed it to be the truth?" Lydia asked.

"I didn't have a job, and I had two small children. What choice did I have?"

"Oh, Eva."

"What was I going to do? I couldn't leave him. I had no other option but to stay. At that moment I felt like I was stuck in Mama's shoes. I understood why she never left the old man."

"I'm serious, Eva, I wish you had told me." Lydia said. "Manuel and I would have helped you any way we could."

"You and Manuel had just gotten married. I couldn't ask you for help."

"We don't have much, but we'll try to help you now. I'll talk to Manuel and see what he says."

Though Eva was grateful for her sister's offer, she knew the burden of what to do next rested squarely on her own shoulders.

Eva finally calmed down and was able to compose herself. The thought of her sweet children coming in and finding her crying helped to sober her up. She was a boiling pot of emotions at that moment – broken-hearted, angry, sad and feeling a profound sense of worthlessness. But she could not let it show, not any of it.

She had to stuff those feelings down and once again find the inner strength to do whatever she had to do. As much as Lydia wanted to help her, she knew she had to rely on herself to get through this, for the sake of her children and the sake of her own future.

CHAPTER 21

ATTEMPTED ASSAULT

NOW THAT MOVING TO GERMANY with Richard was no longer an option, Eva decided to move out of Lydia's house and into the rustic cottage behind her mother's house. She would have to share the big bed with Rory and Angie, which wasn't ideal. But, staying in the cottage, she felt, would at least give her time to think about her next move.

Since her brother, Mateo, had been kicked out of the house by Carlos at sixteen, he had been living with their brother, Eduardo, and his wife for the past year. They had taken him in shortly after they got married. Now that Eva was living in the cottage, he asked if he could sleep on her couch and give them some privacy. She agreed to let him stay with her.

Early one morning, a couple of days after moving back in, Eva went out to the front yard to water the flowers her mother had recently planted. She always loved the quiet and crispness of the first part of the day. With the rubber garden hose in her hand, she was lost in thought about her circumstances and her future, drenching the daisies and the mums.

"Eva?"

She was startled from her daydreaming and turned quickly in response to her name, splashing water on Alex's pants and shoes. He jumped back and laughed.

"Oh, man. I wasn't expecting that," he said, shaking the water off one of his shoes.

"Oh, I'm sorry, I'm so sorry," Eva said, quickly turning the hose away. Her cheeks became hot with embarrassment. "You surprised me. What are you doing sneaking up on me like that?"

"I didn't mean to. I just got home from my shift and saw you over here, so I came to say hello. You must've been so deep in thought you didn't hear me or my car."

"I suppose you're right. My mind was somewhere else."

"I thought you'd be in Germany with your husband by now."

"No, the kids and I aren't going to Germany now."

"What? Why not?"

"It's a long story," she said, looking down at the drowning flowers. "I don't want to talk about it." Alex noticed her eyes looked sad and her voice tensed.

"Well, I was just so surprised to see you, I wanted to come over and say hello." Alex felt badly for Eva. He could tell something was wrong, that something had happened between her and her husband to change their plans. He read it on her face, heard it in the tone of her voice. "I'll be around if you ever want to talk."

"Thanks. I appreciate the offer." Eva answered. She didn't want to talk about her unfaithful husband right now. Her feelings were still raw. She moved the hose to more flowers in another part of the yard, and Alex recognized that was his cue to leave.

"It was nice to see you again," he said as he walked out the gate and back to his house.

Eva returned to watering the plants and trying to think through her situation in the stillness of the early morning. But Alex kept cropping up in her thoughts. He had disrupted her quiet with his sudden presence, but she had to admit it was not unwelcomed. He was a good friend, and he watched over Sofía, just like he promised. If only she had married someone like him, instead of Richard, she wouldn't be in this mess. Someone honest and hardworking. But what's done was done, and there was no going back to change things.

While she pondered her options, she decided she had better get a job to bring in some money. She would need it, she decided, no matter what her next move was going to be.

* * * * *

Eva found a job as a waitress at a diner just a block or so from her mother's house, on Main Street at the bottom of the hill. She worked mostly in the evenings, so Grandma Sofía and Lydia took turns watching her kids as they were available from their jobs at the cannery.

The diner was connected to the gas station next door, and there were plenty of customers. Eva's boss, Victor, was an older Portuguese man that looked out for her, especially when men came into the café and tried to get fresh with her.

Two or three times a week, Alex came in for lunch or dinner and sat at the counter so he and Eva could visit as she served him his food and refilled his coffee cup. It wasn't a very private setting, so she was careful not to share anything too personal because others could overhear. Occasionally, he came for a late supper and stayed long enough to walk her home after she finished her shift. It was a short walk, but it was a nice gesture.

The second night he walked her home, Alex asked her about Richard.

"Eva, do you mind if I ask you something?" Alex said casually, as he looked up and down the street before they crossed.

"Sure," she replied, following him across.

"Something personal?" he pressed.

"Okay," she responded, with trepidation. They began to walk down the alley to the cottage.

"I know something happened between you and your husband that stopped you from following him to Germany, but you've never talked about it." He looked over at her as she kept up with his gait.

"I know, it's hard."

"But I'm your friend, Eva." Alex stopped and turned to face her. "I hope you feel comfortable enough to tell me anything." The truth was that he hoped they could be more than friends, but he needed to know what was really going on between her and Richard.

She stopped, too, and looked up at him. "Yes, I do feel comfortable talking to you. You've been a good friend." She could see gentleness and concern when she looked into his deep brown eyes, and she knew he truly cared about her and what she was going through.

"So, what's the situation with you and your husband? Why did you decide not to go to Germany with him?"

Eva took a deep breath to steady herself before proceeding. "This is hard to admit, Alex, but here it is. Right before I moved into the cottage, Richard sent me a letter telling me he was in love with another woman, someone he met in Germany."

A rush of tears was very near the surface, but she was determined to hold them back. She didn't want Alex to see her dissolve into a weepy puddle right there in the alley.

Alex was shocked. He wondered how any man could do this to someone as kind and as lovely as Eva. Though he felt sad for her because of how her husband had hurt her, he was surprised by his own feelings of outrage. He wanted to knock Richard's head off. Not wishing to make her feel worse than she already did, he attempted to mask how he really felt.

"Oh, Eva, I'm so sorry," he said, offering his sympathy. "How could he do this to you? That son of a…" Alex was disgusted by the thought.

Eva couldn't answer that question. She didn't want to keep talking about Richard. She wanted to tell Alex to stop. But, no words would come. All she could do was look down at the ground, shrug her shoulders and shake her head.

"Are you going to divorce him?"

"I don't know. I haven't decided," she replied, weakly, raising her head to look at him.

"How could you stay married to a man who admits he's two-timing you?" Alex asked in disbelief.

"It's not that easy. We have two children together. I have to think of them."

"But, Eva…" Alex started to say, but she cut him off.

"As for Richard and me, we're done. But the children, well, I need to think about what will be best for them. I need some time to work that out."

"I didn't mean to press the issue and upset you like this." Alex reached out and put an arm around her shoulder as they started walking again. His touch weakened her resolve and a few of her tears escaped.

When they got to the cottage, they paused at the door.

"I'm going inside for a few minutes to calm down before I go up to Mama's to get my kids. Thanks for walking me home." She opened the door and stepped inside.

"I really am sorry, Eva," Alex told her as she nodded and slowly closed the door. He shoved his hands in his pockets and walked home.

Eva stood just inside the door, leaning her back against it. She knew Alex was just trying to be a good friend, but it hurt to talk about Richard and what he had done to her. She couldn't go on and on talking about it. Not only was it painful, it was humiliating.

She knew it wasn't Alex's fault she was so upset. They were becoming close friends, and it was only natural he would want to know what happened. So, she decided that the next time she saw him she would let him know that she appreciated his caring so much about her.

* * * * *

Now and then, Alex was invited for dinner at Sofía's house. There were always lots of people there – family, friends, and their children. Alex wanted a chance to get to know Eva better, but they couldn't seem to find much time to be alone and have meaningful conversation. One evening at the diner, Alex asked her if she would go on a date with him so they could spend some time alone, just the two of them.

"What do you say, Eva? Dinner Sunday night? At a nice, quiet restaurant? Your pick."

"I'd love to, Alex," Eva replied, as she poured him a cup of coffee. "But I'll have to see if there'll be someone home to watch my kids that night." She wanted to get to know him better, too. They'd been friends for quite awhile, but she had always been guarded, wary of sharing with him the brutal details of her life growing up and her bad marriage.

She assumed, though, he must have learned a few things about her stepfather from the night he arrested Carlos. He probably had formed some idea of what her home life might have been like, she thought. But her spilling all the gory details was a different matter.

"If we can't swing it Sunday night, then you find out when you can get a sitter and let me know."

"Okay, I can do that." She was excited at the possibility of there being something more between them than simply friendship.

"Now, what would you like to order for dinner tonight?"

* * * * *

The next evening three young men came into the diner about five-thirty, and Victor seated them in a booth. They had obviously been out drinking half the afternoon and stopped in for a bite to eat before drinking more that evening. Eva came to their table and attempted to take their orders.

"What can I get for you fellas?" Eva asked with a smile.

"How about a date?" one of them said.

"The special tonight is pot roast and mashed potatoes. Does that sound good to you?" she tried to suggest.

"You know what sounds good, honey, is if you slide on in next to me. You look like the kind o' girl who could show a man a *real* good time," another one said, noticeably intoxicated.

"Okay, okay, are you guys going to order any food tonight?" Eva asked loudly, trying to get them to focus on their order.

"Is everything all right here?" Victor asked, as he walked up to the booth.

"Yeah, yeah, everything's okay, old man," the third tipsy man said, waving Victor off.

"I'll handle it," Eva told Victor.

So, Victor walked away, but he kept his eye on Eva and the men. She fended off their advances and eventually took their orders. As she was walking back to hand their order slip to the cook, Lydia came in with little Rory and Angie. Victor let Eva bring her kids in for dinner sometimes at a greatly-reduced rate, to help her make ends meet.

The young men saw Eva pick up the little blonde-haired girl and smother her with kisses. They overheard Eva call the girl her daughter. Confused why this Mexican woman was saying this little blonde girl was hers, they began speculating among themselves about how she might have gotten white kids. Too much alcohol was clouding their thoughts and leading their conversation down a nasty path.

Lydia and the kids finished eating, and she took them back to Grandma's house. Sofía would be home by this time from the cannery, and Lydia could put the kids to bed at their grandmother's house until Eva got home from work.

Eva worked until eight that evening. She said goodnight to her boss and left to walk home. Watching for possible traffic, she crossed Main Street and strolled down the alley a short distance, the back way to the cottage. She didn't know that one of the flirtatious young men from the diner was lurking in the shadows, waiting and watching her, following to see where she lived.

She picked her kids up from Grandma Sofía's house and put her sleepy little ones to bed in the cottage. Leaning over to turn off the lamp, she was startled by a forceful knock at the door. She heard several male voices talking and laughing outside, which scared her. They had clearly been drinking and were looking to make trouble for her. The young man that followed her home had gone and gotten some of his buddies and showed them where she lived.

"Hey, let us in!" one guy hollered, staggering around. "You know what we want. Come on! Open up!"

Eva left the children to sleep in the bedroom and closed the door. She stood in the living room, frozen with fear, hoping the children could not hear the men from the bedroom.

"Go away," she cried out frantically.

"We saw the little white kids you have, honey. We can tell you really go for us white guys."

The young men were laughing and drinking outside, yelling out the graphic sexual details of what they would like to do to her. They thought she was a Mexican whore with illegitimate white children.

"Go away, I said," she repeated, "you'll wake my babies!" But they would not relent. They continued pounding on the door. Each of the men was inciting the others, urging them to break the door down. Eva heard a beer bottle crash against the cottage.

She was near hysteria, her body trembling. The ruffians outside continuing to beat on her door, spewing out sexual and racial slurs.

"You know you want it, chiquita," they kept taunting.

"Mommy, Mommy!" Rory cried, standing in the doorway to the bedroom. They woke him up with their hollering and pounding on the front door.

"It's okay, honey. Mommy's right here," she tried to soothe him, without much success. She checked on her daughter and found her surprisingly sound asleep. She carefully closed the bedroom door and sat on the edge of the sofa with Rory and put her arm around him. Stroking his soft brown hair, she tried to stay calm. She hoped her brother Mateo would come home soon.

Eva yelled at the door again, "You guys better get outta here! The Gonzalez brothers are coming!"

Either they were yelling too loudly to hear what she said, or they were too drunk to fully understand what she meant. The Gonzalez brothers were known in Hollister for sticking together and protecting their own, ever since grade school, and they weren't afraid to fight to do it.

Eva got up from the sofa and carefully peeked out the window from the corner of the curtain. She recognized a couple of the young men as sons of the owner of a large farm outside of town named Williamson.

"Get out of here!" she cried again. "The Gonzalez brothers are coming, and you're gonna wish you'd gone!" Over and over she kept yelling the same warning. Finally, what she was screaming sunk in to some of the men, and they convinced the others it was time to beat it out of there.

Shortly after they left, Mateo came home. With tears streaming down her cheeks, Eva relayed the frightening events she just experienced. She tried to tell him in a soft, muffled voice so she didn't scare her children, but the details and tears just spilled out uncontrollably.

Red-hot anger began to boil in her brother. He told Eva he would round up the other brothers and they would take care of this. It was their duty to protect their sister, he said. He promised her they would find those white devils and make them pay for what they'd done.

Before he left, Mateo helped his sister gather up her children and go up to Mama's house until she was sure the men were not coming back. Eva tried to telephone Alex, but there was no answer. He had gone in to work early that evening.

After searching different bars and hangouts, Eva's brothers caught up with the Williamson boys at a bar on the outskirts of town. Blind with pent-up rage, the Gonzalez brothers went in. They scanned the dimly-lit, smoky room for the Williamson boys and found them clustered at the end of the bar. Their eyes zeroed in on their targets, and they rushed in to deliver the first of many blows to the Williamson boys and their friends.

A huge fight broke out and the bar owner called the police. He had no alternative but to tell the police that the Gonzalez brothers started the brawl. The policemen handcuffed Eva's brothers and put them in the back of the squad cars and took them to the county jail.

In the morning, the Gonzalez brothers were released from jail. Mr. Williamson, the father, told the authorities his sons were not going to press charges, once he learned why the brothers beat up his sons. He was a hard-working, honorable man, but his success had made life too easy for his boys, and their irresponsible behavior time and again brought disgrace on his name. He wasn't going to let his sons hold the Gonzalez brothers responsible for their beating. He hoped this would teach his boys a lesson.

Eva didn't sleep a wink that night. Pacing the cottage floor, she wondered how much more drama she could take in her life.

There was a soft rapping on her door. She pulled the curtain back a little to see who it was before opening it. She was relieved when she saw it was Alex. He had heard about the incident at the police station and came over as soon as he got off duty.

She quickly opened the door for him. In a moment his arms were around her, and he held her close. Eva felt safe in his arms, and she laid her head against his strong chest.

"Mommy?" a little voice said.

Alex and Eva quickly released their embrace and felt a little embarrassed.

"What is it, Rory?" his mother asked, as she sheepishly flashed Alex a quick, guilty grin.

"I had a bad dream. I dreamed there were mean men pounding on the door and trying to break in."

Alex got down on one knee. He reached out and put his hand on Rory's shoulder. "It's okay, big guy. There's no need to worry. I'm here now." Alex looked up at Eva, hoping she understood he was there for her, too. She gave him a little smile and mouthed a silent thank you, confirming she understood, letting him know she was glad he had come.

CHAPTER 22

A SECOND CHANCE

ALEX AND EVA SETTLED on a Tuesday evening for their first date because it was one of her nights off. Sofía agreed to babysit her grandchildren while her daughter went out with "a really nice young man", as Grandma Sofía put it.

Little Angie excitedly watched her mom get ready for her date in her grandmother's bedroom. Eva had chosen a short-sleeved sheath with a small floral print in various shades of red that was strategically fitted to show off her curvy figure. She wiggled into the dress and asked Angie to stand on the bed and help her zip it up the back.

Then Eva went into the bathroom to finish her makeup. Angie stood next to her mother at the bathroom sink and looked on with rapt attention while Eva applied her lipstick and mascara.

Sofía came fluttering past the bathroom. "Aren't you ready yet? Alex is almost here."

"I'm almost done," she replied, fingering her hair into place.

There was a crisp knock at the front door, and Sofía quickly opened it.

"Hello, beautiful," Alex said to Sofía.

"Oh, Alex." She giggled and feigned embarrassment. "Come in, come in. Eva is almost ready. Sit, sit," she said, motioning to the sofa.

Before he could sit down, Eva and Angie walked into the room, and Alex's eyes lit up.

"Wow, you look beautiful!" he said to Eva.

"You don't look so bad yourself, mister." Eva replied. She hadn't seen him in a sport coat and slacks before. *He really looks handsome*, she thought. "Just let me grab my coat."

Alex took Eva to an upscale steakhouse in the nearby city of Gilroy. He wanted their first official date to be memorable. A valet parked the car and the doorman courteously opened the large wooden door for them. The maitre 'd checked the reservation list and found Alex's name. He grabbed a couple of large maroon and gold menus and escorted them to their table.

Eva looked around, taking in all the finery. She had never been to any place this elegant. The deep maroon carpet felt plush beneath her feet and the golden candlelight danced off the linen tablecloths and the rich wood paneling. She wanted to ask Alex if he could afford this place, but she stopped herself, not wanting to offend him.

"Oh, Alex, this place is wonderful. I'll bet the food is really good, too."

"It is. My parents brought me and my brothers here after I graduated from high school to celebrate." He opened his menu to read the offerings.

"So many things on the menu look good. I don't know what to choose." Eva commented.

"Welcome to Chandlers," the formally-dressed waiter said as he approached their table. "Have you had an opportunity to peruse the menu?"

Alex and Eva made their selections, with the help of the waiter and his suggestions, and they enjoyed their delicious food along with good conversation.

"Eva, I'm so glad you agreed to come tonight."

"Me, too. I'm having a wonderful time."

"Do you remember the first time we met?" Alex asked.

"Yes. You followed me to Piedmont Park in junior high and we had lunch together."

"Do you know why I followed you that day?"

"No. Why?"

"I followed you because you weren't the same as the other girls. I noticed you in class and wondered what you were like, what your life was like. You seemed interesting and mysterious."

"Me? Interesting and mysterious?" she asked, incredulous that anyone would think her interesting and mysterious.

"Yes. And I was right. You were smart and strong...and pretty, too."

"What do you mean 'were'?" she asked jokingly.

"You're right, you're right. You *are* smart and strong and pretty."

"Thank you." Eva smiled sweetly at him. "Do you mind if I ask you something?" A question had been nagging her for awhile.

"Sure."

"Why is a great guy like you still single? I mean, why hasn't some lucky woman already snatched you up?"

"Well, someone did once," Alex replied.

"What do you mean? What happened?"

"After you married Richard, I went off to college at San Jose State University. I dated a little, but then I met a great girl named Mary in my junior year. We dated for quite awhile, and I asked her to marry me during the last semester of our senior year. We both graduated and the wedding was planned for the beginning of September. But two weeks after we finished school she was killed in a car accident."

"Oh, Alex. Oh, Alex, I'm so sorry."

"Thanks, it was hard, but over time I worked through it. I entered the police academy in San Jose and became a cop. I poured myself into the job to help get over my grief. A couple of years ago I decided to come back to Hollister. I missed the small town life. I've dated a little since coming back, but there was never any spark with those girls."

"Spark?"

"Yeah, I had spark with Mary. I had it with you, too, from the very first day."

"You felt a spark with me? All those years ago?"

"Yes, all those years ago. I still do." Alex watched the reflection of the candlelight dance in Eva's eyes, and he reached across the table and gently took her hand in his. At his touch, a warm sensation radiated from her hand up her arm, then to the rest of her body.

"Oh, man, Eva, I had such a crush on you," he said, grinning at her.

"Are you kidding me?" She was surprised to hear he had had feelings for her even when they were in junior high. "I was the one who had a huge crush on *you.*"

The realization of their mutual feelings suddenly hit them both, and they had a good laugh about it. From that point on, the conversation flowed freely and easily. The spark had become an ember, and their attraction to one another fanned the flame.

* * * * *

While living in the cottage, Eva received a letter from the German woman for whom Richard had professed his love. The letter read:

"Dear Eva,

You don't know me, but I am the woman Richard is in love with in Germany. He told me he wants a divorce from you so he can marry me. We are very much in love. Please give him the divorce so he can marry me.

Greta"

Eva thought this woman had a lot of nerve. If she wanted Richard, Eva felt she should know what she was getting herself into. She promptly wrote back to Greta:

"Greta,
    You can have my husband. I'm done with him. But, you should know that he does have 2 small children that he's responsible to support until they turn 18.
    Eva, the mother of Richard's children"

A few weeks later, Eva received a letter from Richard, who was still in Germany, saying that he had made a mistake and wanted her to forgive him. He realized, he wrote, that it was Eva he loved, not Greta, and that he wanted her back. Greta, the letter went on to say, was not the woman he thought she was. She had left him and run off with another American soldier.

That was it. Eva knew it was time to move forward with filing for divorce. She met with a divorce lawyer to get the process moving. She needed to protect herself and her children. However, she found out from the attorney that she could not divorce Richard until he returned to the United States.

She couldn't believe this was happening. As she sat in the leather chair in her attorney's office, her body violently reacted to the news. At first, she felt sick, like she was going to throw up. Her head started to pound.

"Are you all right?" the lawyer asked with concern. He could see the dramatic change in her countenance.

Eva was beyond disappointed. Words could not describe the depth of her despair. She needed to cut Richard off like a gangrenous limb. But he was outside of her reach at the moment. She was forced to be patient and wait for the right opportunity.

"I will be," she said as she gathered up her purse and coat and walked out. What she needed now was yet another plan.

Numerous thoughts swirled around in her head as she drove home. She knew she needed the child support from Richard to help cover their living expenses after the divorce, especially if she hoped to start a new life. She couldn't earn enough on her own. Besides, the kids were his responsibility, too. If he wanted to play around with other women, fine, but he would pay to support his children.

Rory's and Angie's sweet little faces danced in her mind. Eva knew she needed to focus on what was in their best interest. It was on her shoulders alone to build a new life for them, to give them a childhood that would be better than what she had known. What she had to do was bide her time until she received confirmation that Richard was back on U.S. soil.

A few months later, Eva got another letter from Richard.

"Dear Eva,

I miss you all so much. I'm back at Fort Ord now, and I want to come and see you and the kids. Write me back and tell me when I can come. I love you.

Richard"

With a satisfied grin, Eva quickly shot off her response to him:

"Richard,

I do NOT want to see you ever again. I don't want you to come and visit the children either. They are better off without you – we all are. By the way, divorce papers are on their way to you.

Eva"

Eva sighed with relief. She was finally free of her no-good husband and able to pursue true love and happiness. This time, though, she decided she would take her time.

She and Alex had gone on a few more dates while she waited for her final divorce decree, mostly opportunities to talk and get to know each other again. Eva could sense he was falling in love with her, and her affection for him was growing, too; but she wasn't ready to jump into anything yet. She enjoyed the long walks in the country with him and the quiet dinners they shared, but she remained guarded until the divorce was final.

Once the divorce was behind her and she was no longer bound to Richard, Eva was eager to let Alex know her better. She wanted to share with him what her life was like growing up, how she escaped that life, and what she wanted for her future and her children's future. She had always been rather tight-lipped about the harsh conditions in which she had grown up. But now, she had come to the place where she was willing to be vulnerable and open up to him.

One afternoon, Alex took Eva on a picnic in Piedmont Park. He brought the blanket and drinks, and she had packed a picnic basket with sandwiches and fresh fruit. She even slyly included a couple of cold bean burritos in the basket, for old time's sake.

"This looks like a nice place," Eva said, pointing to a flat, shady spot under a mature oak tree.

They spread out the blanket, set the basket down, and each found a comfortable place to sit. Eva set out the paper plates and cups and then dug around in the basket for the napkins.

"Here," Alex said, "let me help you get the food out."

He pulled out the sandwiches and the bag of bananas and grapes, then he noticed there was something else in the bottom of the basket. It was a dish towel folded into a neat little square, tied with twine, which looked oddly familiar to him.

"What's this?" he said, raising one eyebrow as he held the little bundle up to Eva.

"It's a surprise. Open it."

Alex looked at her suspiciously, then looked down at the mysterious fabric-covered packet in his hand. He untied the twine and let the cloth fall open. There sat two cold bean burritos. He looked puzzled for a moment, his brows knit together and his head cocked to one side. Then a huge grin spread across his face and his eyes lit up. He realized what those burritos meant.

"Oh, Eva…this is great!" he said with a chuckle.

"I wasn't sure you'd remember."

"Me? Not remember? How could I forget the day we met?"

Eva was pleased that Alex understood what the burritos symbolized. They were starting over, getting reacquainted as if they were back at the beginning.

"I'll swap you half of my sandwich for one of your burritos," Alex said, reminding her of that first day.

"You really want a cold bean burrito?" she asked jokingly.

"Sure. I like Mexican food!"

"Do you? Why?" she asked, as if she didn't know.

" 'Cause I'm one-fourth Mexican," he said proudly. "My dad's mom was Mexican. She passed away last year, but she used to make fresh tortillas and tamales and all kinds of good stuff."

"Oh, Alex, I'm sorry. I didn't know your grandmother passed away," Eva told him. She was so touched by him losing his beloved grandmother that her eyes started to glisten with tears.

He reached out and put his strong hand gently on hers. "It's okay. She lived a good, long life. No regrets. My grandpa loved her for over fifty years, and they had five children together."

He gave her a little smile to reassure her that it really was all right.

"Wow, he loved her for over fifty years. I can't even imagine that kind of life." Those tears that were so near the surface began to spill over. She was embarrassed by them. She took a napkin and stood up, turning away to hide them.

Alex quickly got to his feet, too, and lightly grabbed hold of her forearm.

"I don't understand, Eva. Why does that make you cry?"

"I don't know," she replied, shaking her head slightly. Alex was perplexed. He couldn't see why his grandmother's death would cause Eva to react like that.

"Come on," Alex said, as he took Eva's hand. "Let's go sit on that bench over there," he offered, noticing a park bench less than ten feet away. He led her over to it and they sat down.

"Talk to me, I don't understand," he said again, holding her hand in his.

"You must've figured out that Mama and Carlos didn't have a good marriage, with her divorcing him and then you having to arrest him for drunkenness and trying to break into her house."

"Yeah, I assumed things weren't great between them. But, how bad was it?" he asked, not realizing he had opened a flood gate.

Even though Eva hated talking about her harsh and abusive life, she was ready to open up to Alex and let him in all the way. Starting her story from as far back as she could remember as a small child, she spilled out all the horrible and painful details of her life.

He tried to take it all in, but the misery and brutality of it was overwhelming to him. He had never known anyone who had endured the things Eva and Sofía had. Alex was a man with a profound sense of right and wrong, and he couldn't understand how Carlos was allowed to get away with abusing his family all those years.

Just listening to Eva's stories about her family – enduring the violence, fighting to go to school, breaking free of her abusive life and rescuing her mother – made Alex's feelings for Eva grow even stronger. He wanted to protect her so no one would ever hurt her again.

"I'm so sorry, Eva." He put his arms around her and pulled her in. Resting her head against his chest, she breathed in his scent, which smelled of strength and love. She dried her tears and rested in his arms for a few moments. Her body relaxed against his. She felt safe.

What Alex felt was a twinge of guilt. He had his arms around Eva, trying to comfort her. But holding her against him made him want her, it made his whole body ache for her. She wanted to take things slowly, she had told him, but he didn't know how long he could hold back his passion for her.

* * * * *

Eva could sense her relationship with Alex growing deeper, their feelings for each other growing stronger. But she wanted to be especially careful not to let her children get too attached to Alex. If things didn't work out between them, she didn't want her children hurt. At this point, she only told them that Alex was a good friend.

But keeping them from getting attached was impossible to do, because he was crazy about them. And the feeling was mutual. They loved the attention he gave them, and he was often willing to play with them in the yard before he went to work in the evenings.

One night, after a family dinner at Grandma Sofía's house, Alex and Eva stole a few minutes for themselves and sat on the front porch talking. It was a mild spring evening, and the sky was clear and studded with stars and a bright, full moon. There was a warm glow from the living room lamps shining through the screen door, illuminating the porch. The air was filled with the scent of jasmine that Sofía had planted in the yard. Alex slipped an arm around Eva and pulled her in close to him.

"Eva, I love you."

Eva turned her body to look him in his eyes, and she cupped his face in her hands. She gazed at him and could see he unquestionably meant what he said, which warmed her down to her toes.

"Alex Messina, it seems like I have been waiting my whole life to hear you say that. What took you so long?"

He looked a bit surprised at her response, after all it was her that wanted to take things slowly. Then he gave her a little smile, pleased at her reply. He enveloped her with both arms and held her tenderly. Her arms slipped around his neck. His face was close to hers and their lips almost touched. Alex studied her face for a moment, then passionately pressed his lips to hers. She had never been kissed like that before – purely, deeply, totally.

When she was good and kissed, he slid off the step and onto one knee. Her heart started to beat wildly as she sensed what was about to happen.

"Eva, I love you with my whole heart. I love you, and I love your kids. Will you marry me?"

"Yes, we will! We will!" Rory and Angie squealed in unison. They were standing just inside the screen door and had watched the proposal.

Alex and Eva were so surprised by them that they burst out laughing. Rory and Angie opened the screen door and ran out to join them. They were all hugging and laughing on the front steps. Sofía heard the laughter from inside and came to the door.

"What's all the noise out there?" she asked.

"We're getting married!" Angie announced.

CHAPTER 23

MAMA SAVED THEM ALL

EVA AND ALEX WERE OVER THE MOON for each other, happily planning their wedding. Eva was thrilled to have Alex back in her life. He made her feel loved, cared for, and protected. She never had that before. Neither had Sofía.

One evening, Alex was at Sofía's house for dinner, and he and Eva were going over some of the details of their wedding. It was going to be a small family affair, but Eva wanted it to be memorable. Trying to blend her Mexican family and his Italian family shouldn't be too hard, she thought.

She had spoken to Alex's mother, Lucia, and she and some of the women in her family were happy to make their traditional Italian dishes for the reception. Sofía and Lydia, and some of their friends, were already planning to make the Mexican food. But other details still needed to be discussed and decided on.

It was getting late, so all the children had already been put to bed at Grandma Sofía's house, except for Hector, a teenager, who was staying the night with friends. Eva and her mother planned to sit around the kitchen table and talk more about the wedding plans as soon as Alex left to work his ten o'clock night shift. Eva walked Alex to the door, and they paused for a moment.

"I wish I didn't have to go," Alex told her, as he took her hand and kissed it gently.

"I wish you didn't either, but I'll see you tomorrow." She pushed herself up on her tip-toes, smoothed out the collar of his uniform, and threw her arms around his neck. He lovingly responded by putting his arms around her. She gave him a long, deep kiss good-bye.

"Please be careful out there," she reminded him as they released their hold on each other.

"I will, I will. Don't worry so much. I'll see you tomorrow," he promised as he walked out the door.

Eva went back to the kitchen table and continued talking with her mother about the guest list and decorating ideas. A few minutes later, there was a knock at the front door.

"Oh, it's probably Alex," Eva assumed. "He must've forgotten something."

She got up from her chair and started for the door. "Why don't you pour us some coffee, Mama? It should be ready by now. I'll be right back."

Eva swung the door open, expecting to see her fiancé. But it wasn't Alex. Fear gripped her for just a moment, but soon that fear mixed with anger.

Standing in the doorway was her stepfather, Carlos, wearing a cheap white dress shirt and faded blue jeans. His face was gnarled in an angry scowl and his eyes were dark with hate. He reeked of sweat and alcohol. Having been released from jail that afternoon, followed by a few hours in a local bar, he had come to Sofía's house to get even with her.

"What are you doing here?" Eva demanded. Even though her initial reaction to seeing him was fear, she resolved to stand her ground against him.

"Get outta my way, puta!" he shouted, as he shoved Eva aside, sending her flying to the floor.

"Sofía!" he hollered in a gruff, raspy voice as he stomped his way back to the kitchen. He spotted her at the stove, with her back to him, about to pick up the coffee pot to fill the two mugs sitting on the counter. She froze in terror at the sound of his voice, unable to even turn around.

Eva scrambled to her feet and ran after him. She was small but fierce. She would not let him hurt her mother again.

"No! You leave her alone, old man!" Eva screamed.

His strong left hand clamped onto the back of Sofía's neck, and he spun her around. He clutched a hunting knife in his right hand that he drew up to her throat. Sofía was terrified. She was certain he was going to kill her this time.

"Get away, muchacha! I'm gonna show your mama she can't run from me," Carlos growled.

"Please, Carlos, no. Let me go," Sofía pleaded.

Carlos had been thinking about this moment since he was sent to jail. The last time he was at this house, he had been arrested. Because Sofía and Eva had testified against him at his trial, he was sentenced to one year's confinement.

"You got me locked up, now I'm gonna make you pay!" Carlos threatened.

"Let her go!" Eva warned, "or I'm going to call the cops and you'll be going back to jail!"

"Go ahead, call 'em, you whore! She'll be dead before they get here." In his drunkenness, he didn't seem to care if the police came or not. He was set on doing what he came there to do.

"No, please. You don't have to do this." Eva tried to reason with him to save her mother's life. "You can walk away right now, and no one will ever have to know you were here."

"You think I'm stupid?" He paused, like he expected an answer. "No, you think I'm a coward. You don't believe I'll do it, do you? You don't think I have the guts. Well, I do. See, it's real easy...like this." He ran the sharp blade lightly across Sofía's neck as she winced in pain, just to torment her. He left a two-inch slice that started to bleed.

"Mama!" Eva shrieked as she stepped forward.

"That's far enough, girl!" Carlos shouted. "Say good-bye to your mama."

"Let her go!" Eva demanded again.

In the commotion, Eva and Sofía had forgotten the children were asleep in the bedrooms. The noise had awakened little Angie and she sleepily wandered into the kitchen.

"Mommy, what's going on?" the six-year-old asked, rubbing her eyes. Unaware of the danger, Angie innocently stepped between Eva and Carlos, and he tried to take full advantage of it.

"Go back to bed, Angie," Eva instructed her, masking the terror she felt, trying to sound calm.

"So, is this *your* little girl, Eva? That's perfect," Carlos snarled, his eyes narrowing. "You took my family from me, I'm gonna take yours from you."

Momentarily pulling the knife away from Sofía's neck, he pointed it straight at Angie in a threatening motion. The tip of the blade was not more than a few inches from her angelic face.

"As soon as I'm done with this worthless woman, I'm gonna slice this little one up, from ear to ear." Angie's eyes widened with fear. Eva was panicked and quickly moved forward to pull her daughter away.

"You know, niña," he said to Angie, "I should have done that to your mama when she was a baby. I never did like her."

As Carlos' attention was temporarily diverted to Angie, Sofía felt his grip relax a little from around her neck. A fierce anger rose up in her against this vicious man, she was not going to let him have his way. She saw she only had a small window of opportunity if she was going to do anything to fight back. *God help me*, she prayed.

Swiftly, with her left hand, she grabbed the pot of hot coffee off the stove. She swung it around at his face. The lid flew off from the centrifugal force. Scalding liquid covered him from his grizzled face to his muscular chest. He released his grip on the back of her neck and drew his hand up to his face as he screamed in pain. In a flash, Eva pulled Angie behind her.

Sofía spun around quickly. She saw he was still grasping the hunting knife in his other hand. In a split second, she grabbed hold of Carlos' right hand with both of her hands and plunged the knife deeply into his abdomen.

She released her grip and jumped back, stunned by what she had just done. He stared at Sofía in disbelief, she had never really fought back before. Whenever she had tried to, it cost her dearly. But this time, she had no choice. This time, he would be the one to pay.

Carlos staggered around and slumped against the cabinets, then slowly slid down to the floor. He groaned a few times, then he fell silent.

Sofía stood motionless. She was in shock, the color draining from her face.

Eva quickly turned her daughter's head away so she couldn't see Carlos, and walked her out of the kitchen.

"Go and get back in bed, Angie. Hurry, now. I'll be in to check on you in a few minutes." Eva struggled to keep an even tone in her voice, trying not to scare her daughter any further. The little girl whimpered and clung to her mother.

"Everything will be okay, honey, I promise. But I need you to be a big girl right now and go back to bed. I'll be in to see you in a little while." The frightened girl reluctantly did as her mother asked.

Then Eva pulled out a chair and motioned to her mother to sit down, as she went to grab a towel from the kitchen drawer to stop Sofía's bleeding.

Suddenly, Alex kicked the front door open and stormed in, his adrenalin pumping and his gun drawn. Startled, Eva carefully peered around the doorway of the kitchen, into the living room. Fear gave way to relief when she saw it was Alex. He cautiously rushed to her, not knowing what to expect.

"Are you all right, Eva?" he asked. Before she could answer, he saw the whole bloody scene in the kitchen – Carlos slouched on the floor with a knife in his gut, blood soaking his white shirt, and Sofía sitting in a daze with blood running down her neck, her glassy eyes staring blankly into the distance.

"My God, what happened here?" Alex questioned, as he holstered his gun.

"It was Carlos, he busted in and said he was going to kill Mama!" Eva hastily tried to explain, battling back her tears. "He said he was going to kill Angie, too." She was shaking all over, doing her best to stay calm.

"Oh, man! Who stabbed him?"

"Mama did," Eva replied. She took the towel, quickly ran it under the faucet to dampen it and held it to her mother's neck.

"Sofía," Alex said softly, as he knelt down on one knee by her chair, but she didn't respond. "Sofía," he repeated with a little more force. "Can you hear me?"

Slowly, she moved her eyes and looked at him.

"Are you okay?" he asked. "You're bleeding."

"I'm okay," Sofía replied flatly. Alex stood up and put a reassuring hand on her shoulder for a moment, then he looked over at Carlos.

"Is he dead?" Eva asked nervously.

Alex crouched down and felt Carlos's neck for a pulse.

"No, I'm sorry to say, he's still alive. I better call this in and get an ambulance here." Alex used his radio and called for the ambulance and for the assistance of another police officer.

"Help will be here in a few minutes," he reported. "Now, how about you? How are you doing, Eva?"

"I'm all right. I just want to take care of Mama, then go check on Angie."

Eva was able to stop the bleeding from the gash on Sofía's neck, which wasn't very deep. Fortunately, Carlos was only toying with her when he cut her, apparently trying to terrorize her first, before he slit her throat.

"How did you know to come back, Alex?" Eva asked.

"Well, as I was driving down the hill to Main Street, I saw a pickup turn and start up the hill. The truck seemed familiar, but I couldn't place it. Just before I got to the station, though, it dawned on me. I hadn't seen that truck for a year or so, but I remembered it was Carlos's truck. So I flipped a u-turn and flew back here. I knew something was wrong when I saw his truck out front and your door ajar. That's when I stormed in."

He wrapped his strong arms around Eva, and she melted into his embrace.

"I don't know what I would do if something happened to you, Eva, or to any of you."

"Don't worry, we're fine now," she reassured him, resting her head against his firm chest.

"But it could have ended very differently."

"Yes, it could have," Eva said, "but it didn't. Mama's courage saved us all."

DEBRA BURROUGHS

CHAPTER 24

A GLORIOUS DAY

ALEX AND EVA DECIDED to have their wedding in Piedmont Park, in the heart of Hollister. This was where they had gone to lunch together in junior high and where their love for each other was kindled. The setting for the ceremony was a lovely expanse of lawn decorated with a brass archway covered in billowy white toile and lavender and white flowers. The lush green grass was freshly mowed and white folding chairs were set up for the guests. It was a perfect summer day.

When everyone was seated, the small group of musicians began to play. Alex and the minister took their places under the archway and stood facing the guests. Alex's brother escorted their parents to the groom's side of the front row, then Mateo escorted Sofía to her seat in the opposite front row.

Little Angie, dressed in a pretty white party dress with a deep purple sash, meandered down the center aisle, scattering white rose petals from her basket that was covered in purple ribbon. Then, she stood impatiently at the front to wait for her mother.

After that, Rory, in a handsome gray suit and lavender tie, which matched the groom's, dutifully carried the rings down the aisle on a white satin pillow and proudly took his position next to Alex.

The musicians began to play a new song, signaling the bride to enter and the guests to rise. Eduardo, Eva's first brother, wearing a black suit, escorted her down the aisle in a pale lavender cocktail dress, carrying a simple spray of white roses.

Alex watched Eva coming toward him with an expression of pure joy on his face. He was finally marrying the love of his life, and he couldn't wait for them to be man and wife. Eva was giddy with excitement and ready to be loved, cherished, and protected.

The minister led them in reciting their vows and pronounced them man and wife. Alex kissed his bride, gently but thoroughly, and Angie and Rory squealed with pleasure. The minister asked Alex, Eva, Angie and Rory to turn and face the guests.

"I would like to introduce you to Mr. and Mrs. Alex Messina and family!"

The musicians started up a lively song and the family walked down the aisle to a burst of applause. Alex's mother and Sofía were both crying tears of joy and were escorted down the aisle next.

The minister invited everyone to head over to the reception area, which various family members had set up with tables and chairs. Some of the men had strung lights across the area, as the reception was expected to go well into the evening. As the musicians continued to play, the parents encouraged the guests to dance.

With sweet music filling the air, Alex's uncle Mario, a widower with wavy black hair and a neatly-trimmed mustache, invited Sofía to dance. At first she tried to decline, but he was very charming and persuasive. He took her by the hand and led her in a slow dance.

As Eva and Alex were wandering among the guests, they noticed Sofía dancing with Uncle Mario. Sofía looked over at them, raised her eyebrows, and gave her daughter a questioning look, not sure she was doing the right thing. Eva winked back at her mother and gave her a big smile of approval before continuing on to greet more guests.

Some guests were already lining up at the two long buffet tables that were located at one end of the reception area. The tables were well laden with trays of enchiladas, chicken mole and carnitas, as well as lasagna, antipasto, rigatoni and plump meatballs. Papa Messina made sure wine and beer flowed freely to toast and celebrate the new couple.

The beautiful three-tiered white wedding cake sat in its own place of honor, on a lace-covered round table with a view of the festivities, just waiting for its turn to put a sweet ending to this glorious day.

The End

ABOUT THE AUTHOR

Debra Burroughs grew up in the San Francisco Bay Area during a tumultuous time when the Civil Rights Movement was gearing up and racial tensions were mounting. Her parents moved the family to a more peaceful town in the Central Valley of California.

Starting college, she majored in broadcast journalism, but over time she changed her major to business. Even though she moved her focus to business, she never lost her love for writing. She always hoped one day to return to it.

Over the years, with a large Mexican family, she heard many stories about their history, particularly from her mother and grandmother. As she would relay these colorful and heart-wrenching family stories to her friends, many times she would hear them say, "You should really write a book about that."

After continual encouragement and gentle prodding from her husband, she finally decided to do it. Now that their children are grown and gone, Debra has found a quiet place to write in their home in Boise, Idaho.

Visit My Blog: www.Debra@DebraBurroughsBooks.com

Contact Me: Debra@DebraBurroughsBooks.com

I'd love to hear from you. Email me! ~ *Debra*

www.ingramcontent.com/pod-product-compliance
Lightning Source LLC
Chambersburg PA
CBHW050031180626
46810CB00002B/667